Thi...

Shelby thought as she gazed at Blaize. "Let's just say my love life hasn't been all that exciting lately," she said.

"Would you want it to be? And if you do, why don't you fix it?"

Shelby snapped her fingers. "Fix it? Just like that? I don't think it's that simple."

"Of course it is. You just have to have desire for the other person." Blaize's eyes never left Shelby's face.

"I hate to sound naïve, but what about love?"

"Love isn't necessary . . . it would be a sort of icing on the cake," Blaize assured her.

"Well, I can't say that I'd always choose to love first . . . but it should be a possibility."

"Many things are possible. But sometimes if we wait for love it could be a long time before we find fulfillment. As I'm certain you can testify."

"Is there a point to this conversation?"

"I think," Blaize said huskily, placing his hand on top of hers, "the point is quite clear."

EBONI SNOE

Wishin' On A Star

AVON BOOKS
An Imprint of HarperCollinsPublishers

This is a work of fiction. Names, characters, places, and incidents are products of the author's imagination or are used fictitiously and are not to be construed as real. Any resemblance to actual events, locales, organizations, or persons, living or dead, is entirely coincidental.

AVON BOOKS
An Imprint of HarperCollins*Publishers*
10 East 53rd Street
New York, New York 10022-5299

Copyright © 2000 by Eboni Snoe
Inside cover author photo by Terry L. Ford
ISBN: 0-380-81395-5
www.avonromance.com

First Avon Books paperback printing: July 2000

Avon Trademark Reg. U.S. Pat. Off. and in Other Countries, Marca Registrada, Hecho en U.S.A.
HarperCollins® is a trademark of HarperCollins Publishers Inc.

Printed in the U.S.A.

WCD   10 9 8 7 6 5 4 3 2 1

*To my Larry,
I said I would know you
anytime . . . anywhere . . .
I'm glad I kept my promise*

Prologue

1985

What good are my tears? Shelby Russau thought. She dropped down on one knee and pretended to tie her shoe as she fought the familiar sting. Shelby was aware of the feet around her, shoes of various colors and sizes, belonging to her classmates and their parents. Her own shoelaces blurred as she fumbled with the tie. *Where do I fit in? I have no family. I have no home. I don't belong with these people. I don't belong to anyone.*

Shelby heard her friend Linda's voice above her. "Hey Dad, Shelby and I are going to the Indian mound over there."

"Go ahead. I won't be far behind," Mr. Johnson replied before he continued his conversation with another parent.

"C'mon Shel—"

Before Linda could call her name, Shelby started running toward the mound. As she ran the wind streaked her tears across her face. Shelby tried to outrun her sadness, her fears and her tears. She didn't want Linda to see her cry. She didn't know how to explain her persistent grief. Shelby was sure, no matter what she said, Linda wouldn't really understand. How could she? She *had* a family. It would be impossible for her to know what it felt like to be alone.

Shelby reached the top of the mound and looked out toward the water below. Her breaths were deep and painful because of her asthma, but not as painful as the hurt in her heart. She attempted to shout at the sky, but only a whisper emerged. "I'm twelve years old and I'm alone. How can that be?" She spoke into the wind. "Wasn't it enough for you to take away my parents? No, it must not have been, because two years ago, today, you took my brother, Cleophus, away." Shelby felt dizzy. She could barely breathe, but her mind continued to churn. "What did I do to deserve this kind of life? What did I do wrong?" she demanded, sinking to her knees.

She clenched her eyes. She told herself to open them, but moments later she felt grass beneath her face after she collapsed on the mound. When Shelby looked out again the scene had changed drastically. What had been an empty dock was speckled with ships, while the white sails of other craft billowed beyond them against a perfect blue sky.

Shelby watched as crowds of people who appeared to be from various lands bought and bartered goods. The sound of their laughter and disagreements floated up to her along with the smell of spices, fruits, fresh meat and flowers. She watched a small crowd gather in front of a magnificent black-and-red ship. Abruptly, the group parted, and Shelby could see a cloud of petticoats fluttering around a set of kicking legs. A man carried a woman in his arms, and although she appeared to resist him with all her might, he walked as if the woman were as light as a feather. They were an odd pair, Shelby thought as she compared his colorful clothing with the woman's plain white skirt and blouse.

"What do you think you're doing?" the woman shouted. "Put me down!"

Shelby heard the woman's words directly in her ears, as if they were coming through a headset.

"You don't know what you want," the man said as he strode forward. "I am taking you back with me where you belong. I am your family now. My people are your people." He started across the plank and held her firmly against his chest.

"You let me go right now, you hear me!" The woman pushed against him.

"When are you going to admit the truth to yourself?" he replied. "When are you going to have the courage to reach out for what you want?"

"Don't you question my courage." She stopped flailing long enough to challenge him with her eyes. "I know what I want, and you can believe, it isn't you."

The man stopped in his tracks. He stared into her eyes before he began to release her. Finally her feet touched the wooden dock. The man paused, then said, "If I leave you now, I am never coming back."

Shelby could sense the woman's fearful indecision. She looked into his face, then looked away, giving no response. Without glancing back, the man boarded the vessel and crossed to the other side of the deck.

Several sailors made ready to sail. One walked over to the plank and prepared to remove it. Shelby, like the crowd that had gathered, held her breath as the woman turned toward the shore. She took one step, closed her eyes, then released a gasp before she ran toward the ship and into her lover's arms. They embraced as if there would be no tomorrow.

As the ship pulled away from the shore, the man held the woman in his arms and looked over at the mound where Shelby lay, before the vessel disappeared into a thick fog. . . .

"Shelby, are you all right?" Linda asked, standing above her.

"Yes . . . I'm fine." She watched Linda's concerned expression turn to irritation.

"What in the heck did you do that for?"

"Do what?" Shelby responded, distracted.

"Run off like that. You know you've got asthma. What are you trying to do? Pass out?"

"No." Shelby focused on her friend's face. "I just felt a need to run. That's all." She looked down at the water. Once again the beach was empty. The wharf gone.

Shelby decided not to mention the dreamlike experience. She wasn't certain what to make of it, and if she said anything, Linda would probably tell her foster father. He was a preacher and Shelby was certain he would not understand. She had enough strikes against her. It was one thing to be known for losing your family. It was another for losing your mind.

"C'mon." Shelby got to her feet. "Let's check out the other mound." She took Linda's hand and led her down the hill.

Chapter 1

Fifteen years later

"Would you go stand over there, please?" Shelby smiled at the elderly man and motioned toward the line of people that was forming in the park several yards away. The man smiled back, showing a mouth full of perfectly uneven yellow teeth, but he didn't budge. "Go over there." She emphasized each word, pointing. He nodded his head and continued to smile. "How in the world did I let Linda talk me into this?" Shelby mumbled beneath her breath.

"You let me talk you into it because you know you needed to do something else besides go to work and go home." Linda came and took the man by the arm. Shelby watched her as she led him to his proper position in the parade line before returning to her side. "Your social skills are pitiful, Shelby," Linda declared. "But I guess that's something you know by now." She shook her head, looking out across the park. "Absolutely the pits."

"No, they're not," Shelby defended herself.

"Yes, they are. When do you get to practice them?"

"Every day when I go to work."

"Work. Okay. I'll give you that. But that's the extent of it. And that says it all. How well-rounded can you be when all you do is go to work?"

"Exactly *what* are you saying about me?" Shelby crossed her arms and looked at her childhood friend.

"I am saying—" Linda put her arm around Shelby's shoulder and paused with her mouth wide open "—I'm glad you decided to volunteer to work with the Parade of Cultures. I think through the Pinellas County Millennium Celebration you will meet a lot of different people. Perhaps—" she smiled too sweetly "—just perhaps, you'll expand your horizons when it comes to other members of the human race."

Shelby rolled her eyes. "Meaning . . ."

"I have to spell it out for you, do I?" Linda looked over the rim of her glasses. "You don't go anywhere besides work. You never meet any new people. *Your life* is totally boring. So, working with the parade is a great opportunity to do something different."

"Linda, we live in St. Petersburg, Florida. How many new people am I going to meet here? It's not the biggest city in the world, you know," Shelby said, offended.

"But that's just it. It's not the biggest city, but people come here from all over the world to enjoy the Florida sunshine. To enjoy the beaches. There are all kinds of people coming here everyday, Shelby. Some of them stay. But you've got to make a special effort to meet them. That's all I'm saying." Linda spread her arms wide. "Look at the diversity of people that are participating in this parade. Did you have any idea that we were such an international city?"

Shelby looked at the myriad faces that were haphazardly lined up in Straub Park. She had to admit she hadn't realized it, and the variety was impressive. "No."

"And here you are, playing a significant role in the biggest event in the history of Pinellas County. The Pinellas County Millennium Celebration."

"Significant . . . Linda." Shelby had to smile. "Cut the crap."

"Hey! It's all about perspective, girlfriend."

"Well, I'm going to perspective my butt right on over there and rest for a while. It's hot as I don't know what out here." Shelby wiped her forehead with the back of her hand.

"You know what it is as hot as." Linda started walking away. "But being the church-going woman that I am, I simply won't say." She turned her nose up meaningfully and smiled.

Shelby found a tree near a collection of hibiscus shrubs and sat down on the grass. Even though she never would admit it to Linda, Shelby thoroughly enjoyed the hours she spent volunteering. Sometimes communication was a problem, but the smiles and camaraderie that resulted made up for all the shortcomings.

Still, Shelby admired Linda's winning ways with people. True or not, she believed those ways were the product of a close-knit family. Shelby was the product of foster homes, which had not nurtured her people skills.

A familiar discomfort stirred within her. *You would think after all these years I would have come to terms with being orphaned.* In many ways Shelby had. But just the thought of being the only one, despite the Florida heat, still left a cold feeling in the pit of Shelby's stomach.

Perspiring, Shelby glanced around to see if anyone was watching. Certain there wasn't, she pulled the elastic waist of her skirt below her navel and raised her top. She sighed as the lazy breeze caressed her abdomen. "Thank God for small favors." She relaxed and enjoyed the reprieve. Shelby extended her neck back, allowing herself to cool off thoroughly, but when she did, her gaze fell on a man looking down at her with intense black eyes from the opposite side of the hibiscus bush. Quickly, she righted her position and pulled down her top. "May I help you?" she asked.

The man did not respond. He walked around the flowers then planted his feet firmly in front of her.

He looked like someone straight out of the adventure movies, adorned in a flowing pants set of white gauze that gleamed in the sunlight. His dark hair had a shadowy halo above it.

"May I help you?" Shelby repeated. She was breathless and more than a little irritated. The man had caught her completely off guard, showing more than she had shown to anyone in a long time. And now he was looking at her as if she were a specimen under a glass. Did he sense the butterflies that were fluttering in her stomach?

The conversation with Linda was fresh in her mind as Shelby got to her feet. "I suppose you don't speak English either," she said to him with a false smile on her face. Although he was far from an old man, Shelby decided to take the initiative and guide him to the proper place in the parade lineup. "Let's see, you look like you could be from the islands." She surveyed his reddish-brown skin, muscular frame, and locks that reached just below his shoulders. "But if you were, at your age—" she guessed he was in his mid-thirties "—you probably would be able to speak some English." She looked directly into his eyes.

His eyes were dark and compelling, but as Shelby looked deeper, her heart lurched at the volatile emotions she saw there. She had never seen so much fire inside the eyes of another human being. Shelby took a step back.

"Do you have a brother named Cleophus?" The man spoke for the first time.

"Say what?" Shelby was stunned.

"Do you have a brother by that name?" He spoke with a heavy island accent.

"You *can* speak English, and you let me go on all that time as if you couldn't." Shelby felt heat rising to her face.

"You were so sure of my shortcomings. It's an unattractive trait that many of you Americans possess."

"Unattractive trait . . ." Shelby was confused. What was going on here? She didn't know this man from Adam's apple, but he was berating her. And didn't he say something about Cleophus?

"Cleophus Russau. Do you have a brother by that name?" His voice held an unfriendly edge.

He *had* asked about Cleophus! "What if I do?" Shelby replied, her eyes narrowing.

"I need to talk to him right away. We've got some important business to discuss."

Shelby's defenses locked in. She didn't like the vibes the man was giving off. Here he was asking about her brother, Cleophus, who had died sixteen years ago. And he wasn't being nice about it either. Shelby crossed her arms and sized up the stranger. From the tone of his voice, she would think Cleophus had committed a crime or something. "I don't know who you are or what this is about—"

"I am Raphael Blaize." He said his surname as if it should ring a bell.

"Well, Mr. Blaize, if you really knew my brother, I don't think this conversation would be taking place."

"I think it is you who does not really *know* your own brother."

Shelby was taken aback. "How dare you?" she replied with anger and hurt. He had no right to talk about her family. By now Cleophus was the only family member that she could truly remember, and to Shelby's dismay, as the years increased, those memories became more and more vaporous every day.

Blaize looked at the wounded expression on the woman's face. She was an attractive woman, he thought, actually beautiful in a restrained kind of way. He watched her lips tremble ever so slightly as her soft brown eyes became far too bright, as if she were fighting back tears. Blaize knew his words had caused more pain than he had intended. "Ma'am—"

"Ms. Russau to you." Shelby's fists involuntarily balled up at her sides.

"Ms. Russau, I didn't come here to start any problems with you."

"Well, if you didn't, you sure have a strange way of showing it."

"I just want to speak to your brother," he declared with hooded eyes.

"That's something I can't help you with."

"Can't or won't?"

"I'm not even going to answer that." Shelby tilted her chin up stubbornly. "Good-bye." She turned and walked rapidly across the park. She stopped next to Linda, who was rifling through a pile of papers.

"Was he trying to find out about the parade?"

"I don't think so," Shelby said looking back at Blaize, who remained at a distance.

"Did you ask him?"

"No, I didn't."

"Shelbeee."

"He was not interested in the parade, Linda."

"Oh." Linda's eyes brightened. "He was interested in something else, huh?"

"Not in a million years."

"He wouldn't be interested in a million years, or *you* wouldn't?"

"Take your pick."

Linda shielded her eyes against the sun as she watched Blaize walk away. "He looked really good from here. What was wrong with him? Bad teeth? Skin?"

"Linda, you have a one-track mind," Shelby said, exasperated.

"Just trying to bring you into the loop, that's all."

"Well, let me save you some work. He's not the one." Shelby massaged her hands.

"Really?" Linda stared at her friend's bright

eyes. "Something he said got you going."

"It's not what you think," Shelby said softly.

"Want to tell me about it?" Linda examined the serious lines that etched Shelby's face.

"Not particularly."

"Okay." Linda threw her arms up in the air. "Have it your way. We're about to discuss the floats and performances. You want to join in?"

"Nope. I think I've had enough for one day." Shelby tried to smile, but she couldn't forget the look in Blaize's eyes when he had asked about her brother. Why was he asking about him now? "I'll talk to you later," Shelby said before she headed for her car.

Chapter 2

Shelby stood in her dining room and looked at the gladiolas she had bought at the supermarket. They were beautiful. Nothing could lend a special touch to a room like flowers, she thought, except, perhaps, scented candles. Shelby inhaled the lavender scent that lightly coated the air. She'd lit the candles minutes after she arrived home, trusting the aroma that normally relaxed her would do the trick. It hadn't.

Shelby went back to the living room and picked up the book she had been reading. Moments later she found herself staring into space. The incident in the park with Raphael Blaize plagued her. It wasn't just because he had asked about her brother. She didn't know how to explain it. There was almost something familiar about him, but Shelby couldn't put her finger on what. It was strange. She bit her lip. If Shelby had met Blaize before there was no way she would have forgotten him. He wore his masculine appeal like an amulet.

She placed the book on the cocktail table. Trying to read was useless in the state she was in. Her restless gaze fell on the entertainment center. Maybe some music would change her mood. She rose from the couch.

After going through stacks of CDs, Shelby found some oldies but goodies. It was only after the first CD began to play that she realized Donald Byrd's "Fallin' Like Dominoes" had been one of her brother's favorites. "Cleophus." She said the name softly. It had been her father's name as well.

As Shelby wandered over to the window, she wondered what her brother would look like now, had he lived. Absentmindedly, she peered through the blinds. To her surprise and chagrin, the man from the park, Raphael Blaize, was stepping onto her porch. Shelby couldn't believe it. He had come to her home! Well, this time he had gone too far.

Shelby went to the door and flung it open. "I'm going to call the police."

"Call them." Blaize's voice was teasingly cool. "It still won't solve the problem."

"Problem. What problem? From what I can see, *you* are the problem."

"No, your brother is. He is the one who left without taking care of his responsibilities. I don't have a problem with you, Ms. Russau." Blaize paused. "I simply want to talk to your brother. This is where he can find me." He placed a hotel business card on the windowframe.

Shelby looked at the card. "You're going to be waiting for a mighty long time."

"So you don't plan to tell him."

"I can't tell him. He died sixteen years ago."

Blaize's eyes narrowed. "What?"

"You heard me. So I can't imagine what kind of urgent business you could possibly have with my dead brother."

"So he died when he returned home from Grenada?"

"How did you know that Cleophus served in Operation Urgent Fury?" Shelby was more distrustful than ever.

"I know. I also know he fathered a child by my sister during his stay. That's why—"

"No. No." Shelby shook her head. "Wait one damn minute. You're saying my brother had an illegitimate child by your sister?"

Blaize appeared to smart at the word *illegitimate*. "Call it what you want. He is the boy's father."

"How do you know that?"

"Marlene told me."

"Marlene, meaning your sister?"

"That's right. She was eighteen years old when he got her pregnant. And instead of doing the right thing and marrying her, he left her behind and returned to America."

"I don't believe a word of it." Shelby crossed her arms protectively in front of her.

"So what are *you* saying? My sister is lying about who fathered her child?" Blaize's handsome features turned hard.

"I don't know who is lying." Shelby showed Blaize her palms. "You pop up out of nowhere, stalk me in the park, then show up at my house, telling me I have a nephew." Her thick head of twists bobbed emphatically. "My brother would never leave his child behind without caring for it. Family meant too much to us for him to do that."

"That's not how I see it." Blaize's voice was a rough whisper. "I see that your brother had his fun with some island girl, got her pregnant, and took the first opportunity that came his way to forget the whole mess." He reached inside one of his jean pockets.

"And it took you sixteen years to come to this conclusion?" Shelby placed her hands on her hips.

A thick eyebrow shot up. "I am here now to right this wrong," Blaize announced. "Take a look at this." He held out a piece of paper between them.

Shelby's heart lurched as she stared at the creased object. *What if Blaize is telling me the truth?* she thought. *That Cleophus left his child behind. It would destroy the image of how I thought Cleophus felt about family. About me.* Shelby was not up to facing that possibility. "I'm not taking anything from you," she retorted, tightening her arms about her. "And I don't know if you've righted any wrongs today, but as far as I'm concerned you've had your say. Now, I'm warning you. Get off of my porch, or I'm going to have you arrested."

They stared at each other.

Shelby watched as Blaize sized her up with a look that could burn. She nearly winced from the heat of his gaze, but she didn't dare show him how he affected her. And affect her he did in more ways than one, for despite their battle she was quite aware that Blaize was a superb specimen of a man. Her awareness of that peeved her. *He is vilifying my brother. I've got some nerve finding him attractive.*

"All right, Ms. Russau." Blaize folded the paper and returned it to his pocket. "But I'm going to tell you something." His tone turned silky, but there was a knife beneath the cloth. "I come from an ancient line of Grenadian people who believe a family's blood connection is very sacred. And when that sanctity is dishonored, horrible things can occur."

His eyes bore into hers as he stepped within a foot of Shelby. "My nephew is sixteen now. It is almost beyond the time when he should have gone through a rite of passage. A rite that my family has performed for many generations. He has fallen physically ill because this rite, which requires the presence of his matriarchal and patriarchal lines, has not been honored. The doctors say he has chronic anemia. And this may be true. But the root of this disease is in the spiritual realm. That is where everything starts. The disease is the physical result of the spiritual ailment."

"Look, I've warned you—" Shelby tried to interrupt.

"No, you must listen. I would not have come here if there had been a way around it. The boy needs a blood transfusion, and none of the blood types of my family members match. He is AB−, and it must come from the father's side of the family."

"I know it is extremely rare. I am AB−." The realization struck her. Shelby laughed in Blaize's face to keep from screeching. "I don't believe you're standing here telling me this."

"But I am. You or someone in your family may be able to save him. Without the transfusion or the rite, my nephew . . . your nephew could die."

Blaize's intensity frightened Shelby. She edged back inside the doorway. *I shouldn't have opened the door. He could be insane!* She looked down the street to see if any of her neighbors were walking their dogs or taking their evening stroll. She was comforted by the sight of two shadowy figures coming up the public sidewalk. "If you don't leave now"—she stepped inside the house—"I'm going to call the police."

Blaize noticed how quickly Shelby's full breasts were rising and falling beneath her summer smock.

He knew she was frightened. For a moment he had forgotten how different her culture was from his own. He wondered what was going through her mind. She probably thought he was lying, or that the rite of passage sounded barbaric, to say the least. He watched her closely. Blaize could see the flight or fight in Shelby's eyes. Alluring eyes. Blaize wondered which she would choose if she were pushed to the limit. Fight, he decided. He could sense the fire in her. *But why do I care about Shelby Russau?* he silently wondered. *She is not my concern. I am here to save my nephew. And that means I must not frighten her any further or she may never come around. Since the boy's father is dead, Shelby Russau must be the one to come to Grenada.* "I'm leaving, Ms. Russau."

Blaize backed away. "But if you do not come to Grenada soon, *our* nephew might die." The words dropped like stones between them. "And his death would be on your family's hands." Blaize let his words sink in before he opened the porch door and disappeared up the street.

Shelby went inside and stood with the door pressed against her back. What had just transpired was almost too much to bear. Her gaze searched the familiar surroundings, but she saw nothing. Could it be true? After all these years of thinking she was alone, she had a nephew? Shelby shook her head. No, it was impossible. Cleophus would not have abandoned his baby.

Shelby didn't remember much about her brother, but she remembered how strongly Cleophus felt about family ties. After their parents died, Cleophus had promised her nothing would come between them. Nothing did—except death.

Looking back, Shelby knew Cleophus was speaking out of the pain of being parentless and left with the responsibility of taking care of his little sister. But he took that responsibility oh, so seriously. Shelby knew he would never have left a child behind.

"This guy must be mistaken. When Cleophus returned from Grenada he barely talked about the country." Shelby looked around her as she spoke aloud. "But there is the possibility that he thought I was too young to deal with what had happened over there. Then, of course, it wasn't long before he became ill." She went back to her bedroom and sat on the bed. "Blood transfusion." Shelby looked at the veins in her arms before she looked in the mirror. "Rite of passage. Nobody does that kind of thing in this day and age, do they? It sounds like something out of the Dark Ages."

Shelby started to put on her nightgown, but she thought of Raphael Blaize and decided to give the house one last security check. Although she didn't feel he would harm her, she could never be too careful.

When Shelby felt confident Blaize had not returned and couldn't get in, she put on her nightgown and climbed into bed. She tossed and turned as she thought about the things he'd said. Perhaps Blaize suffered from delusions. Or perhaps the Cleophus he sought was not her brother. On and on she attempted to reconcile the Pandora's box Blaize had opened, but the unsettling thoughts would not be appeased and they flowed over into Shelby's dreams.

Chapter 3

In her dream, the heated sound of drums had called Shelby to the bedroom window. It was as if her heart was keeping time with the staccato beat, making breathing difficult. It had been a long time since she'd had an asthma attack, and Shelby flung open the window hoping to gulp the cool night air. To her surprise, when she drew her first deep breath hot air singed her lungs. Shelby's hand went up to her throat. She realized the air was aflame from a fire that burned several yards away. "Oh my God, there's a fire in my backyard."

Before Shelby knew it, she was outside and in her yard. She reached down to turn on the garden hose spigot, but a large, strong hand covered hers.

"The fire is within you," the accented voice spoke in her ear. "It is your need to know the truth. It is your need to live your life like a blazing flame."

Shelby turned around and there stood Blaize.

"Why have you come back?" She spoke with her face mere inches from his. Like the air around them, his body exuded heat, causing Shelby's temperature to rise even further.

"I am the Blaize," he said with the fire roaring behind him, his thick locks outlined by a golden glow. "Through me you will taste life like you have never tasted it before. It is your desire and your destiny." Blaize took both of Shelby's hands and began to lead her toward the fire. Her feet moved of their own volition as she stared at his naked chest.

"The truth is in Grenada, Shelby." Blaize stood aside but held on to her hand. Together, they stood staring into the flame. "Like you, perhaps your brother did not know his future was in my homeland."

Shelby watched the flames dance and leap. She was pleased to hear Blaize acknowledge that he might have misjudged Cleophus. A peace settled within her as the orange-and-red tongues turned to gold and images swirled within them. At first they were hard to discern, but soon one materialized in the flame; seconds later she could see a ship with a couple standing on the deck. Instantly, Shelby recognized the scene. She felt it was only fitting that it was the couple from her childhood vision, but this time it was Blaize's eyes that looked back at her, and she was the woman in his embrace. . . .

Shelby suddenly awakened. When she collected

her wits, and although she had slept nearly an entire night, she felt tired. She sat on the side of the bed with her head hanging down. Vestiges of the dream swarmed in her mind like wisps of smoke. The implications of the images were unclear. *What did it all mean?* she wondered—a question she hadn't asked herself for years. As a child she had determined there were no meanings, no explanations. It was the safest answer for bad things happening to good people and little children.

Shelby looked out the window at the sun peeking over the horizon. Perhaps, even in her sleep Raphael Blaize's presence was overwhelming.

As Shelby dressed, the dream and the man consumed her thoughts. She couldn't remember anything in her adult life that had affected her more.

On her way to work Shelby realized one thing weighed heaviest on her mind. In the dream, Blaize had said, like her, Cleophus did not know his future was in Grenada. She looked in the rearview mirror. Was it possible Cleophus had fathered a child but never knew it? Shelby drove away as the traffic light turned green. She knew the answer to that question. Of course it was *possible*.

"I will be glad when five o'clock gets here," Shelby's coworker at the county court clerk's office complained to nobody in particular. "This has been one long day."

"I know that's right," another female chimed.

Shelby heard the remarks but didn't look up from her desk. She was accustomed to the women's chatter. During her five years of work there, the talk had remained the same: men, money problems, weight gain. The young women seemed to complain more than the old.

"What are you going to do tonight, Mary?" a female in a tight yellow dress asked.

"Nothing if I don't get out of here," the fed-up woman replied.

"Let's go back to the club where we went the other night."

"That's a possibility." Mary looked at the large wall clock. "I swear, y'all, somebody fixed that clock. It's been a quarter to five for the last ten minutes."

Silence filled the office before an expressive "oh" erupted from Mary's throat. "May I help you?" Her voice turned into syrup.

It was always the same, Shelby thought, continuing to look at her work. Whenever a good-looking man entered the room the women put on their best faces.

"I need information about obtaining dual citizenship for someone born in another country," a familiar, accented voice replied.

The quip, "You can marry me, sweetie," was hurled across the room. It was followed by laughter and affirmations.

Shelby's stomach dropped as she watched Blaize

glance at her assertive coworker. His lips hinted that he might be amused, but his eyes remained as cold as steel.

"I guess you're not his type," one of the women teased.

"I can be whatever type he wants," the sassy female insisted, but in a lower voice.

Blaize's gaze met Shelby's. Their eyes locked, then Shelby looked away, but not before Mary, who was assisting Blaize, made a note of the interaction.

"You're in the wrong office." Mary pulled herself up to her fullest height and wriggled just a tad. "You've got to go to Tampa for the immigration office. We don't have one here in St. Pete."

"I see." Blaize continued to look at Shelby.

With her hand on her hip, Mary looked from Blaize to Shelby. "Sorry we can't help you." Her tone reflected her irritation.

Slowly, Blaize turned and walked out of the office.

"O-o-oh, honey. I didn't know they made 'em like that," one of the women said. "And I'm surprised at you, Mary. Normally, with a man that good-looking, you would have given him the address to the Immigration Office and anything else he might need."

"We-ell . . . it was obvious he wasn't interested in me," Mary insinuated. "Maybe Shelby should have got it for him."

"Say what?" her accomplice chimed.

"Didn't you see them making goo-goo eyes at each other?"

"Not Ms. Russau. She'd never stoop to anything that low." The office vibrated with sniggles.

"I wasn't making goo-goo eyes at anybody," Shelby spoke up.

"What would you call it then?" Mary inquired.

"I'm not going to validate this with a discussion." Shelby began to stack the folders and papers on her desk.

"Now I know something's up." Mary wouldn't let go. "When has Shelby prepared to leave before anybody else? It's five minutes to closing time and she's already getting ready to go." She pursed her lips. "Russell says, sometimes you're still here while he's trying to clean up."

Unnerved that Raphael Blaize was the source for the ribbing, Shelby's temper flared. "Why don't you all stay out of my business?"

"Mary, I think you've stepped into something now," Mary's friend remarked. "You better leave Shelby alone. I've never seen her this riled."

With her peripheral vision Shelby saw one of the women poke the other. She grabbed the stack of file folders, pulled her purse strap up on her shoulder and walked across the room. She dropped the files on top of a file cabinet before she turned toward the door.

"See you on Monday, Shelby," one woman said.

"Have a good weekend," another added.

"You do the same," Shelby replied with her back facing them.

"It's about time she had some business for us to butt into," one of the workers quipped, not quite out of hearing range. The office erupted in laughter.

Chapter 4

Shelby sat back from the restaurant table. "When did you get back?"

A smile curved Linda's lips. "We got in late last night."

Shelby examined her friend's face. There was a special air about her. A kind of peace Shelby had never sensed before. "It must have been two weeks of fun, huh?"

"It was wonderful, Shelby. Simply wonderful." Linda looked at her with sparkling eyes.

For a second Shelby felt a spark of jealousy. It was quickly doused by happiness for her childhood friend. Shelby knew that Linda had found something special during her year-long relationship with James. She only wished she could say the same for herself.

"Shelby . . ." Linda said, her voice full of joy.

"What is it?" Shelby leaned forward

Linda opened her mouth to speak. Then she

broke into a huge smile before she showed Shelby her left hand.

Shelby looked down at the small stone twinkling up at her. "James asked you to marry him?"

Linda nodded enthusiastically. "And you *know* what I said."

"Oh, my God. You're getting married." All Shelby could think about was how Linda's marriage would change their twenty-year friendship. She tried not to look shocked, but she knew that what she was feeling and thinking was written all over her face. "Congratulations." Her voice trembled.

"Aw-w, Shel." Linda grabbed her hand. "We'll still see each other."

"I know." Shelby's hand went up to her mouth. "I'm pitiful, aren't I?" She batted back the tears that were forming.

"No, you're not pitiful. We've been friends for a mighty long time. And my marrying James won't change that."

"You're right." Shelby's twists bobbed as she nodded. "We'll still get together and do things. It's not like you're leaving or anything."

Linda looked down. "No. At least I won't be leaving right away."

Shelby's eyes widened.

"James' parents are getting old," Linda rushed on. "And he's been looking into moving back to his hometown of Ft. Pierce. He thinks he has a pretty hot lead on a job there." Linda started bubbling again. "He's expecting a call from the company tomorrow. And if things go as we've planned, we'll get married in six months, and I'll start my new life with James in Ft. Pierce."

"It all sounds wonderful, Linda." Shelby couldn't stop a wayward tear that escaped from the corner of her eye.

"Shell, don't be sad." Linda clutched at her hand.

Shelby felt a guilty pang. "I'm not sad. Look, these are tears of joy." In a way she was telling the truth.

"For real?"

"Of course, girl. What kind of friend would I be if they weren't?" Shelby tried to ignore the feeling that James was taking her friend away.

"Wow." Linda sighed with relief. "That's all I needed to hear, Shelby. I was so worried about you. We've been like sisters. You know, in a way I feel like I'm the only family you have. I couldn't be happy knowing that you were hurting."

"I know that." Shelby patted her friend's hand. "So don't even think about it. Enjoy." A real smile crossed Shelby's lips. "You're getting married, woman. To a man you love. There's nothing more wonderful than that."

Linda beamed, but as she searched Shelby's eyes a worried look creased her brow.

Shelby placed both her elbows on the table and

rested her chin on her crisscrossed fingers. "You know something else?"

"What?" Linda replied.

"You're underestimating me, a-as usual." Shelby presented what she hoped was a smug look. "You're not the only one with special news."

"Really?" Linda put her hands on her hips, then narrowed her eyes. "Don't tell me you went out with that guy from the park."

Shelby was surprised by a nervous whirring in her stomach. "No, I didn't go out with him. But he's connected with what I've got to tell you." She paused meaningfully.

Linda stared at Shelby. "I've known you for a long time and you've never been this cagey." A leery look crossed her features. "Are you doing this just because I told you I was getting married and you don't want me to worry about your being lonely?" Linda cocked her head.

"No." Shelby was a bit offended by Linda's implication, even though a part of her felt Linda was right. To her surprise, in response, Shelby blurted, "I've got a nephew."

"You've got a what?" Linda's eyes narrowed.

"A nephew." Shelby held her head high. "At least there's a big possibility that I do."

"How do you figure that, Shel?" Linda was skeptical.

"It's rather amazing when I think about it." Shelby began to assuage her bruised pride. Linda wasn't the only one who had exciting things happening in her life. "The guy you saw in the park. He's from the country of Grenada. Grenada is in the Caribbean, you know."

"I know that." Linda leaned forward. "Isn't that where Cleophus served in the army before he died?"

"Yes, it was." Shelby swallowed. She could feel her heart pounding. "Well, Raphael Blaize, that's the guy from the park, he told me his sister had a baby by Cleophus after he left the country."

"My goodness." It was Linda's time to be shocked. Shelby was pleased. Linda started shaking her head. "Is he sure? Are you sure? You know you didn't have a good feeling about that guy the first time you met him. Maybe he's trying to run some kind of scam or something. Did he ask you to help get him a green card?"

"No, he didn't." Shelby was truly offended. "Maybe you hadn't noticed but I'm not stupid, Linda. I didn't jump on this with both hands and feet the first time he told me about it."

"Of course you didn't. I'm just surprised," Linda explained. "Aren't you?"

"Shocked would be a better word," Shelby said quietly.

"Did he show you some kind of proof that this baby is your nephew?"

"He's not a baby anymore. He's sixteen years old." Shelby glanced at the couple in a nearby booth. "And no, he didn't. I didn't give him a chance. My reaction was similar to yours. Skeptical. But maybe a bit more dramatic," Shelby confessed.

"I can imagine it was. So when was the last time you talked to this guy? What did you say his name was?"

"It's been two weeks." Shelby recalled how Blaize showed up at her job. That was the last time she had seen him. She thought about the hotel card he'd placed on her windowsill. Now it was sitting on the mantel in her living room. "His name is Raphael Blaize."

"Wow, Shelby. I don't know what to say." They lapsed into silence before Linda started up again. "Did your brother ever mention a girlfriend or anybody special in Grenada? I mean, I don't remember him as the kind of guy that would just sleep with a woman without having some feelings for her. I know being in the service and away from home can bring out interesting qualities in a man, but we all kind of looked up to Cleophus. Especially after he was called for Operation Urgent Fury."

"You know I looked up to him. He was my big brother, and because of that he probably felt I was too young to talk to about personal things like the women in his life."

"It's kind of strange that we are having this conversation. I mean about Cleophus and all, because guess who I saw at the African Festival Market this morning?"

"Who?"

"Willie Wesley."

"Cleophus' friend?"

"Yeah."

"I thought he moved up north."

"Evidently, he did. He came back when his mother died and moved into the house where he grew up. But he says he's been back in St. Pete for a couple of months now, although he doesn't have a telephone."

"He told you all that?" Shelby asked, surprised.

"No." Linda shook her head. "He wouldn't know me from Adam's housecat. I'm sure if he remembers me at all, I would be some pesky kid that used to gawk at him all the time."

Shelby smiled slightly.

Linda continued, "He was talking to one of the guys running a booth at the market, and I overheard."

"Willie Wesley." Shelby repeated the familiar name. "Everybody had a crush on him. Is he still handsome?"

"Sort of. His face is real puffy now, but you can see traces of how good-looking he used to be. I think he drinks. . . ." Linda made a face. "Heavily."

"Why do you say that?" Shelby frowned.

"Because it was ten thirty in the morning and he smelled like a distillery."

"Oh. How sad," Shelby replied. "Cleophus used to visit him an awful lot when he came back from Grenada. And if my memory serves me right, it was right after Cleophus died that Willie moved away."

"Maybe Willie knows some intimate details about your brother's life in the Caribbean," Linda suggested.

Shelby thought about it for a second. "That's a possibility."

"You said Cleophus was over there all the time after he came back. If Cleophus had a woman that meant anything to him, he probably would have told Willie."

"I think you're right."

"You should go by and see him," Linda suggested.

"Maybe I'll go by tomorrow." Shelby looked down at her watch. "Actually, I could go by after we finish eating."

Linda sat back as the waitress placed a chicken-and-vegetable plate in front of her. "I would if I were you."

Shelby inhaled the aroma of clam chowder that drifted toward her from the table. "Right now, Linda, you'd probably agree with everything."

Linda looked puzzled. "Why do you say that?"

"Because you're getting married." They looked at each other and shared a familiar squeal.

Chapter 5

There were cars lined up and down the sidewalk, but Shelby was only vaguely aware of them. It had been awhile since she had visited the neighborhood near Jordan Park. The entire area was on an upswing after experiencing the downward spiral many neighborhoods and government housing projects had suffered.

A bit uncertain, Shelby approached Willie Wesley's house. Willie's frame house was a bit more in need of repair than those of his neighbors. It looked quiet and somber with the blinds closed. The yard was overgrown and untended, but the humid Florida weather had insured a profusion of blossoms throughout the thick foliage. Feeling uneasy, Shelby knocked on the door.

"Go around the back," a voice shouted from inside.

"Around the back." Shelby mumbled, but she did as she was told. To her surprise there were several groups of young men standing around talking. From the expressions on their faces they were just as surprised to see her. Shelby fortified herself and made her way through the human clusters.

"Hey, Baby. You came to see the action, huh?"

Action. What action? Shelby glanced at the young man, who had a mouth full of gold teeth. She gave a slight smile, but continued to move forward. *What in the world have I gotten myself into now? There's no telling what they will say if I turn around and head back to my car,* she thought as she eased past a heavy-set young man and climbed the stairs. *Where is Willie?* Shelby's gaze searched the open doorway.

A man standing just inside the door had his face averted. He was listening to the fellow behind him. Without looking at her, he held his hand out in Shelby's direction. She stood staring at his up-turned palm.

"That'll be five dollars."

"Five dollars?" Shelby looked around the kitchen. There was a scattering of men throughout the room. The man asking for money turned and looked at her. A smirk materialized on his angular face.

"You here for the dog fight?"

Shelby couldn't answer. She just stood there shaking her head.

"You're not here for the pit bull fight?" This time he was openly laughing at her.

"No." Shelby found her voice. "I'm looking for Willie Wesley."

"You sure you don't want to see the fight?" he asked teasingly.

Another guy yelled, "Hey Willie. Willie." All of the men stood and stared.

"What's zup?" A voice increased in volume as Willie drew nearer.

"Someone's here to see you, man."

"Who is it?" Willie asked as Shelby saw the vaguely familiar face appear in the doorway. Willie squinted. "Can I help you?"

"Hi. You don't remember me but I'm Cleo—"

"Shelby?" A dawning look of pleasant surprise blanketed Willie's street-worn features.

"Yes." A tremulous smile touched Shelby's lips. All she could think about was that this was Cleophus' friend. This was someone who cared about and really knew her brother.

In a couple of strides Willie was across the room holding Shelby in a bear hug, his eyes glistening with unshed tears. "I can't believe this. It's been such a long time."

"It sure has," Shelby said hugging him back, overlooking the smell of liquor.

Willie let go and looked down into her face. A reminiscent smile surfaced before he looked around the kitchen. "Y'all excuse me," he announced. "This was my homeboy's little sister. He died awhile back. But when I looked into her face, I could see him there." Willie looked at Shelby again.

"That's all right, dawg," one young man said. "It's all good."

"That's for real," another man echoed.

Willie smiled. "What are you doing here?"

"I came here to talk to you," Shelby replied, feeling out of place.

"Well." Willie glanced around. "We can't talk in here. Let's go outside." He started toward the door. "Y'all give me a few minutes, but if I'm not back in a reasonable time, start without me." They walked through the backyard and around to the front of the house, where Willie sat down on the steps. Shelby followed suit.

"So how you been?" He shook her shoulder. "You lookin' good."

"I've been fine. I work at the County Court Clerk's Office. I've been there for five years now."

"Really." Willie nodded. "Time really goes by. I remember you as Cleophus' little sister who always wore a ponytail, not some woman who works in an office. Cleophus would be proud of you."

Shelby didn't know if that was true, but found herself smiling anyway.

"So you never left St. Pete?" Willie continued.

"No, I didn't. But you know there aren't many people that are born here who leave. At least that's the way it seems." Shelby watched as a middle-aged man nodded to Willie, then walked to the back of the house. She tried to concentrate on the conversation at hand. "But I heard you had moved up north. I was surprised to hear you were back in town."

"Yeah, I lived in Detroit for awhile. Tried my hand there." Willie ran a soft-looking hand over his salt-and-pepper hair. "But it was too cold and too much snow for me. I was ready to come back after the first winter. I kept saying I was going to move back, but I didn't have the resources, so the years kept rolling by. And then my mother died. I came back here for her funeral." Sadness shadowed his face. "I've been here ever since. I wish I had come back sooner."

They sat in silence.

"So what made you look me up?" Willie asked.

"I've been thinking about Cleophus a lot lately," Shelby replied. "I realized because I was so young I really didn't know how he felt after he came back from Grenada. The things he thought about during his last days. I know he used to come and visit you a lot. So I thought you might be able to help me remember my brother a little more clearly."

"Oh. I see." Willie nodded his head for awhile. "To tell you the truth, Shelby, Cleophus was basically the same after he got back. He was glad to be back, even though from the very beginning his health wasn't good." Willie squinted his eyes. "He talked about the things he saw over there and the people he met. He said things were different in that country. But he seemed to manage okay."

"I thought he was glad to be home," Shelby replied. "As far as I could tell he seemed satisfied." She searched for a way to find out more. "But of course, like I said, I was pretty young back then. I might not have been able to tell if anything was bothering him."

"I wouldn't say anything was bothering him. He formed some relationships while he was over there. But he knew you were here and, in his mind, you were his first obligation. I guess you know how Cleophus felt about family."

Shelby nodded. "But he did leave some friends behind in Grenada?"

"The main friendships he made were with guys in his outfit. But he did mention a woman that he had gotten rather close to. Cleophus said she was a little on the young side, and although she wanted to come back to the States with him, he felt she'd be better off there. Said she had some issues with her family that he felt she needed to deal with."

"Really?" Shelby bit her lip. "Do you remember how old she was?"

"I think Cleophus said she was seventeen or eighteen years old."

"Eighteen," Shelby said quietly.

"So he told you about her?"

"No. Someone else did." The front door opened behind them as Shelby thought of what Blaize had said.

"Hey, dawg. We're having some problems back here. That dude with the Lac and the purple-and-red chameleon paint job claims he betted on the white pit with blue eyes. You know, the one that won the last time. He says he gave you quite a bundle and he wants to be paid."

Willie turned halfway around. "I don't know what he's talking about. That man didn't give me no money."

"Well you better come in here and talk to him because he acts like he's about to flip out if he don't get paid."

"All right. I'll be there."

Shelby stood up. "I don't want to keep you, Willie. I can see you've got business to tend to."

"Yeah. It seems like I need to see what's happening back there." He stood up.

"It was good talking to you. And you've been more help than you'll ever know."

Willie squeezed her arm. "It was good seeing you too. So don't be a stranger. Come around and see me sometimes. Things aren't always this busy."

Shelby glanced at the man standing inside the house as Willie opened the creaky screen door. "You take care now."

"You do the same," Shelby replied.

Willie closed the door behind him.

Chapter 6

Blaize was aware of the people scattered along the beach, watching the sunset, but he kept his gaze riveted on the sky. At first the sand felt hot beneath his feet, but as he drew closer to the water, it cooled with each step. Finally, he stood where the sand was dark and moist, and the surf began to lap at his ankles. He closed his eyes to imprint the colors of the painted sky, orangish yellow, mauve and indigo, onto his memory. There was one thing that was always the same no matter where you traveled, Blaize reminded himself—the sky and the stories it told. This evening, like every evening, it revealed the never-ending cycle of light giving over to the dark, and the dark giving in to the light.

Blaize opened his eyes when a giggling child brushed against his leg. He watched the boy regain his balance and continue on to the water.

"Be careful," a woman said, following at a protective distance. She stopped near Blaize. "I'm sorry. I hope he didn't get sand on you."

"No problem," Blaize replied.

"We don't get to go to the beach that often. We're on vacation."

Blaize nodded.

"Are you on vacation?"

He shook his head slightly. "No."

"We try to come here every year," the woman continued, seemingly oblivious to Blaize's distant demeanor. "We're from Philadelphia, but we love coming to the St. Petersburg/Clearwater area." She kept the child within her sight. "So you live here?"

Blaize studied the persistent woman before he answered. She was probably in her mid-thirties. Her body was thick, her brown hair frizzy. "No. I live in Grenada."

"Grenada. Isn't that in the Caribbean?"

He nodded.

"Well, what are you doing here? If I lived in the Caribbean I'd probably never leave."

A genuine spark touched Blaize's eyes. "It was difficult, but what I came here to do was very important."

"Oh. Look at that!" the woman exclaimed as the sun slowly sank below the water's edge. "That is amazing. Absolutely amazing. It's like you can actually see the sun going down." She began to fold the towel that had been hanging on her arm. "Come back up this way now, Brian," she shouted. "I don't want you going too far out into the water. It will be dark in a few minutes, and we have to go see Daddy." She looked around. "The light from the hotels doesn't reach this far. It probably gets really dark down here."

"But that is a powerful time. That's when the stars come out." Blaize gazed upward. "A glittering road map in the sky."

"I like the way you said that." The woman smiled. "And with that accent. A road map in the sky. But a road to what? I guess only God knows."

"My grandfather and my father knew."

"You're kidding me." She held the towel against her breasts.

"No. For generations members of my family were known as Stargazers."

"You mean like in astrology?"

"Not quite." Blaize thought of his family and the timbre of his voice thickened. "The constellations were the base of their knowledge, but when they stared at the sky they would notice how certain stars grew brighter or darker, or appeared to drift. They would read the message within the subtleties."

She threw her head back and laughed, totally impressed. "You're too much. What kind of messages?"

"Things about our lives. Our past. The future." Blaize looked at the first pinprick of light that twinkled in the north.

"Now I know I've got to go to the Caribbean.

That's unbelievable," the woman exclaimed. "But it takes a little more money to go there. And we're barely making it down here. C'mon Brian," she called. "It's time to start heading back." The little boy ran toward his mother and wrapped himself around her leg. Her body jerked at the impact. "You know, I'm going to start paying more attention to the stars. But since Brian was born I haven't had much time to do anything." She looked down at him lovingly and patted him on the back before she took his hand. "Daddy's going to start worrying if we don't get back to the house. It was nice chatting with you," she said to Blaize. "And I'm going to make it my business to get to the Caribbean. Even if I don't go to Grenada. I want to go somewhere down there. That was a lovely story," she remarked, walking away.

Story? Blaize thought. *That was no story. It was the truth. It's hard for Americans to believe anything that their scientists have not told them. Everything else is a story. A myth.* He thought about Shelby Russau. *It's been more than two weeks since I've seen her. I made sure I stayed away, but time is running out. I wouldn't have come if I didn't believe I would not be returning to Grenada alone.* He looked up at the sky that was slowly filling up with stars. *I don't have the ability my ancestors had but I'm certain the stars assured me of that.* Reluctantly, Blaize's mind recalled the rest of the message. *This person will teach you the meaning of attachment.*

Blaize could feel a knot form in his stomach. He didn't want to feel attached to anyone. A guilty pang added, *who is not family. Especially a foreigner.*

For years he had lived as a hermit, and his desire for human contact had dwindled with each passing day.

He stared at the emerging stars. Perhaps his interpretation had been inaccurate. It had been a long time since he had attempted stargazing. There had been no need for it. He hadn't cared about the future.

But then Marlene returned to Hummingbird Island with the boy, and Blaize knew the way he had been living had to come to an end. Cleophus symbolized a new chance at life. A new beginning for the Blaize family. The rift between Blaize and Marlene was wide. Perhaps Cleophus would build a bridge between them, and provide a way for Blaize to fulfill the promise he had made to his parents the day they died. "I have finally found the desire to fulfill my promise. I will not let the old ways die."

Shelby unlocked her front door and picked up the business card Blaize had left. She walked over to the telephone and placed her hand on the receiver. The telephone startled her when it rang.

"Hello."

"Did you go?" Linda's anxious voice came over the line.

"Yes, I went."

"And?"

"There's a strong possibility Raphael Blaize was telling the truth."

"So Willie knew about the woman in Grenada?"

"He knew about *a* woman in Grenada that Cleophus was involved with. He said she was rather young. Seventeen or eighteen years old. Willie said Cleophus really cared about her, but he felt she had some pressing family issues to resolve before she considered leaving Grenada."

"Still, that could be anybody, Shelby," Linda replied, frustrated.

"I've got a feeling it's not." She looked at the business card. "I feel Blaize is telling the truth."

"Well, there's one way to find out."

"Yeah, I know. I was about to give him a call when you called."

"So where is he staying?"

"At the Heritage House, downtown."

"I don't know, Shelby. If I were you I'd probably try to catch him off guard. I don't know if I would call him and let him know I was coming." There was silence on the line.

"Doesn't your cousin Joyce work there?" Shelby asked.

"The last I heard she was working in housekeeping. That's an idea. Maybe she can help you out."

"Maybe," Shelby replied. "I think I'll pop over there tomorrow. Do a little lurking around."

"Okay now. I know you. Your imagination can run a little wild when you get involved with something. I think it comes from looking at too many old movies and not getting any for such a long time."

"I knew you were going to throw that in there."

"Hey. Those hormones are all bottled up. It's got to be messing with your brain," Linda teased.

"I'm going to hang up on you," Shelby threatened.

"Okay. Okay. I'm done." Linda paused. "So you're going to go over there tomorrow?"

"Yes. I think I'll go right after work."

"Give me a buzz and let me know what you find out."

"I will, Sherlock Holmes."

"Bye, Queen of the Celebates." The line went dead.

Shelby looked at the receiver and shook her head. Linda had such a way with words. Although, in truth, after two years of being alone Shelby felt she deserved that crown.

Chapter 1

"I know *exactly* who you're talking about." Joyce's head emphasized her words. "There's not a woman working here in the hotel who hasn't seen him or been talking about him. But *I'm* the one who gets to clean his room. I don't know what kind of cologne he wears, but it's just right there when you enter the room. Smells so good. But you know what? I don't think it is cologne. I haven't seen any cologne in his bathroom. But I have seen some little bottles of oils."

Shelby stood, listening patiently. She hadn't been able to get a word in edgewise since she mentioned Blaize's name.

"He's in room two-zero-two," Joyce whispered conspiratorially.

"He is?"

"Yeah. But I can't let you in there. I'll get fired."

"No." Shelby shook her head vehemently. "I never expected you to let me in his room. I'm just trying to find out a little bit more about him. Does he seem like a regular guy? Or does he have weird people hanging around, or coming to see him?"

"He seems like a loner to me," Joyce said quickly. "I haven't seen anybody visiting him. And there surely haven't been any women going in there because I would have heard about that." Her eyebrows went up. "You really like this guy, don't you? I mean, to come down here and ask questions about him, you must."

"It's not about that," Shelby explained. "This is strictly business."

Joyce gave a clear impression that she didn't believe her, but she kept her mouth shut. She unbuttoned the top of her uniform. "Well, I'm about to get on out of here. I'm so glad it's Friday I don't know what to do. And,"—she beamed—"I've got the weekend off."

"Sounds good," Shelby replied. "And thanks again." But Joyce was already heading through the door.

Shelby looked around the lobby, then walked toward the elevator. She wasn't quite sure what she was going to do, but once she was inside she punched the button to the second floor. With a tiny jerk the elevator headed upward. Moments later the doors slid open and Shelby stepped out into the hall. It was quiet as only an empty hotel corridor can be. She looked at the signs that explained what rooms were where, before she headed toward

Blaize's room. As Shelby approached the door, she slowed up and listened for noises inside. She couldn't hear a thing. She glanced up and down the corridor, then backed up and leaned in. Shelby pressed her ear against the metal.

"What are you expecting to hear?"

She jumped. Her mouth remained open as she turned and faced Blaize. He was holding an ice bucket.

"I—I was just . . . I was just—"

"It's obvious what you were doing. You were trying to hear inside my room." He stepped up and unlocked the door. "I'll make it easy for you. Why don't you come inside?"

Embarrassed and surprised, Shelby automatically stepped into the hotel room. When Blaize closed the door behind her she realized the precariousness of the situation. All of Shelby's senses were on guard as she watched Blaize place the ice bucket on the counter. He proceeded by dropping a couple of ice cubes into a glass. Then he poured pineapple juice into it. His serious gaze swiveled to Shelby, who was still standing. "Would you like some?"

"No." The word was breathy. Shelby took a hold of her voice. "No, thank you."

"Why don't you sit down."

Shelby looked at the couch, but didn't move.

"I thought for sure you would take advantage of this opportunity. It is much better than lurking outside my hotel door." A condescending look marred his handsome features. "But of course I don't know if it is in you Americans to be on the level."

Shelby's eyes turned into instant slits. "What I was doing is no worse than your stalking me in the park." She started counting the incidents off on her fingers. "At my house. On my job."

"I wasn't stalking you. It was my intention to approach you. I did that at the park and at your house."

"You came to my house without an invitation, I might add."

"That is true," Blaize said calmly. "But when I came to that office, I didn't know you would be there. It was a strange coincidence I must admit. But sometimes when things are meant to be, those kind of coincidences happen."

A wary look surfaced in Shelby's eyes. It was a little bit too much of a coincidence for her. Shelby's distrust mounted as they locked gazes.

"Why are you looking at me like that?" Blaize asked.

The look in his eyes was so serious Shelby couldn't imagine lightheartedness ever being there. "I don't know if I believe you," she replied. "And if I can't believe that, most certainly I shouldn't believe my brother has a son, and your sister is his mother."

Blaize put the glass down and walked across the room. When he returned he offered Shelby an envelope and a folded piece of paper. "Let's try this again." He held the objects out between them.

Shelby knew it was the same paper she had refused to take on her porch over two weeks ago. She stared at it, her heart pounding. Slowly, she took it and unfolded the creased square. It was a birth certificate for a Cleophus Blaize dated June 5, 1984. Cleophus Russau appeared as the father's name. Marlene Blaize was the mother. Shelby's eyes grazed the rest of the information before she opened the envelope. Up to that second her brain had been operating on cruise control. Everything was functioning on an even keel. She was taking things in without judgement.

But when Shelby saw the photo inside the envelope her brain stopped and her heart took over. It was Cleophus smiling at her. A young Cleophus. But how did Raphael Blaize get this picture? Alarmed, Shelby said, "As far as I know there have only been two pictures of Cleophus as a little boy. How did you get this one?"

"That *is* Cleophus," Blaize replied, softly, "but it is *not* your brother. It is his son."

"What?" Shelby stared at the photo, confused. It had to be her brother. The eyes and the lips were exactly the same. But as Shelby studied the details, she realized the backdrop was unusual. And there was something about the clothing that wasn't quite right. "You mean this really is my nephew?" She looked up at Blaize, her lips trembling.

"Yes."

The solitary reply was enough to plunge Shelby into emotional turmoil. Maybe it was all of those years of being orphaned, or the feeling of knowing she was totally alone that broke her down. But when Shelby looked at that photograph and realized she was not the last of her bloodline, she heard herself sob. A sound, as an adult, she had never heard before. "Oh my God, it is Cleophus' son. It's true. Cleophus has a child." Her knees started to buckle and she would have landed on the floor had it not been for Blaize.

"You should have accepted my invitation to sit down." His breath was warm against her ear as he cradled her, sitting with her gently on the couch. "What greater surprise can life hold than finding out you are one by blood with another human being? My ancestors believe it is one of the miracles of physical life."

Blaize's gentle, understanding words gave Shelby license to cry. She wanted to halt the flow of tears. She was not accustomed to crying. This made her emotional display in front of Blaize all the worse. But for Shelby, discovering after all those years that she had family tapped a reservoir of feelings that was old and deep. Nothing could stop the waterfall from her eyes.

Silently, Blaize allowed Shelby her release. Finally, he murmured, "So we do have something in common. The importance of family." He reached toward a pile of napkins and handed Shelby a square.

She accepted it eagerly, so painful was her awareness of how she must look. After she had done the best she could to dry her face Shelby looked at Blaize and mumbled, "Thank you."

"That's not necessary," he replied, looking into her misty eyes mere inches away. Blaize thought they were hauntingly beautiful in their misery. Vulnerable, with a history of sadness. Beautiful, but never having accepted their beauty.

"I can't stop crying," Shelby attempted to explain her behavior. "This has never happened before." She took a deep breath and was suddenly aware of the rich fragrance that hung about Blaize's person like a cloud. It filled her nostrils, and seemed to warm her as well as calm her down.

Blaize watched Shelby's discomfort with a growing unease of his own. He had reached out to comfort her, but now, as he sat close to her side, there was a desire to do more. It had been a long time since he had been this close to a woman, and the smell of Shelby called all of his senses to attention. Blaize's gaze trailed over her face, instinctively missing nothing. He found he yearned to touch it. To see if the skin was as smooth and soft as it appeared.

"I think I'll be okay now," Shelby said softly, trying to collect herself. She was pointedly aware of Blaize's muscular thigh pressed against hers and his strong arm draped around her shoulders. Once again, Shelby was also aware that she was alone with him in his hotel room.

Although Blaize heard Shelby, his mind did not focus on what she said but on the movement of her lips as she spoke. He had forgotten how inviting the nearness of a woman could be, and for a split second Blaize was only aware of the flash of pink as she formed the word think, and how full and soft her bottom lip became as Shelby spoke the word now.

"I can't believe I'm acting like this." She looked down at her lap, embarrassed even further as she thought about the entire scene. "I can imagine what you must think of me." She looked into Blaize's eyes. For a moment the intensity there shocked her. But almost like magic a veil was lowered, and it was gone. The transition was so smooth Shelby wasn't sure she had witnessed his raw emotions.

Blaize slid his arm from behind her back. "Would you care for something to drink now?"

"Like what? Pineapple juice?" Shelby's heart was racing.

"If you like. But I have something stronger if that suits your taste." Blaize kept his back to her.

"Pineapple juice will be just fine." Shelby watched his back muscles move beneath the thin T-shirt, and she wondered if he were keeping his face averted for a reason. But when Blaize walked toward her and handed her the glass, his eyes were steady and void of emotion. "So it's obvious, you believe me now."

"Yes." Shelby nodded her head. "Yes, I do."

"And you will come back with me to Grenada?" Blaize waited because Shelby didn't answer right away. He watched indecision play across her face, and Blaize found his hand tightening on his glass. He knew the exact moment Shelby made up her mind.

"Yes, I will," she stated with resolve.

Blaize felt his body relax. It unnerved him to realize, deep inside, that his eagerness to know if Shelby would be coming to Grenada extended beyond his concern for his nephew. He sat back and crossed his legs. His large hand stroked the condensation forming on the glass with light, long movements. "How soon can you leave?"

"I'll have to give notice at work," Shelby said, attempting not to stare at the way his fingers moved. "But I've got plenty of sick days that I haven't used. They've piled up over the years." She swallowed, but it almost felt painful, her mouth was so dry. "I should be able to leave by the middle of next week."

"That will give us time enough to prepare for the ritual," Blaize announced.

"The ritual . . ." Shelby's eyes widened. "I forgot about that." Her fingers curled around the edge of the couch. "Let me make something clear. The reason I'm going to Grenada is because Cleophus needs a blood transfusion. My blood type matches his. I haven't agreed to any ritual."

"You would stand in the way of his being healed because you do not believe in our customs?"

"If I didn't want the boy to get better, I wouldn't be going. And who's to say the ritual will help him anyway?"

"Is it your place to say it will not?" Blaize challenged.

"No, but—"

"Don't discount what you do not understand."

"I'm not discounting anything." Shelby could feel herself going on the defensive. "I'm just going by what you told me at my house. You said the boy needs a blood transfusion. It was a matter of life and death."

"That's exactly what I said," Blaize replied, his eyes hooded. "But I also said the root cause of his sickle cell anemia is not in the physical. It is in the spiritual."

"I'm sorry. I don't mean to put your beliefs down or anything, but I don't see the need to wait for you to do this ritual when the transfusion could be over and done with. Cleophus could be on his way to recovery. In my opinion, the transfusion should come first."

"Dr. Minor is a specialist in blood disorders. He won't be back to Grenada for another week and a half. I've scheduled the transfusion the day after he arrives."

"You did?" Once again Shelby was surprised. "How could you be so sure that someone would be returning with you to Grenada?"

"I have my ways of knowing," Blaize said quietly.

Shelby felt as if she were being drawn into an uncanny web. She tried to introduce some logic. "I guess you figured once the proof was presented there was no way you would be turned down."

"That among other things." Blaize's voice held a hint of mystery.

"Like what?" Shelby pressed, her curiosity and vexation rising with his vague answers.

"I don't think this is the time to discuss it," Blaize said, then paused. "Maybe there will never be a time when you will understand." He watched her closely.

"I don't think I like the sound of that." Shelby looked away. She knew Blaize was studying her, but she refused to be intimidated. "I think perhaps, if you really want me to come to Grenada, you shouldn't be so mysterious."

"I'm not being mysterious. I am being as forthright as I think you will permit me to be. It is obvious the gap between my culture and your understandings is wide. Let's leave it at that."

He placed the empty glass on the table. "You have the proof that you need to come to my country and help the boy. That is enough for now."

Shelby made a fed-up sound. "Where do you get

off telling me how much is enough? I guess you
think you know so much about Americans because
of your contact with us through Operation Urgent
Fury. But we are as individual as every other human being on this planet. I don't presume to know
what makes you tick, and it would suit me fine if
you weren't so presumptuous about me. I can tell
you, you have not figured me out in the fifteen
minutes that I have been here in this hotel room,
when nobody else has been able to in all these
years."

"Was that by choice, or have you just been difficult?" Blaize's voice was low.

Shelby rose from the couch. "Why don't I just
let you find out?" she replied with a fake smile.

"Who said I was interested?" Blaize retorted.

"I can see this is going to be one hell of a trip."
Shelby jerked her purse strap up on her shoulder.

"You never know." Blaize's voice turned to a
silky whisper. "Perhaps it will be your first taste of
heaven."

Startled, Shelby looked into his eyes, but Blaize
continued to talk, his words taking a totally different direction. "Contact me once you know the exact
day you will be able to leave. I will make our travel
arrangements on American Airlines. That's the air-
line that I used in flying here. All of your accommodations in Grenada will be taken care of by me,
of course."

Shelby looked down at him. "I haven't allowed

anyone that much control over my life since I was a little girl. I don't know if I like it."

"Perhaps it's time to find out." Blaize stood up and towered above her.

The energy between them was real and they both knew it. It was unnerving enough for Shelby to make a quick exit. "I'll call you and let you know," she said, closing the hotel door behind her.

Chapter 8

"Look, I'm going to meet this man before you get on some plane with him." Linda studied the people gathering in the American Airlines check-in line. "He's going to know that he's got somebody to answer to if you don't come back here in one piece. You can't trust people these days. Underneath that handsome exterior he might be a weirdo." Linda tilted her head purposefully, a familiar indicator for Shelby to take a look.

A tiny man in a colorful shirt was carefully watching everyone in the line. His crusty skin looked as if it had been burnt by the sun.

Shelby smiled at the obnoxious look on Linda's face. "I don't know how much more checking is possible. You had James' police buddies run him through the system to see if he wasn't some brother from Chicago running some island scam. But when you think about it, Linda, what good would it do him to scam me? I don't have any money." Shelby removed her driver's license from her wallet.

"I don't know. But it does seem like you have some other treasures he might be interested in. At least temporarily." Linda gave Shelby a knowing look. "And you know you're not a temporary girl."

Shelby thought about the scene in the hotel room. She knew Linda was thinking of it as well. She had told her everything. "This is not the kind of man that would have to jump through hoops to get a woman. Fight them off, yes. Get one, no. The only reason he's probably single is because of his attitude. You'd have to put up with a lot to be with a man like that."

"He sounds like the kind of guy that likes being single. It allows for a wider variety. You know what I mean."

"I don't know." Shelby threw up her hands. "And I'm not about to jump to conclusions about the man's sex life. It is not my concern." She didn't look at Linda because that wasn't exactly true.

"That's what you're saying now. But any woman spending a couple of weeks with a fellow like that is bound to get stirred up some kind of way. I just want you to be careful." Linda placed her palm over her heart. "Remember the C for commitment that's carved into your chest. Don't get out there in the rain forest and think he's Tarzan and you're some freewheeling Jane, because you're not, and you never will be."

"Next," the attendant called. Shelby was glad for

the reprieve. She rolled her luggage up to the counter.

"This will be the first test, you know," Linda said, carrying Shelby's carry-on bag. "I've never heard of an e-ticket."

"I have," Shelby replied, "although I've never used one."

"How do you know so much?" Linda challenged.

"I read about it someplace."

"I'm not talking about the e-ticket. I'm talking about how do you know it would take a lot to put up with a man like this Blaize?"

"Oh." Shelby placed her purse on the counter. "I can tell. I hate to admit it, but perhaps I see a little bit of the loner in myself in him. Hi," Shelby spoke to the attendant. "I've got an e-ticket on flight one-two-three-five, flying to Point Salinas International Airport in Grenada."

"Your last name, ma'am." The attendant's fingers flew over the keyboard.

"Russau."

"Shelby Russau?" The woman looked over her glasses.

"Yes."

"I've got you right here," the agent said, before going through a routine security spiel that ended with "May I see some picture I.D., please?"

Shelby offered her driver's license and turned back to Linda. "Now will you relax? Ever since I told you I was going to Grenada you have been more of a pain in the butt than usual.

I was already uneasy about the situation, but you've just made it worse."

"Somebody's got to look out for you. You're operating on pure emotion." Linda tried to talk softly, but the attendant's eyebrow went up anyway. "I can only guess how deeply you feel about helping this boy."

"My nephew," Shelby corrected her. "And I'm very capable of looking out for myself. I've had to be."

Linda ignored Shelby's last remarks. "*Possibly* your nephew. And going to a foreign country is a big step."

The attendant interrupted them. "You've got one bag, Ms. Russau?"

"Yes. One." Shelby pushed the suitcase on the metal bin before Linda started up again.

"I had no idea that you would actually consider going there," Linda exclaimed. "You've never been outside of this country. You've only been on an airplane twice in your life. And now you're going to some island with a man we hardly know." Linda wagged her finger. "That's why I'm going to make sure I look him directly in the eyes and tell him you better come back here safely, or he'll have me to answer to."

"Here is your ticket, Ms. Russau," the attendant announced. "The four fifty-five flight is on time and you'll be boarding at Gate E thirty-one.

"Thank you." Shelby took her ticket and left the counter with Linda in tow. "I appreciate your concern, Linda. But I'm telling you, you're not helping me by being neurotic."

"Ms. Russau."

Shelby recognized Blaize's voice instantly. She turned and saw him walking toward them with a shoulder bag. She thought he moved as if he owned the place. All he needed was a name-tag that verified it.

"So you've already checked in?" The answer was obvious, but Shelby didn't know what else to say.

"Yes, I checked in about thirty minutes ago."

"Hello." Linda pulled her five-foot frame up to its full height. "I'm—"

"I'm sorry. I forgot to introduce you," Shelby cut her off. "Raphael Blaize, this is Linda Johnson, a good friend of mine. Linda, this is Raphael Blaize, the man that I will accompany to Grenada."

Linda took a step back and let her gaze trail deliberately from Blaize's shoes to the top of his head. "I'm just getting a good look at you because if anything happens to my girlfriend, I'm going to be able to tell the authorities everything about you."

Shelby's eyes rolled upward. She wondered where all those people skills Linda had honed over the years had gone.

"You don't have to worry, Ms. Johnson. She will

be fine. But if you feel like you want to get in touch with her you can leave a message at this inn." He began to write down a name and a phone number.

"Why can't you give me your number?" Linda pressed.

"Because there are no telephones on Hummingbird Island."

"Say what?" Linda looked at Shelby with disbelief. "Did you know that?"

"No," Shelby answered, as shocked as Linda.

"No, she didn't know it," Blaize echoed in a nonchalant tone. "By choice, Hummingbird Island has been isolated for years. But it won't be for long. An order has been placed. The island will be connected shortly."

"What does shortly mean?" Shelby inquired, flabbergasted.

"Anywhere from a week to a couple of months," Blaize replied. "In the islands, we do not concern ourselves with time as much as you do in the States."

Linda wasn't having any of it. She crossed her arms. "Maybe you should wait until he gets a telephone."

"That's impossible." Shelby's eyebrows knitted with concern. She'd never thought Blaize's home would be so isolated. "Cleophus needs the medical treatment now."

"What else don't you have?" Linda asked, flustered.

"We have all the other modern conveniences," Blaize assured her, but Linda was armed with another question.

"Who else lives on this island?"

"My sister, my nephew, a man who has worked for my family through the years."

"You mean your family owns the island?" Linda's eyes brightened.

"Hummingbird Island is mine."

"Excuse us for a moment." Linda took Shelby by the arm and stepped a couple of feet away. "Are you sure you still want to do this?"

"Yes, Linda. What is the worst thing that can happen?"

"Don't make me answer that."

"Look, you just keep me in your prayers and everything will be fine."

Linda looked wary, then looked at Blaize. "The man does *own* an island."

Shelby smiled. Linda would always be Linda. "Everything is going to be just fine," Shelby insisted. "Now, give me a hug and I'll see you in about three weeks."

Shelby and Linda hugged. Afterwards, Linda went over to Blaize. All pretense of toughness had disappeared, and only concern lay on her face. "Please look out for my girlfriend. We've known each other for a long time, and I don't want anything to happen to her. I want her back here." Linda tugged Blaize's hand. "Safe and sound, in time to be the maid of honor in my wedding."

"I will make sure of that," Blaize pledged.

"Okay. I'm going to trust you to keep your word." Linda gave Shelby another hug before she joined the airport crowd.

Shelby took a deep breath. "I guess it's time to go."

"Yes," Blaize replied. "The plane is scheduled to leave in less than an hour." They started walking.

"Wait." Shelby turned to pick up the shoulder bag Linda had been carrying. Out of the corner of her eye she saw quick movement. It was the man in the colorful shirt. It appeared he had stepped out of the corridor leading from the men's bathroom. The quick movement was him turning his back. *Did I really see that?* Shelby thought. She watched the man act as if he were searching in his pockets.

"It's that way to Gate E," Blaize announced.

"I'm right with you." Shelby grabbed her bag and caught up with him.

Chapter 9

Shelby tried to catch a glimpse of Grenada from her aisle seat but it was rather difficult to see around the large man who sat between her and Blaize. Shelby wanted to lean toward the airplane window, but whenever she did she rubbed up against his thigh.

Blaize was oblivious to her plight. He gazed out the window as if he were already on his secluded island. His nephew and no one else seemed to matter, and Shelby wondered what was going on in his mind. She recalled how Blaize had told Linda he owned Hummingbird Island, so it must have been his choice to keep it isolated. Shelby also wondered why, and tried to imagine how his sister and Cleophus had dealt with the solitary life.

The conversation between them had been nonexistent during the flight. When they were being seated Blaize offered her the window, but Shelby had quickly declined. She didn't want it to appear as if she would be seeking special favors. This was not a pleasure trip for her. She was going to Grenada to help her brother's son. Her nephew. Whenever it was possible she would hold her own as she had done all of her life.

Shelby closed her eyes as the plane made its final descent. At the speed it was flying she felt it would be impossible to make a safe landing, but the aircraft touched down on the runway with barely a bounce. Shelby was the first to set foot in the airport. Blaize was a distance behind her. His progress had been slowed down by their neighbor, who had difficulty removing himself from the small space between the seats.

The waiting area was alive with activity. Islanders returning to their homes were greeted in a variety of accents, while tour guides wearing bright hats held up signs in order not to be missed. Shelby had always felt that living in Florida had prepared her for cultural diversity, but she knew she was in another country now. She was actually in Grenada; she was excited and apprehensive. The country that had taken her brother had given her a nephew.

Shelby was deep in thought when Blaize emerged from the jetway, but he quickly gained her attention as he moved in her direction. People turned and looked as he passed. It reminded Shelby of how ruggedly handsome Blaize was. As if she needed to be reminded.

Although the attention seemed not to faze Blaize,

Shelby couldn't say the same for herself. It was difficult to look at him and not think what practically every other woman was thinking, *What would it feel like to be with a man like that?* Even more, to be loved by a man like that. The latter was what dominated Shelby's mind. She couldn't have it any other way. Commitment was so important to her. Knowing that a person would be there and never leave. At least not have that intention . . . because Shelby knew the future was not guaranteed.

Blaize focused on her face as he approached, and Shelby was glad he could not read her mind. She tried to appear casual, as if her thoughts and the unusual circumstances were just like another day at the office. Blaize had almost reached her when he was intercepted by a man with a newspaper under his arm. He was holding a pen and notepad.

"Raphael Blaize, I am Henry Roydon with the *Grenadian Voice*. I want to talk to you about your coming out of seclusion."

At first Blaize gave the man a look that could kill, then he blatantly ignored him. "This way," he said, touching Shelby on the arm.

"Mr. Blaize, we think your change of heart after, how long has it been?" The reporter looked at his notes. "Sixteen years, is quite intriguing. Can you tell me what influenced you?"

"I don't give interviews," Blaize retorted, walking.

"But that couldn't be true." The man whipped

open the newspaper that had been under his arm. "The *Spice Sentinel* has an extensive article about you and your family that begins on the front page."

Blaize stopped. The story headline read: Heir of the Blaize Empire Hermit No More. He glanced at the article along with the old photographs. There were pictures of Blaize, his mother and his father. "I don't know anything about this." He took a shocked Shelby by the arm and continued on his way.

The reporter stayed close on their heels. "Obviously, this is the first time you've seen that story and I'm sure you want to give your account." He took a small tape recorder from another man who was following with a camera.

"What I want is for you to leave me alone."

"Will you comment on the rumors about your sister? That you two have reconciled? That it's because of her illegitimate son that you have resurfaced," the reporter pressed.

Blaize's temper flared. He abruptly turned around. "What happens in my family is none of your business."

The reporter stepped back and the cameraman took a picture at that exact moment. They did not follow when Blaize and Shelby took off again.

Shelby was out of breath by the time they reached the baggage claim area. She wanted to ask what this was all about, but the muscle twitching in Blaize's cheek kept her quiet. She looked at the people who were standing nearby. A couple of the women had seen the scene and were whispering. Shelby wondered if they were as curious as she was, or if they too knew Blaize's family history. If it was enough for the local papers to write about, Shelby thought, it must be quite a history indeed. *What kind of family had her nephew been born into? What kind of man had brought her to Grenada?*

Shelby yearned to learn the answers, but Blaize gave the distinct impression he wouldn't be open to telling her. It took all the self-control Shelby had to stand beside him in silence, waiting for her suitcase to surface. Finally, the piece emerged. Shelby went to retrieve it. Blaize stopped her.

"Which one is it?"

"The speckled beige one," she replied.

Blaize grabbed the luggage. "It's too late for us to start for the island tonight so I've made accommodations at a place in Grand Anse." She could tell there would be no further explanation. It was as if she didn't deserve one. *He acts as if he hired me to accompany him*, she thought wryly.

They got in a taxi outside the airport. Shelby slid in first. Blaize climbed in behind her.

"Spice Island Tourists Resort," he said, closing the car door.

"Spice Island Resort," the taxi driver repeated as he studied them through the rearview mirror.

"Yes," Blaize replied.

The driver raised up to get a better look at Shelby. He paused before he started shaking his head. "That's going to—"

"Don't even think about it," Blaize interrupted him. "I may know the back roads better than you. And I know exactly how long it should take us to get to the resort. So don't try to hike up the price."

"Hey mon, I wouldn't think of doing that," the driver came back quickly. "I was just admiring the beautiful woman at your side. Any harm in that?"

"No harm at all." Blaize looked out the window.

Shelby hated to admit that she felt offended by Blaize's obvious lack of interest. The driver gave a big smile and started up the cab.

"You look familiar." He glanced at Blaize. "Maybe I know your family."

"Grenada is small. You may be family," Blaize replied with a hint of humor beneath his rich voice.

The driver broke into musical laughter. "Ahh, you are a slick one. And what about you, Miss? Might you be family too?"

"I don't think so. I'm from the U.S.A.," Shelby replied.

"You never know. We Grenadians get around." He raised his eyebrow meaningfully. "Family or not, I hope he shows you a good time while you're here." He paused. "If he doesn't, you just remember my cab number. I'll gladly be at your service." His teeth glowed in the rearview mirror.

Shelby gave him a hesitant smile. She had heard

that West Indian men could be very friendly, but she thought this fellow was outright brash, considering he had no idea what kind of relationship she and Blaize shared. But Shelby guessed it was obvious from Blaize's silence that it wasn't an intimate one.

"Spice Island Tourists Resort is a very luxurious place. You must have big bucks to stay there." The driver turned his attention to Blaize again.

"I can hold my own," Blaize replied.

"It's too rich for my taste and my pocket," the driver confessed, obviously hoping to get a response out of Blaize, but there was none.

Around ten minutes later they were being dropped off in front of the property. Shelby had lived in St. Petersburg all of her life and was accustomed to tropical breezes and beaches. But living in St. Pete proper was nothing like staying at a place with a mountain view nestled on a beach. Despite the driver's comments Shelby hadn't expected such luxury. Somehow, she had gotten it in her mind that her trip to Grenada would require pants, shorts and T-shirts. Shelby was sure the resort would accept the clothing she had, but from the attire of the women milling around, she would be far underdressed to say the least.

"I don't think I brought the proper clothes for the occasion." Shelby stepped up to the check-in counter where Blaize was standing.

"It doesn't matter. We'll do dinner here tonight

and be on our way in the morning." He signed the paper the attendant placed before him.

"It matters to me," Shelby piped up, feeling like the country bumpkin who has been told she must attend the ball.

Her irritated tone got Blaize's attention as well as the hotel attendant's.

"Good evening, ma'am. You're going to love your rooms." The attendant threw back his shoulders with pride. "They both have ocean views. And ma'am, I have given you the royal private pool suite, at the gentleman's insistence." He nodded his head toward Blaize. "He will have the adjoining one, equipped with a whirlpool tub."

"Thank you," Shelby replied, feeling like an ingrate with an attitude when she took the key.

"Your rooms will be down the hall on the left." He motioned, and then as an afterthought added, "I heard you mention dinner, Mr. Blaize. It might be good to call down and see if there will be any tables available tonight. We have a small tour group staying here for a few days." He looked at the ladies standing near the entrance. "If you have any problems please let us know and we'll be glad to direct you to other fine restaurants in the area."

"Thank you," Blaize replied.

They started down the hall. Shelby's anger caused her to walk faster than Blaize despite her shorter stride. She didn't know exactly why she was upset. She only knew she was. Maybe it was because she felt like a fish out of water with no one to care. Shelby stuck her key in the door and tried to unlock it, but there was no cooperation there either.

Blaize stood in front of his door as Shelby mumbled and jerked the key around. He came back and stood beside her. "Is there a problem, Ms. Russau?" he asked as Shelby popped the door open.

"Are you going to call me Ms. Russau for the next three weeks?"

Blaize's eyes became hooded. "What do you want me to call you?"

"Whatever you want to, *Mister* Blaize." Shelby stormed into the room. "I mean you've been so warm and welcoming, I guess I'm overwhelmed," she announced sarcastically.

Blaize followed slowly behind her with a wary expression on his face. He watched Shelby as a man might watch a tiger that has burst out of its cage.

Shelby whirled around and faced him. "I've heard of the strong, silent type, but you take the cake." She crossed her arms.

"I was trying to show you the proper respect." Blaize spaced his words out carefully.

"Respect is one thing. The invisible servant is another."

"I haven't been treating you like a servant. I've had people in my employ before and I have treated you quite differently."

"Oh. You mean you talk to them." Shelby flashed a fake smile.

"What?" Blaize shifted his weight to one hip.

Shelby shook her head with exasperation. "You don't get it, do you? You convinced me that I should come to your country for *our* nephew's welfare, but you act as if you brought me along to carry your bags." She paused, but Blaize just continued to stare at her. "At least I've got your full attention now. You're looking at me. I can probably count the words on my fingers and my toes that you have said to me since we left Miami and came into this hotel room. Not that I expected you to talk my ear off. But a little bit of conversation would have helped."

"I'm sorry if I'm not very social," Blaize replied in an even tone.

"Is that what you call it, not very social? I'm sorry, *Mister* Blaize, what I've gotten from you shouldn't even be mentioned in the same breath."

Blaize looked down. When he looked up again, it was as if he intended for Shelby to see into the very depths of his eyes. "I'm sorry, Shelby." Blaize's tongue lingered, ever so slightly, on the L. "Perhaps I have been a little too distant. I've got a lot on my mind."

"Like I haven't." Shelby made a comical expression. "I'm in a foreign country. I don't really know you. I'm going to some island that doesn't have a telephone to see my nephew that I didn't know existed a month ago."

Blaize raised his hand to stop her. "I don't want you to feel unwelcome. The incident at the airport caught me off guard. I wasn't prepared to see my parents' faces plastered in a newspaper like that."

"What was that all about?"

"It's a complicated story." Blaize walked over to the sliding glass door. "At one time my family was very much in the social scene here. I guess I put an end to that and people are just curious."

Blaize faced Shelby again. She knew there had to be more. Much more. But she did not feel this was the time to dig deeper.

"I've spent a lot of time alone, Shelby. Perhaps with a little oiling my social skills can be re-claimed."

"Okay, so I guess since you have decided to call me Shelby, I should call you Raphael."

"Take your choice," Blaize replied. "But my mother was the only one who called me Raphael. To her I was an angel. Others choose to call me Blaize, including my father, who was afraid my mother was going to make me too soft."

Shelby laughed lightly. It was hard to imagine anyone thinking this man would ever be soft. "Blaize it is then. I can't quite categorize you as an angel."

Blaize's eyes softened but his lips never smiled.

"Dinner will be rather late tonight. Do you feel up to it?"

"I'm hungry. That's for sure."

"I'll check and make sure we can get in to one of the restaurants. I'll get back to you with the details."

"That sounds fine."

Blaize walked to the door where the bellman was standing with Shelby's bag. "Excuse me," he said as he exited.

"Where would you like for me to put this?"

The bellman spoke so quickly and his accent was so thick that Shelby was unsure of what he had said. She hesitated for only a split second. "You can put it right over there." She pointed to a space beside the TV stand.

The bellman set the bags down, then waited, smiling.

"Oh. Just a moment." She grabbed her purse. "I only have U.S. dollars."

"No problem," the man responded. He took the bills from Shelby's hand and left.

"Well I guess it was no problem." She turned around and took a real look at the room for the first time. "This is huge," she exclaimed. Then she wandered from the living room to the bedroom, into the bathrooms and the private fitness area. "It's a shame I will only be here for one night," she said minutes later. Shelby considered unpacking her bag, then decided it wouldn't be worth it, as someone knocked on the door.

"Who is it?" Shelby called.

"Ms. Russau, it is Henry from the front office. I have a package and a note for you."

"A package?" Shelby opened the door.

"Yes, ma'am." The man gave the box to Shelby, smiled and walked away.

"What is this?" Shelby walked over to the couch. She opened the envelope first. In a scripted writing Shelby read: We have nine forty-five reservations for the restaurant here in the hotel. I will knock on your door at that time. Blaize.

Shelby put the note down and lifted the lid off of the box. Inside was a bright island dress that tied around the hips. *Blaize sent this?* Shelby stared at the dress. "I can't believe it," was her initial reaction. Then she added softly, "How considerate. I wouldn't have expected it in a million years." Then Shelby looked at the lush surroundings Blaize had secured for her and realized she had no clue what made a man like Raphael Blaize tick. A man who could obviously afford luxury but who had chosen a solitary existence. Most likely, giving up many extravagances to which his family was accustomed. Hadn't he said his family was very involved in the social scene on Grenada? That would mean Blaize had made a choice to end ties and shut doors that had been open to him. Shelby pulled the dress out of the box and ran her hand across the soft material. This was a very complicated man indeed.

Chapter 10

Blaize knocked on Shelby's door. Moments later she opened it.

"Hi," she said as she held it open. "I see you're a man of your word."

"How is that?" Blaize looked confused.

"You said nine forty-five." Shelby looked at her watch. "And it's nine forty-five on the dot."

"The truth is I didn't have to go that far to be timely."

It would have been a light remark if Blaize didn't look so serious as his gaze ran over Shelby's body in the dress. She felt uncomfortable beneath his unabashed scrutiny. Finally he said, *"Oui foot."*

"Pardon me?"

"Oui foot. It's a local *patois* for 'You're looking good.'"

"Oh." Shelby smiled, but she felt a little flushed because the words sounded so sensuous. Letting out a tremulous breath she said, "I guess we should go on over."

Blaize nodded. Shelby stepped into the hall and closed the door.

"Thanks for buying me the dress. It was quite a surprise." She gave him a genuine smile. "And it fits perfectly."

"I can see that. And this is the first time I've truly seen you smile," he replied.

Blaize's unorthodox remark caught Shelby off guard. "I-is it?" She looked away. He had so easily cut to the heart of things. *Or is he simply messing with my head?* "Maybe it is," Shelby replied cautiously.

They walked to the restaurant in silence. This time Shelby was glad for it. Blaize's simple statement had touched her. During her longest relationships Shelby had felt the men had never really paid attention to the things that were important to her. Blaize had seen below the surface effortlessly. Still, with plenty of practice a man like that would know exactly what to say to touch a woman's heart, Shelby reminded herself. Perhaps it was because he was the Casanova Linda painted him to be.

Shelby and Blaize were seated at one of the outside tables. A trio played mellow reggae, and a full moon provided a shimmering view of the ocean. Shelby picked up the menu and tried to concentrate.

"There's quite a variety of foods offered here."

She spoke just to hear herself speak. *I feel like I'm in a movie. Here I am on a Caribbean island with a gorgeous man, but there is nothing between us. It's the perfect setup.*

"Anything to your liking?" Blaize asked.

"What?" Shelby's eyes were doelike, because of the uncanny timing of Blaize's question.

"Do you see anything on the menu that might interest you?"

Shelby's curly lashes came down quickly. *I'm the one who's been alone too long.* She could feel the heat rising to her face. "I'm sure there will be. I love seafood and there's plenty of seafood here." She added a nervous laugh.

The waiter appeared from out of nowhere. "Would you care for anything to drink?"

"I'd like some kind of tropical fruit punch."

"Sure." The man nodded and turned to Blaize.

"Planters punch."

"Of course," the waiter replied and walked away.

"Of course, he says." Feeling more in control Shelby relaxed in her chair. "Does that mean Grenadians drink a lot of Planters punch?"

"An awful lot," Blaize replied lazily.

"What's in it?" Shelby leaned forward, unaware of the hint of cleavage that was showing.

"Basically, fruit juice, rum and nutmeg," Blaize replied, tilting his head up slightly. "Grenada is known as the Isle of Spice. At one point in our history Grenada's spices were the source of our prosperity. That isn't so now. Our share of the world's market in nutmeg has been lost, and prices are low," he said in a reminiscent voice. "But it is still a profitable business."

"For a man who has been in solitary confinement for . . . I think that reporter said sixteen years, you seem to be very knowledgeable."

"Some people took it upon themselves to keep me informed by mail. There would also be the occasional newspaper."

"I can't imagine choosing to do that, living away from everything. Didn't it bother you?" Shelby looked directly into Blaize's eyes. She admired the thick, dark lashes that traced the edges.

"No," he said quietly. "Keith was very loyal to my parents. He still lives on the property. He tried to keep me company, although I must say I wasn't very open to it."

"What about Cleophus and your sister? How did they deal with being isolated?"

"Their situation was quite different," Blaize said as the waiter returned.

"May I take your orders now."

"I think I'll try the *dango*." Shelby looked uncertain. "The menu says that's fish cooked in a ginger and coconut sauce?"

The waiter nodded.

"Okay. And I'll have that with some plantains." She handed the waiter her menu.

"I'll do *tatou* and *calloloo*." Blaize passed his menu to the waiter.

"Certainly." The man smiled. "Anything else?"

Blaize looked at Shelby. She shook her head. "Not right now."

The man bowed and left.

"What did you order?" Shelby couldn't wait to ask.

"I ordered *tatou*. You would know that as armadillo. And *calloloo*. It's a soup with okra, plantains, *dasheen*, which is a kind of root, and scallions. It's got other things in it as well. It is very Caribbean."

"And good?"

"I think so."

"I'll have to learn about your foods, your customs and your ways if Cleophus and I are going to strike up a relationship."

Blaize sat back and eyed Shelby. "That is a very open-minded way of approaching it."

"Sounds like you expected otherwise."

Blaize paused, then gave a solid, "Yes. I did."

"Why? *That* seems very close minded to me." Shelby turned the tables on him.

"I'm just speaking from experience."

"We've all had good and bad experiences. I think it's rather presumptuous to categorize a whole nation of people or race of people by the actions of one, or even a few. My brother must have had a very tough time with you."

"Not necessarily."

"I find that hard to believe." Shelby accepted her drink from the waiter. She watched a couple advance toward the dance floor. The woman was dressed in a spandex top and skirt and she had the body to set them off. It was clear her partner thought so as well. When they reached the floor he pulled her to him in an embrace that ensured he would feel every move she made.

A sensuous reggae tune vibrated with a swaying hypnotic beat. Shelby glanced briefly at the amorous couple, but she was more aware of Blaize's reaction than anything else. He was outright staring at them. Shelby wasn't sure if it was the couple's dance technique or the woman's slowly gyrating bottom that held him.

Blaize's eyes had narrowed ever so slightly. Everything except for his chest, which was rising and falling slowly, methodically, was still as stone. Shelby could feel her breath synchronizing with Blaize's.

"Tell me if I'm wrong"—she had to break the uncanny connection between them—"but it seems like it's been a long time since you've seen someone dance?"

"It's been a long time for lots of things." Blaize's gaze slid over to Shelby's face.

"Oh." She swallowed hard at his candidness. "Really?"

"Yes," was his silky reply.

"Not sixteen years, I hope." Shelby had to make light of the situation before she picked up the napkin and started to fan herself. The image of Blaize's unleashed virility was scorching. And her own dormant sex life was beginning to spark.

"Not quite."

"Well . . . so much for that." Shelby sat up straight. "Ah. Rescued by the food." She watched the waiter approach. He placed their dishes on the table.

Moments later, as he was cutting the armadillo, Blaize asked, "And what about you?"

"What about me?" Shelby couldn't believe he was continuing on the same vein.

"Has your life been very full in that way?"

In her mind she could hear Linda saying, "I told you so." But her response to Blaize was, "For a guy who I could barely get to talk to me, I see you have no problem talking about very personal things."

"It is all a part of life. I have no problem talking about that." He took a drink of Planters punch, then rested his elbow on the table.

"I can tell." Shelby placed a fork full of food in her mouth to buy time as Blaize watched and waited. "Let's just say my life hasn't been that exciting lately."

"Would you want it to be?"

This is a man with an agenda. "Would I want it to be?" Shelby gritted her teeth and looked to the side. She snapped her finger. "Fix it. Just like that? I don't think it's that simple."

"Of course it is. You just have to have desire for the other person." Blaize's eyes never left Shelby's face.

"I hate to sound like some naïve youngster, but what about love? What about caring for the person that you're planning to share such an intimate act with?"

"Like you said, you're not some naïve youngster, so I'm sure you know love isn't necessary. It would be a sort of icing on the cake, but it is far from necessary," Blaize assured her.

"Of course I know that." Somewhere inside Shelby felt disappointed, and she didn't like that disappointment. "It's a matter of choice."

"And you choose to love first?"

"I can't say that, but it should be a possibility."

"Many things are possible. But sometimes if we wait for love it could be a long time before we find fulfillment. As I'm certain you can testify."

With aplomb, Shelby placed her fork and knife on the table. "Is there a point to this conversation?"

"I think the point is quite clear, Shelby," Blaize said huskily, placing his hand on top of hers.

Shelby looked down. It was a large hand, but amazingly soft. "Oh. That's what I was afraid of."

"Afraid. Why should you be afraid? I'm a man and you're a woman. I think I can safely say there is a definite attraction between us. I could feel it in my hotel room back in the States. At first I was a little uncomfortable with the idea. I don't know why. It is so unlike me. But now I can say, in looking at you tonight, I have put those demons to rest."

It is so unlike you. So that means normally you have no problem bedding any and every woman. Shelby slowly reclaimed her hand. "You're moving really fast for me, Blaize. It's amazing how well that name fits you. Whoosh! Burnt up in a blaze of smoke. Now to the next one."

"I think you are joking. I am serious."

"I know." Shelby bit her lip. "Too serious for me. I think you need to drink a little more of that rum punch." She leaned over and peered into his glass. "It'll loosen you up a bit." *How dare he just want me for that? I deserve more. Much, much more.*

"You continue to make light of what I'm saying. Do you not know how to approach this subject head-on?"

"I'm approaching it as head-on as I can. But I don't do things this way. Call me a small-town girl or whatever you wish, but operating like this *ain't* my cup of tea." Shelby's mouth formed a tight line. "Perhaps you're in a rush and you feel like you need to make up for lost time, but I don't think I'm the woman for you to do it with."

The table went quiet. Blaize concentrated on eating. Shelby just sat and watched him until she couldn't handle it any longer. "So that's it? You can't talk about anything else?

"Of course I can, Shelby." Blaize paused for a moment, closing his eyes. "Maybe it is the music. Or maybe it is the way that dress hugs every curve of your body. Maybe I have been alone for too long." He took a deep breath before he opened his eyes. "But please forgive me if I have offended you. I didn't bring you here for that. My first concern is the boy, and I don't want you to think otherwise."

My God. Was that supposed to make me not think about the things he said? "You haven't offended me." Shelby could feel a tightness in her stomach. "But I must say I am glad to hear you speak of your concern for Cleophus."

"You will get to meet him tomorrow. I plan to rent a car. It won't take us long to get there." Blaize signaled for the check. "Grenada is a small country. We will ferry over to Hummingbird Island."

"I tell you the truth, I can't wait to meet him."

"He is a fine boy. Together we will do what we can to ensure his health and his happiness."

Shelby liked the sound of the word together. How long had it been since she had shared a feeling of togetherness? Ever since Linda started dating James, the time they spent together had been cut drastically. Of course, the time she spent with Linda was quite different than what she was feeling now.

"Would you like for the meal to be put on your hotel bill?" the waiter asked ceremoniously.

"Yes," Blaize replied.

"I just need your room number and your signature, please."

Blaize did as he was asked.

"Have a good night, sir. Ma'am."

"Well, it's just about my bedtime," Shelby said, rising from the table. "Thank you for dinner. Now I guess I'll head back to the room and get comfortable."

"I think I'll take a walk down the beach." Blaize stood up beside her.

"Sounds lovely." Shelby glanced at the sand that gleamed with mellow gold compliments of the moonlight. "I would think, since you live on an island, you would have become bored with that kind of thing."

"Bored?" Blaize looked up at the night sky filled with stars. "How could one ever become bored with this?" Shelby looked up as well. "No. It is quite the opposite, Shelby. The more it is a part of your life, the deeper it is in your blood. I walk the beach at night to feel the sand and the stars. Between them I connect the heavens and the earth. As we all do. We only have to be aware of it."

"How beautiful," Shelby said softly.

"It is that and much more," Blaize said in an enthralling whisper before he touched her temple with his lips. The warm moistness lingered for a moment and then it was gone. "Good night, Shelby."

"Good night, Blaize." Her knees were weak but Shelby managed to walk toward the hallway. Blaize struck out for the beach. Shelby turned to see him but he was nowhere in sight. She guessed he had become one with the shadows. Shelby wondered if Blaize saw her take one last look.

Chapter 11

The next morning a loud *caw* had Shelby searching the trees outside her sliding-glass doors. She spotted a large, colorful parrot perched on a branch. Shelby took a sip of coffee and marveled at how much the patio gave the impression of being nestled in a tropical rain forest. The air was alive with animal sounds and fragrant aromas of the lush flowers outside. With it was a moistness that Shelby could taste with her tongue.

Deliberately, she had awakened early. She wanted to experience the beautiful surroundings in the daytime before they headed for Hummingbird Island.

Smiling, Shelby walked back inside and turned on the stereo. That's when she noticed a yellow envelope just inside her door. She picked it up and went back outside. Taking another sip of coffee she shook the contents out onto the table.

There were a couple of newspaper articles and a

photograph. It was the picture of her and Blaize that had been taken at the airport. Shelby was shocked to see a red circle drawn around her face.

The clippings were stories about Blaize's parents' deaths. They explained how they died in the unrest in 1983. But it was the typed message on a plain sheet of paper that stunned her.

THE OLD WAYS ARE DEAD, AND YOU WOULD BE WISE NOT TO AWAKEN THEM. IF YOU DO NOT HEED THIS WARNING, NOT ONLY YOU, BUT THOSE WHO ARE CLOSE TO YOU WILL REGRET IT.

Shelby sat there and stared at the pile of papers. "What in the world is this?" Moments later she was knocking on Blaize's hotel door.

"Who is it?" His voice was heavy with sleep.

"Shelby."

Blaize opened the door. His locks hung thick on his shoulders above a bare chest. White muslin drawstring pants encased the lower half of his body.

Shelby waved the papers in front of him. "What have I gotten myself into?"

"What are you talking about?" Blaize slid his hands over his locks.

"I'm talking about this." She rattled the papers again. "You know that picture of us that was taken in the airport? I have it right here. But for some reason somebody felt the urge to draw a red circle around *my* face."

Blaize's eyes were suddenly alert. "Why don't you come inside." He allowed Shelby to pass before he looked up and down the hall.

"Why are you looking up and down the hall? Are you expecting someone?" Shelby's voice went up an octave.

"No. I'm not expecting anyone." Blaize took the papers and sat down on the bed. He examined the clippings and the photograph closely, then he read the message.

Seeing the picture again, Shelby's fear mounted. "What's going on here?"

"I'm not sure," Blaize replied with a stone face.

"What do you mean, you're not sure? I'm sorry, but right now that's not good enough." She pointed at her face in the newspaper clipping. "Somebody is trying to make a point. But none of this makes sense to you?"

Blaize clasped her hand. "Try to calm down, Shelby."

She shook her head. "Considering what this might mean, I don't think I can."

Blaize walked over and poured a glass of water. "Here, drink this." He gave the glass to Shelby and looked at the pile of papers. "It appears someone isn't happy with my coming out of seclusion."

"Why?" Shelby held the glass. "And what's this stuff about no more old ways?"

"Drink the water, Shelby."

"You think this water is going to calm me down? Uh-uh. The only thing that is going to calm me down is your positive explanation for my face appearing in a Grenadian newspaper article that someone has cut out and placed a red circle around it."

"They are assuming that you are someone close to me. It's got to do with the timing of everything," he said in a silky, calculating voice. "Most likely, whoever is responsible for this is aware of how quickly I resurfaced, went to the United States, and came back with you. They probably think you have something to do with my coming out of seclusion."

"Lucky me." Shelby made a face before her brow wrinkled with worry. "But so what? What if I did? What is the big deal about that?" She threw her arms up. "Why are you being monitored?"

Blaize walked across the room and leaned on the edge of the desk. "They think I will gather the people and start performing some of our ancient rituals." He squinted into the distance. "Those are the old ways they are referring to."

"And that's exactly what you plan to do, right?" Shelby's eyes widened.

"Yes. It is."

"You said the rituals are a part of your culture. So why wouldn't they want you to perform them?"

"I don't know." He looked at her. "I don't have all of the answers."

Shelby looked around the room in frustration. "You want my opinion?" she asked, but had no intention of waiting for an answer. "I think you shouldn't perform the ceremony."

"The ritual is necessary for Cleophus' well-being," Blaize replied in a low, controlled tone.

"Ahh c'mon. What's necessary for his well-being is the blood transfusion that I am willing to provide. In my opinion, my coming to this country to do that is dangerous enough. Being on someone's hit list because of some ritual is more than I bargained for."

"No one has mentioned a hit list."

"They didn't use those words, but there's a threatening note with a picture that has a circle around *my* face."

"I promise no harm will come to you, Shelby." Blaize's tone was low, predatory.

Shelby's heart began to beat faster. "It won't if you don't perform the ritual."

Blaze glanced at the article with his parents' pictures. "The ritual will be performed on Hummingbird Island in three days." When he looked at Shelby again his eyes were like stone. Shelby's fear exploded.

"I won't be a part of it." She sliced the air with her hand.

"Then, as I said in St. Petersburg, your family will be responsible for Cleophus' death."

Shelby was across the room before she knew it.

With tears in her eyes she drew back her hand to slap Blaize. "How dare you threaten me?"

He grabbed her wrist before her hand reached his face. "Be careful, Shelby."

She gritted her teeth. "I came to Grenada because that boy is the only living relative I have on this earth, and you threaten me with his death. Damn you!" Her eyes welled up but she refused to cry.

Blaize looked into her tortured face and saw the pain and loneliness that had plagued Shelby's life. He saw the little girl that had longed for a family, and the woman who had recently hoped to claim one. He saw a beautiful woman with passions that ran deep, but who had never excavated them. "We will be your family, Shelby," he declared as a single tear escaped her eyes and his lips descended on hers.

A taste of salt mingled with the sweetness of Shelby's lips. Blaize waited to see if her mouth would open in invitation. And when it did his tongue greeted hers in introduction. Blaize's arms went around Shelby and pulled her close. Soon a haze of desire formed within him.

Shelby floated on the sensations Blaize's mouth created. At first it was annihilatingly sweet. His lips and tongue comforted her and the possibility of life coming to an end was the furthest thing from Shelby's mind. But soon she could feel the mounting need in Blaize. The need of a man who had needed too long. Shelby drew back from the kiss with downcast eyes. "You don't have to worry," she said softly. "I'm no longer dangerous, but I don't know about you."

"To me you're more dangerous now than you've ever been," Blaize said huskily.

Gently, Shelby placed her palm against Blaize's chest. "I think we both got caught up in the moment."

"Yes, and I'm still caught," Blaize said, kissing her forehead and then her temple.

For a moment Shelby closed her eyes, drawn in by the softness of his lips. But she knew she couldn't let it go any further. Shelby knew she would regret it. "Considering the circumstances I don't think we should go any further." Shelby put pressure on his chest. "Being caught up isn't always the best beginning. Making a conscious choice is."

Blaize held back what he wanted to say. *I don't care about right beginnings. I don't care about conscious choices. You Americans think too much. You should follow what you feel and I can feel your desire, Shelby, as you can feel mine. But you believe you have to master your desires, unlike we islanders who believe we should use them masterfully.*

Blaize didn't want to let go, but he knew he had to, so he released her. He fought a small feeling of resentment as he walked over to the bed. Resentment that he could want Shelby so badly, and she could so easily turn him down.

Shelby watched him cross the room. His sudden withdrawal created a chill in the room.

"I'm going to get dressed. Then I'm going to go ask some questions at the front desk." Blaize looked at the clock. "There's no need to stay here any longer. It's early, but we should be able to get a rental car. It will take us about an hour to get to Levera Beach. From there we'll ferry over to Hummingbird Island."

Blaize's switch from intimacy to the business at hand startled Shelby. She had expected he might acknowledge and address what had occurred between them. But it was obvious to Shelby that Blaize was like a light switch. Easy on. Easy off. "All right." She replied but made no attempt to move.

"You should go back to your room and get ready. I'll come and get you as soon as I can." Blaize turned toward the bathroom.

"Do you think the people are still in the hotel?"

"It's possible someone is keeping an eye on things around here."

"So you think it's safe? I mean, we've both got these sliding-glass doors leading out into the patio. Someone could easily hide in the tropical garden out there." Shelby looked at the lush greenery beyond the glass partition.

"The note only threatened harm if they had evidence that I was digging up the past." Blaize's jaw tightened with the mention of it. "Right now, they don't have that. We should be safe enough."

Shelby nodded, but she felt far from certain.

"Unless you want to bring your things over here and prepare to leave from my room."

Shelby looked at Blaize's well-formed chest, and the feel of his kiss flashed right through her. She had resolve, but not that much resolve.

"I think it would be best if I got dressed in my own room."

"Suit yourself," Blaize replied. The corner of his mouth turned up in what Shelby assumed was supposed to be a smile.

Chapter 12

"So they had separate rooms?" George Keegan said, wiping his mouth with a handkerchief.

"Yes. But their rooms were right next door. It was easy for them to do whatever they wanted to do and no one would be the wiser."

"But why go through that if he's banging the woman like you claim?"

"Who knows? I've never understood rich people anyway."

"Raphael Blaize isn't like any rich or poor person you or I have ever known. Don't you forget that. The man managed to live on that island without leaving it for sixteen years. With money and influence at his fingertips, he still gave society the finger because of his convictions. Would you do that just because your parents had been killed?"

Dennis shrugged. "Were you in St. George when the massacre occurred?"

"Yes, I was there. It seems strange to look back

because we were one big family here on the island, just like we are now." He formed a superficial smile. "But Blaize can't get over his perception that his parents dedicated their lives to helping others, and in the end, it's quite possible some of those people they so-called helped may have killed them."

"My grandparents said the Blaizes actually helped them," Dennis spoke up.

"Your grandparents would have seen it that way. Back in their time the rituals the Blaizes performed were very important. Ceremonies for births, deaths, marriages, rites of passage. You name it. According to the Blaizes, they had the knowledge of their ancestors, and they were going to honor that by continuing their work."

"Who were their ancestors?"

"Don't ask me. I'm not a specialist in that stuff and I don't believe a word of it," Keegan declared.

Dennis looked down as he spoke. "I know several families that claimed without the intervention of Blaize's parents things would have been quite bad for them."

"Well, I don't believe it," Keegan reiterated. "So I don't feel a thing about stopping him from doing that bush-mentality religion. It's an embarrassment to our people."

Dennis paused then said, "Why are you—"

Keegan cut him off as he sat back in his chair.

"You don't ask any questions. You simply follow directions. You understand?"

Dennis looked away and nodded.

"You say Blaize and the woman plan to rent a car and head north today?"

"Yeah," Dennis replied, his jaws tight.

Keegan studied the younger man. He didn't want him upset. Dennis was smart and he had performed the job in Miami without a hitch. The truth was, he needed him. He was the one with the grassroots connections. People liked talking to Dennis. They liked telling him things. "I bet seeing that news clipping and her face circled in red gave her quite a scare." Keegan paused. "The red marker was a good touch."

Dennis smiled, slightly. "It would scare me."

Keegan nodded. "Shelby Russau." He read the name from the piece of paper lying in front of him. "We plan to see how important you are to Raphael Blaize. Maybe we can weaken his commitment to his parents' dreams if we roust you up a bit," Keegan said, then looked at Dennis. "Go get Alphonso. I've got a job for him to do."

"Did you find out anything?" Shelby asked as she fastened the seat belt in the rental car. She wanted to appear as if she had put the kiss behind them. The kiss along with her fear had turned her stomach to jelly.

Blaize looked at her and it felt like a bolt of

lightning shot between them. But he casually turned away and started the car as if nothing had occurred.

"Not really," he replied. "The guy who checked us in last night got off a few minutes before I went up front. The man behind the desk didn't know anything. He kept apologizing for any problems we may have encountered at the hotel, and he wanted to know what he could do to make things better." Blaize pulled onto the road. "When he couldn't get any straight answers out of me, I think he became a little leery."

Leery . . . at this point I feel like I should have a monopoly on the word. Shelby looked out the window. Although it was early, Grande Anse was buzzing with activity. It was a busy resort town with many hotels and places to eat. If Grande Anse was any indication, tourism was alive and well in Grenada. "Does Cleophus know we will be arriving today?"

"Last night I called and left a message at the inn for my sister, Marlene. I'm sure he will know before we get there."

"What did you tell them?" Shelby was getting excited. She also knew there was safety in talking about Cleophus.

"That we were in Grenada. That you had returned to the country with me." He paused. "That you planned to do whatever you could to help the boy."

Shelby felt instantly hot. She knew Blaize meant the ritual as well as the blood transfusion. Shelby diverted the subject. "Has Cleophus asked many questions about his father over the years?"

"That's something you'll have to ask my sister," Blaize replied in a detached fashion.

Shelby wondered about the change in the tone of his voice. She felt it meant he was guarding something. She started to ask why, but changed her mind. Shelby didn't think she would get very far.

Once again she looked out the window, this time at a gleaming lagoon. It felt strange, with Blaize driving on the left-hand side of the road and cars passing on her right. Just something else to make her feel out of place, more aware that she was a stranger, among people with ways that were foreign to her.

It wasn't long before they arrived at another city. Shelby noticed, as far as she could see, that unlike Grand Anse, there were no wooden structures. Many of the stone and brick edifices painted in soft pastels sported red tin roofs or roofs made of small orange tiles.

"What city is this?" Shelby asked, leaning toward the front window.

"It is St. George. The capital of Grenada."

"Oh yes," Shelby replied. "It's quite pretty."

She watched the people walk up the steep, winding cobbled streets, feeling as if she had stepped back into the past. A policeman in a picture-perfect uniform directed traffic at one of the corners. Shelby turned and watched him through the rear-view mirror as they headed away from the water. As the vehicle climbed, a statue with outstretched arms came into view over the harbor.

"We're going to take Grand Etang Road, which cuts straight through the center of the island. It's rather mountainous, but much of Grenada is," Blaize informed her. "It is a well-traveled road and it will get us to the north coast much faster."

"Isn't Grand Etang the name of the national park?"

"Yes. We'll be driving right through it," Blaize answered with a toss of his head.

"I did a little reading before I came on this trip. I didn't want to be completely ignorant when I got here. Although considering some of the things that have occurred I don't think I did very well in preparing myself." A concerned look crossed Shelby's features before she said, "I just remembered Grand Etang National Park is a rain forest, and there are waterfalls there."

"That's right." Blaize threw her a glance. "There is also a waterfall on Hummingbird Island."

"There is?"

"Yes. Hummingbird Island is a beautiful place," Blaize began. "My family kept it as natural as possible. Our home was built to compliment the beauty that was already there."

The road wound steeply until they passed a sign

that welcomed visitors to Grand Etang National Park. Shelby marveled at the lush greenness of the landscape and at a crater lake that was the center-piece for it all. She watched a stream of people going in and coming out of the visitors' center, while vendors selling drinks and souvenirs con-ducted business from nearby stalls. Blaize and Shelby continued north, and the road descended sharply in many places, gifting them with scenic views of valleys burgeoning with forests.

"My God. It's like a green heaven out here," Shelby exclaimed. "I've never been up this high before in a car. Florida is very flat, you know." She looked over the edge of the road without trepida-tion. "Looking down from here is so different from looking down from an airplane. The details are breathtaking. It makes me realize how beautiful the Earth really is."

"Yes. She is very beautiful," Blaize replied.

"She? Why do you think the Earth is a she?"

"Because life comes forth from her insides. And she is relentless in her giving despite the pain it may cause her. Because with the quaking of her body she could destroy those of us who live on her, mindlessly taking and poisoning the one who allows us life. Who else but a female would be so generous? Who else but a mother?"

There was a moment of silence.

"You have a gift with words. I guess you know that." Shelby continued to look out the window.

"The gift is my love and appreciation for what so many people fail to see. I'm a man that speaks what's in my heart. I think that is something Americans find very difficult."

"Why Americans?" Shelby was fed up with Blaize's narrow view of her nationality. "I'm sure you can find people all over this planet that would find speaking what's on their minds difficult."

"I did not say mind. That is what America and most of its inhabitants are controlled by. And then you feel superior because of it, not realizing how unbalanced a human being who operates totally out of logic can be. I said heart," Blaize repeated.

Irked, Shelby looked at him. "Heart. Mind. Most people would say it's the same thing."

"But it is not the same." Blaize shook his head slowly. "When you speak from your mind you have selected what you think is best to say. The foundation of your thoughts are what the experts, men and women just like yourself from various fields of study, have purported to be true. When you speak from your heart, your words flow from a center of truth. From the center of universal, even spiritual, understanding. If it is truly coming from your heart it is being said out of love, connected to the ultimate source of love." Blaize paused. "Even so, everyone who hears truth may not always agree with it. May not want to accept it."

Shelby heard Blaize, but there was a part of her that didn't understand. She wondered if he knew that he was speaking beyond her experience. She looked at him out of the corner of her eyes. Shelby also wondered if it was Blaize's way of knocking the highfalutin American down a peg. His way of mentally conquering her, because he couldn't do so physically. Shelby pressed her lips together. "I don't know if I agree with that."

Blaize's tone became mesmerizingly low. "I'll give you an example, Shelby. If you tell a child not to touch a flame and he wants to so badly because it flickers and dances, most likely that child will not agree with your directive. He will think you are trying to keep him away from something beautiful, not trying to protect him."

"And so . . . that's different. A child is a . . . child. They're not expected to understand everything."

"That is true." His voice became husky. "But what if it is a woman, and you tell this woman that you want her, and that the joy and memorable pleasure of your moments together is all that you can promise. You tell her that she should not expect more because that more may not be what she needs. May even cause her pain. Most likely that woman will not agree with you," Blaize added softly.

Shelby focused straight ahead. "I think it depends on the woman."

"What if you were that woman? How would you handle it?"

"I am not one for pain," she said, her curly lashes

casting shadows on her cheeks. "If a man tells me he could be a source of pain for me, I want nothing to do with him. It's very simple."

"Um-m." Blaize made a vibrating sound within his throat. "But in passing this scenario through your logical mind, you have forgotten about the pleasure. How sweet the pleasure can be. In all the years of isolation that I spent on Hummingbird Island, I never forgot the pleasure a woman can give to a man. It is a gift from the universe."

"And although you didn't forget, you're telling me you kept yourself from indulging?"

"It was a choice that I made. One that I do not regret. It also means, whenever I come together with a woman, I will have much to give her."

"Much to give her, but you can't give her everything," Shelby clarified. "With all your philosophical meanderings I'm sure you must be aware of that distinction. What about your heart, Blaize? You speak as if it is so important to you, but it appears there are times when you are willing to abandon it."

"I leave it out of this because my heart is so special. I must be careful in sharing the most sacred part of my being."

"And that goes double for me. I must be careful in sharing my heart and my body, since they cannot—or let me phrase that differently—since they will not be separated. You see, I hold myself in no less esteem than you do, even though I am an American."

For a second Shelby could feel Blaize's eyes on the side of her face and then he focused on the road again. After that the car was silent for the remainder of the ride. Shelby was beginning to think that perhaps she liked Blaize as the strong, silent type. She was uncomfortable with how the things he said affected her. Blaize had a musical way of speaking that spoke to her heart. And that was not the part of her that interested him. It was all too obvious that he was a man in need of comfort of a temporary kind.

Shelby read a sign that said Grenville. It preceded a city not nearly as large as St. George. Afterwards they passed another airport, many plantations and a smattering of small towns with an occasional stone church and countless wooden houses. Soon Blaize and Shelby stood beneath several eroded sea cliffs with the Atlantic Ocean to their right and the Caribbean Sea to their left.

"Right now we're on Levera Beach." He pointed. "That island is Sugar Loaf Island. And the ones strung out behind it on the left are Carriacou and the Grenadines. The island to the left of Sugar Loaf is Hummingbird Island. That's one of my ferries over there." He pointed to a makeshift craft with rails and a small motor. "All we have to do is climb aboard and we'll be on our way."

The islands looked like large turtles floating in a

vast expanse of blue water. Suddenly Shelby felt uncertain. Each island looked like a world unto itself, and it hit her harder than ever how isolated and dependent she would be on Blaize and those who lived on Hummingbird Island. It wasn't that Shelby was afraid of Blaize. As a matter of fact she had more respect for him now than she ever had. What Shelby was afraid of was the giddiness in her stomach when she thought of being with him on Hummingbird Island. Shelby was afraid of herself and the feelings she was trying to ignore. She was afraid of how long she would be able to hold out against this man who was more beautiful and deeper than the ocean that spread out before her.

"I am ready whenever you are," Blaize called from several yards away.

Shelby turned and saw him holding a thick rope attached to the ferry that was bobbing at the edge of the water. Apprehension filled her, although the craft appeared to be quite hardy. Shelby looked at her bags on top of the hewn logs. Then she looked back across the water at Hummingbird Island.

"It's not too late to change your mind, Shelby. The mind is an easy thing to change; it's not possible to change your heart." The words carried tauntingly atop a warm tropical breeze. "That is, if your reason for coming was truly born there."

Shelby thought of Cleophus, her brother, then she thought of his son who awaited her across the turquoise expanse, and she knew her love of family was stronger than her fears. "I was just admiring the view," Shelby said, walking across the sand and stepping onto the logs. "What do I do? Sit or stand?"

"Whatever *pleases* you." Blaize's tone caressed the word as a more forceful wave collided with the ferry.

"Then I think I'll sit." Shelby did so and crossed her legs. "I wouldn't want anything to happen to me before my true adventure begins."

Blaize looked down into her eyes. "Your true adventure has already begun. It is only a matter of accepting it." He used the paddle and pushed away from the shore before starting the outboard motor.

Chapter 13

"Let me take your bag the rest of the way," Blaize offered as he ducked another branch.

"No," Shelby replied, breathing heavily. "No. I'm fine."

Although they had not been walking for long the bag felt like a ton on Shelby's shoulder. Perhaps the thick humidity added to her feeling of heaviness. And on Hummingbird Island there were more plants than Shelby had ever seen in a condensed area. The trees, bushes and flowering plants that lined the well-trodden path teemed with life. Shelby felt as if she had stepped off into another world. Another place and time. Once again she focused her attention on switching her luggage to the opposite shoulder. When she looked up, Blaize's home was before her.

It was a large whitewashed building that consisted of two wings with a two-story windowed structure dominating the center. Tropical flowers claimed the earth that surrounded it, creating the vision of a house being held in a floral caress. The structure was in amazingly good repair, something Shelby had not expected. She had envisioned Blaize becoming less and less enamored with his surroundings and therefore the upkeep of his property as the years went by. But nothing seemed to be further from the truth. The property had obviously been maintained with a caring hand.

As far as Shelby could see there were no cars or vehicles of any sort, and as they walked up the pink-and-white shelled road, there was no one waiting to greet them either.

"So where is everybody?" Shelby hoped her disappointment was not apparent.

"In the house, I assume," Blaize replied, but offered no further explanation.

He did not need a key to open the door, and the well-oiled hinges were as silent as the foyer inside. Although Shelby was no antique buff she knew that the tastefully situated ornate furniture was rare and expensive. The area was clean but a quiet, unsettling void permeated the place.

"I'll set you up in the bedroom down here," Blaize said as he led her down a hall in the east wing. "I believe it can be readied the quickest. You can wait in the living room while I prepare it." He turned the knob and gently pushed the door open with his foot. "In the meantime your bags will be fine in here."

Shelby was surprised to see sheets covering everything. It was obvious no one had slept in the room for years. It was even possible that no one had entered it. Alarmed yet also throwing caution to the wind, Shelby pulled back one of the covers. The furniture underneath was of the same quality and beauty as the furniture in the foyer. "I can't imagine leaving this covered up like this. I can't imagine anyone doing so." Searching eyes looked at Blaize.

The room went quiet and apprehension clutched at Shelby. She was overwhelmingly aware of how empty the house felt. It seemed as though she and Blaize were the only people who had been there for a very long time. Was it possible? Or was she suffering from a bad case of nerves? Shelby looked around the room and Linda's warnings came back to her. Was she on an isolated island with a man who had lied to get her there? The incident at the airport and the yellow envelope that had been slipped under her door flashed through her mind. When Shelby looked at Blaize again, naked distrust shone in her eyes. She took a step back. "How long has it been since someone has been in this room?"

"A long time." Blaize's eyes narrowed as he held Shelby's luggage.

"How long? Sixteen years?" Shelby asked accusatorily.

"Perhaps." Slowly, he set her bags down. Shelby

felt he was watching her like a cat watches a cornered mouse.

"How could that be?" Shelby demanded. "Someone had to come in here. Your sister, Marlene. Or Cleophus, even. How did you keep a little boy from playing throughout the house unless you locked the doors?"

"There are no locked doors on Hummingbird Island." Blaize's response had a dangerous, quiet tone.

"Well how did you do it?" Shelby demanded again.

Blaize just looked at her.

Taking a deep breath Shelby straightened her spine and said, "I want to see Cleophus right now."

"What are you thinking, Shelby?" Blaize came and stood in front of her. "That I coerced you to Hummingbird Island for reasons other than our nephew's well-being?" He ran the back of his hand down her cheek and beneath her chin.

"I'm not going to answer any of your fancy questions. And I don't want to hear any of your fancy talk." Shelby turned her face aside. "You convinced me to come to this island, and I trusted you, thought you were a man who cared about his family, and felt he was doing what he had to do to protect it. Now, I'm not so sure." Slowly, she stepped back. "Maybe you cannot be trusted. Maybe family means nothing to you."

Shelby noticed a mask descending over Blaize's

handsome features. She could feel his pent-up emotions. Shelby knew her words had connected in a profound way, but she continued to forge on. "All I want is to see the boy that you showed me in the picture. The boy that you claimed was my brother's son."

Shelby wasn't certain if it was a partial smile or a smirk that turned Blaize's lips. His hooded eyes told her nothing. But there was a coldness between them now that she had not felt before.

"You want to see the boy." It was both a statement and a question, and Blaize had no intention of allowing Shelby time to respond. "Follow me."

Shelby felt helpless as she fell in behind him. But what else was there to do? She could stand there and out of her apprehension refuse, but then where would she be? Yes, Blaize could be leading her to God knows where, or he could be leading her to her one and only nephew. The only way for Shelby to find out was to go with him.

Their footsteps echoed in the house as they climbed the center staircase. Blaize's pace was swift and determined. Not once did he look back at Shelby. He finally stopped in front of a door at the end of the hall. Despite the rigidity of his body, the tapping sound he made on the door was amazingly gentle. "Marlene?" There was no answer. "Marlene," he called again.

There was a pause before a weak voice replied. "She's not in here."

"It's Blaize," he said, cracking the door and sticking his head inside. "Do you mind if I come in?"

"No," was the singular reply.

"I have someone with me, Cleophus." Blaize stepped inside the doorway. He put his hand up in a halting gesture for Shelby to remain out of sight.

"Who?" The word vibrated with surprise.

"Someone very special. Didn't Marle—didn't your mother tell you I had returned?"

"Yes. Someone came back with you from America?"

Shelby could see Blaize's jaw tighten again. She didn't understand it. Why hadn't his sister mentioned her? Why was Blaize being so careful with what he said?

"Yes. Her name is Shelby." Blaize walked into the room and gestured for Shelby to follow.

With her heart in her throat Shelby stepped inside. The boy lay in a very large four-poster bed with his head propped up on a couple of pillows. Maybe it was the size of the bed that made him appear so small, but when Shelby looked at him, he looked like a child of ten or twelve, instead of a young man of sixteen. Shelby and Blaize walked over and stood beside the bed. Blaize made sure that Shelby was the closest.

"Her name is Shelby Russau, Cleophus."

"Russau?" His round eyes searched Shelby's face. "That is my father's last name."

"Yes." Shelby smiled but her lips trembled. She fought every instinct she had to keep from crying. As she looked at the child, there was no doubt in her mind that this was Cleophus' son. The eyes that looked back at her were her brother's eyes when he was ill, before he died. "I know."

"How do you know?" Cleophus' eyes were riveted on her face.

"Because your father is her brother," Blaize's sister said as she entered the room. "And as you can see, he did not have the decency to come himself."

Shelby looked at the large, shapely woman who held herself rigidly at the foot of the bed. Her straightened hair hung above her shoulders. Her brown eyes were full of resentment.

"No, that's not true," Shelby replied. "Cleophus would have come if he could."

"So where is he?" Marlene spat out. "Married and taking care of his family? Or is he still a puppet of the U.S. Army? Doing what they say do? Going where they say go?" Her eyes flashed although her body stayed motionless.

Shelby looked at Blaize, then at the boy. She reached down and touched his slender hand. "Your father is dead, Cleophus. I believe he died the year you were born. He never knew he had a son. If he had known he would have been very proud."

Shelby looked up when Marlene made a strangled sound, placed her hand over her mouth, then ran from the room.

"What did he die of?" Cleophus asked with his eyes downcast. "The same thing I have now?"

"Oh no," Shelby assured him. "He died of a lung infection. And you are not going to die." She wiped away a tear before Cleophus saw it. "We're going to see to that. I'll supply the blood that you need, and you'll be as good as new sooner than you think."

Cleophus looked up at her and smiled before he closed his eyes.

For a moment Shelby just stood and stared. *Oh my God. This is Cleophus' son. This is my nephew. We are family.* She wanted to reach down and touch his face, stroke his head, but she felt it might be too much too soon. "We should let you rest," she said, looking at Blaize. "It's quite a bit of excitement to find out you've got an aunt, and that you'll be up and on your feet real soon."

Cleophus looked at Shelby and Blaize with tired eyes. "Some days I'm up and about anyway. I'm just very, very tired today. It's not always like this."

"That's good to know." Shelby put on her brightest smile. Blaize started for the door and Shelby knew she should leave as well. "Perhaps I'll talk to you later." She called over her shoulder, but Cleophus was already on his way to sleep.

Chapter 14

Shelby followed Blaize to the first floor in silence. When they reached the bottom of the stair, he motioned to the right.

"You can sit in the drawing room. I'll have your room prepared in no time at all." He turned to walk away.

"Blaize," Shelby called after him. Slowly, he looked at her. There was an awkward pause. "I—I'm sorry, if I jumped to conclusions. It's just that—"

"It's just that you allowed your mind to play tricks on you." Blaize finished the sentence. "In your heart you knew the truth, but it was drowned out by your thoughts." He looked at her as if she were a foreigner. The American incapable of trusting what flows from the heart.

"It all seemed so strange," Shelby replied, trying to recall why she had reacted so rashly.

"You don't have the only stake in the game

when it comes to the importance of family." Blaize's tone was cold. "Just because you have had losses and have suffered doesn't give you the right to believe no one else's experiences have been as powerful. It doesn't give you the right to judge me." He walked away.

Shelby stood there and watched. It was the first time she had seen Blaize react emotionally. It had an effect on her that went deeper than words. He was angry. She was the one who had made him that way.

Wrapping her arms around herself, Shelby entered the drawing room. She didn't know whether to sit or stand. The exchange with Blaize clutched at her heart. She was certain his anger was masking a deep hurt. It was difficult for Shelby to accept that. Blaize appeared so invincible. Immovable. But there he was reacting to a wound that had been reopened by her words.

"I can see you and my brother have gotten off to a good start," Marlene said, entering the room. "I can almost count the times when I have seen such a blatant display of emotion. You have gotten under his skin. That's quite a feat."

Shelby studied Blaize's sister. Her eyes were red and her nose swollen. She had been crying.

"I must admit, we have had somewhat of a rocky road." Shelby glanced toward the hallway where Blaize disappeared.

"He is a difficult man to understand," Marlene

replied. "He is a difficult man to touch."

"I'm glad to hear you say that. I was beginning to think it was just me." Shelby tried to smile.

"I think you managed to touch him. But I am a living witness that touching a man doesn't always mean keeping him."

They looked into each other's eyes, then fell into an awkward silence.

Finally Marlene spoke again. "Cleophus told me he had a baby sister. He always talked about returning to America because he had left you in someone else's care. He said your parents had died years before." She looked down. "I didn't know if he was telling the truth, or simply making up an excuse so that he could go back with a clean conscience."

"Well, as you can see he wasn't lying. I am his sister and our parents died when I was very young. Cleophus didn't want us to be separated. He took care of me for awhile. But he said our father always wanted him to join the armed forces, so we both agreed that he should. Pretty soon he was sent here, to Grenada."

"Did Cleophus ever mention me?" Marlene walked over to a window.

"No. He didn't," Shelby replied softly.

Marlene glanced halfway over her shoulder before looking out the window again. "I guess that says how important I was in his life." She hung her head before lifting it rebelliously. "But I made sure my life did not stop. I made sure everyone knew Marlene would not stop living because your brother had left me behind."

Shelby felt the charge in Marlene's words. She searched for a way to help bring her peace. "I don't think Cleophus didn't mention you because you weren't important. I think he never talked about you because he felt I was too young to understand." She paused for emphasis. "He did talk about you to Willie. A very good friend of his. Willie said Cleophus cared about you an awful lot, but he felt you were too young to come back to the States at that time. That you had some family issues to re-solve. Family has always meant an awful lot to Cleophus and me."

Marlene faced Shelby. "He spoke of me to his friend?"

Shelby nodded.

Marlene's eyes clouded with unshed tears. Shelby knew, this time, when Marlene turned away it was so she would not see her cry. Her pain over Cleophus' death moved Shelby, and she knew no matter what Blaize's sister said, she had loved her brother deeply. And on some level still did.

"How long do you plan to stay?" Marlene asked.

"Around three weeks. Hopefully, by then, Cleo-phus will be showing some progress and will have opened up to me. I can't tell you how excited I was to hear my brother had a son. Perhaps one day he can visit me in Florida. See where his father was from. Understand his culture a little more."

"Why is that necessary?" Marlene interrogated. "What has Blaize told you? That I didn't provide a good life for my son. So now you think you can do a better job by filling his head with all things that are good and American?"

"No." Shelby shook her head, surprised. "No, that's not how it is at all."

"What did you mean then?" Marlene's eyes shone brightly. "Oh-h." She nodded. "Perhaps you're like my brother. Obsessed with the continuation of your family's bloodline. Obsessed with it, but unwilling or unable to contribute to it yourself?"

Shelby was struck by the unprovoked attack. "I don't feel I'm obsessed with anything," she defended herself. "It seems quite simple to me. Cleophus was my only brother. And at this time I don't have any children of my own. I think it's perfectly natural for me to be happy about finding out I have a nephew."

A shadow of remorse crossed Marlene's attractive features. "It may not be the wisest thing for you or Cleophus to become too attached." She glanced at Shelby, then looked away. "After all, you do live in America, and Cleophus lives worlds away."

"I understand your concern." Shelby tried to be agreeable. "But even though our cultures may be different, I think most people want the same things no matter where they live." Shelby offered a tentative smile. "Ultimately, I think we all want to be happy. And perhaps if Cleophus saw the city his father grew up in, and realized how much the same we all are, he will feel that much more whole."

"My son is whole." Marlene stressed each word.

"I'm sorry. I didn't mean that in a negative way." Shelby hurried on. "I just wish I could have seen where my parents grew—"

"I will never allow Cleophus to go to America," Marlene cut her off. "His home is here. His roots are here. There is no need to make him believe otherwise. It will only make him yearn for something more. I can give him everything he needs, and all he really needs is right here."

Shelby sighed. She knew Marlene was speaking out of her past, and she was only trying to protect her child. Perhaps that was why she had not told Cleophus that Shelby had come to Grenada. Shelby realized her stay on Hummingbird Island was going to be complicated in ways she had never imagined.

"The room is ready," Blaize announced from the large archway leading from the foyer into the drawing room.

"Thank you." Shelby looked from brother to sister. "I guess I'll go and unpack my things," she dismissed herself. She needed to be able to close a door and process what had occurred since she set foot on Hummingbird Island.

Shelby was almost to her room when she heard

Blaize say, "Shelby and Cleophus have the same blood type. She can provide him with the blood for the transfusion and represent his father's bloodline at the—"

Marlene interrupted him. "You should have consulted me about this."

"There wasn't time, Marlene. When I found out the boy's father was dead I did what I thought was the next best thing."

"I am in charge of Cleophus' life. I have been all these years and I will continue to be." There was a pause. "And another thing. I am too old for you to try to run my affairs now. Perhaps you are attempting to make up for lost time, but it is too late for that."

As she opened the bedroom door Shelby saw Marlene brush past Blaize, leaving him standing in the middle of the floor.

Chapter 15

"What are you doing here, Keith?" Blaize picked up a papaya and walked over to the kitchen sink. "I thought you had taken the other ferry and were visiting with your family on the mainland."

"They were too much for me." Keith shook his nearly white head. "I'm not feeling too good, so I had to come back here." He placed a glass of rum with lemon in it on the counter. "I'm about to make me up a cold remedy. I ran out of honey." He stepped inside the pantry. "I hope you don't mind my making use of some of yours."

"You know I don't," Blaize replied.

"I think I've become addicted to the calm and quiet of this island. I can't stand too much goings on." Keith emerged with a jar of honey in his hand. "My children act as if I'm too old to make my own decisions. They think I need to come back and live with them in St. George. They think I've spent enough years dealing with you and your family's craziness."

"Is that what they said?"

"Pretty much." Keith took a spoon and dipped it into the honey. "Of course, years ago nobody was complaining about my dealings with your family. They liked the money. They were happy I worked with your daddy and your granddaddy before him. That was before things really took off." Blaize listened to Keith talk about the past for the hundredth time. "Way back then all your granddaddy owned was a small group of nutmeg trees. It was really your daddy who turned it into orchards. I thought about the old times when I drove past what used to be your family's land on the way back from St. George."

Blaize reflected on his unstructured days, and the freedom to do whatever he wanted. Sometimes he didn't know if it was a blessing or a curse. "Things were really different back then," he commented.

"Yes." Keith bobbed his head. "Everyone pitched in and went to the orchards when the fruits split open and started dropping from the trees. You can't let nutmeg stay on the ground. Oh-h no. You got to get it right away or it'll spoil."

Blaize peeled his papaya, allowing Keith his memories.

"But your daddy did the right thing by selling out to that big company. Back then folks laughed at him. Told your granddaddy he was going to destroy what he had worked so hard to build."

"Yes, father was a smart man." Blaize gazed off into the distance. "He cut a hell of a deal. And as long as Spice International stock remains viable we'll be paid. The ups and downs of the spice market won't affect us a bit."

"Who would have thought it?" Keith said. "I didn't know what a stock was back in those days. Your daddy was the one with the vision." His lips turned into a sneaky smile. "And the big ears."

"Yes. What my mother called his nosey ways paid off. Eavesdropping on his White counterparts whenever he went to sell his nutmeg was a good business move. Father's cunning will be taking care of this family for generations to come. And on top of that, through the years I've been able to put away quite a bit." Blaize leaned back on the counter and took a bite of papaya. "I would think you have too."

"Oh-h, I've done good." Keith's eyes sparkled when he smiled. "I've done real good. That's why I don't understand why my folks won't just leave me alone. I'm not hurting anybody up here. And they're still being taken care of." He stirred the honey and a bit of nutmeg into the brew. "Do you know my granddaughter, Danielle, is threatening to come here and give you a piece of her mind? I think my daughter spared the rod too often when it came to her."

One of Blaize's eyebrows went up. "Really?"

"Yes." Keith chuckled. "They think you are making me stay here. They can't believe I stay because I love the place. If they'd ever come visit they'd realize why."

"I guess my reputation precedes me." Blaize cut off another slice of fruit and popped it in his mouth.

"That is a big possibility. Your and your family's reputation."

"Oh yes." Blaize looked down at the fruit and the knife he held in his hand. "What do they think, Keith? No." He stopped his longtime companion before he could answer. "Let me guess. They probably believe I gazed into the stars and came up with a potion that kept you from thinking for yourself?"

A cheesy grin spread across Keith's surprisingly smooth face. "Anything's possible. You know folks believe that's why your family has continued to do well while others have been suffering. You were able to divine when to make the right business moves. They do believe it has something to do with stargazing. Not with your daddy's natural penchant for listening in on other people's conversations."

"Perhaps my father would have been capable of doing that. Determining the proper dates and times for business decisions." Blaize reflected. "But I rarely remember him using his skill for that sort of thing. Mostly he used it to help people with personal growth. Spiritual, family and love issues."

"That's how I remember it," Keith replied.

"I know that's what he encouraged me to do. Whenever I would listen," Blaize said.

"What folks don't understand, they'll make up an understanding," Keith proclaimed. "Or they'll be so afraid to look at truth that they will dare anyone else to look at it." He took a swig of the concoction, then rubbed his throat. "I did my best in the little time I was on the mainland to spread the word about the ceremony."

"I didn't expect you to do that," Blaize replied.

"I know." Keith looked down.

"That's why your family gave you such a hard time." Blaize pointed his finger. "I don't want you taking any flak for me, Keith. If anybody is to suffer repercussions from this it should be me. Reinstating the Rites of Passage ceremony on Hummingbird Island is my idea."

"I know. But I think it is a good one. One that your parents would be proud of."

They fell silent.

"So a woman returned to Grenada with you?"

"Yes." Blaize walked over and placed the papaya seed with several others intended for planting. "I put her in the bedroom next to mine." He paused. "Did Marlene tell you that?"

"Nope. I went to the inn and heard about it. Marlene doesn't have that much to say to me."

"Well, we're in the same boat when it comes to that," Blaize replied. "But don't you take it personally. Her problem is with me."

"Partly. The other part is with herself." Keith made a show of studying his fingernails. "Who is the woman you brought back with you?"

"Shelby Russau. She's Cleophus' aunt. It seems his father died the year he was born. He never knew about the boy," Blaize said, his face turning hard.

"Is that right?" Keith stopped and stared. "I wonder how Marlene's going to feel about that."

"Hearing the boy's father had died hit her pretty hard. I don't know how she feels about the rest of it."

Keith's lips pursed as he went into deep thought. "Maybe she'll let go some now. Both of you made some decisions after your parents were killed that may not have been the best. But it's way past time for you two to come together."

"It's not easy, Keith. I think she resents my going to America and bringing the boy's aunt back."

"Why did you bring her back?"

"She has the same blood type as the boy."

"Does Marlene know that?"

"I tried to tell her, but she was not in a listening mood."

Keith shook his head "Doesn't she know you're just trying to save the boy?"

"She knows that." Blaize looked down. "I can tell she loves Cleophus, and I'm sure deep down inside she is grateful for what I've done. But as she's made it so clear in the past, she still doesn't want anything from me."

"She thinks you still blame her for what happened. Is she right?" Keith finished his cold remedy and looked at Blaize with steady eyes.

"I don't blame her." Blaize returned his gaze. "Yes. There's a part of me that believes if my mother and father hadn't gone to St. George looking for Marlene the day of the massacre they might still be alive today. But I also have to admit that father had seen their deaths in the stars. He felt it was their time. He tried to tell me. Prepare me. But I wasn't ready to hear it. I wasn't ready to accept it." Blaize looked down. "Now I am."

"You haven't been hemmed up on this island for sixteen years for nothing, have you?" Keith said admiringly.

Blaize gave an almost imperceptible nod of his head.

"So how much does Shelby Russau know about what has taken place here?" Keith asked.

"Very little. I told her about Cleophus. I didn't see the need to tell her anything more."

"I guess it wasn't easy to get her to come. You've been gone three weeks."

"No, it wasn't easy," Blaize replied. "She wouldn't listen to me at first, and when she did it took some convincing. But from what happened this morning, I know she wasn't truly convinced until she saw Cleophus with her own eyes. I guess she doesn't find me trustworthy." Blaize gazed off into the distance, a guarded expression descending over his features. "Nevertheless, she is willing to provide the blood that he'll need for the operation."

Keith studied Blaize's change in attitude. "What about the Rites of Passage?"

"She doesn't like the idea. And then some things happened in Grand Anse that turned her even further against it."

"What kind of things?"

"She received a threatening package that was meant for me." Blaize gazed out the window. "One of the local newspapers took a picture of us at the airport, then someone slipped a copy of it along with a note underneath her hotel door. They had placed a red circle around Shelby's face. The note threatened that they would harm me or anybody close to me if I went through with the ritual."

"You're making up a lie," Keith replied, shocked.

"No. I wish I was." Blaize's eyes held a deadly glint. "It really upset Shelby. I wish I could get my hands on the people who are responsible."

"So you and this Shelby got pretty close while you were in America?" Keith lifted his eyebrow meaningfully.

"No." Blaize gave Keith a hooded look. "We didn't."

"Then what made them think that you were close?" Keith's brows furrowed.

"I guess because we came back from America

together." Blaize rinsed his hands in the sink.

Keith stared at his broad shoulders. "It's been a long time since you've been off this island. And unless you made some special stops on the way to board that plane for the U.S.A., I'd say it's been a long time since you've been with a woman."

"And?" Blaize pinned him with a stare.

Keith rattled his head like a bobbing doll in the back of a car. "I just thought that maybe . . . is she ugly or something?" His wizened features turned sly.

"No," Blaize replied softly. "Quite the opposite." Then he flashed a rare smile that didn't reach his eyes. "But no matter your vote of confidence, Keith, every woman who sees me is not bucking to jump into bed with me."

"O-oh. I know better than that. Years ago you had to beat them off with a stick."

"That was years ago. And in some ways another lifetime. I am a different man now than I was back then."

"I believe that." Keith rubbed his chin. "But a man is a man, and every man needs a woman."

"I'm not saying I don't have needs." Blaize remembered how soft Shelby's lips were and how good she felt against his body. "Sometimes a man can act out of his needs before he considers the consequences. But the truth is some women require more than periodic moments of pleasure."

"Is this Shelby one of them?"

"Yes." The word was a prolonged, raspy whisper.

Keith nodded slowly. "Maybe these people weren't so far off when they felt she was someone close to you."

Blaize just looked at him.

Keith cleared his throat. "Who do you think is behind the threat?" He tactfully changed the subject.

Blaize released a breath he didn't realize he was holding. "I have no idea. There were a couple of articles in the paper about my coming out of seclusion. I guess that generated some interest in me and the family. But I don't know what would motivate someone to go so far as to threaten to do bodily harm to those around me if I don't back off of the ancestral ceremony."

"Maybe they feel like you are digging up the past."

"I thought about that. But who would that hurt? I believe certain aspects of the past and the present can exist together side by side. That it could only strengthen our society."

"Obviously, someone doesn't agree with you."

"Obviously." Blaize nodded.

"That stunt at the hotel must have frightened Miss Russau pretty bad, huh? And I am assuming it's Miss." Keith watched Blaize with a steady eye.

"Yes. She's not married," Blaize replied.

"And how long will she be staying?"

"Through the time of Cleophus' transfusion. And a couple of weeks after that to make sure he's doing well, and to spend some time with him."

"That's about three weeks."

"That's right."

"A lot can happen in three weeks. Wouldn't you say?" Keith lifted his eyebrows.

"You better be careful. I might tell your family to come and get you," Blaize replied in a teasing tone as he walked toward the kitchen door.

Chapter 16

Shelby walked down the hall towards Cleophus' bedroom. If she hadn't known there were others in the house, she might have believed she was alone. The place felt so still. Before she reached his bedroom Marlene slipped into the hall, closing the door quietly behind her.

"Is he still resting?" Shelby found herself whispering.

"He is asleep."

"Does he sleep a lot?" Shelby tried to mask her disappointment.

"Sometimes. On other days it's hard to believe he's sick."

They descended the stairs together.

"It must be tough on you to see him like this." Shelby's eyes softened.

"It is difficult." Marlene replied, her back stiffening. "But there are many parts of life that are."

To Shelby's dismay, she could feel Marlene pulling away. But Shelby wanted to get to know the woman who was the mother of Cleophus' son. "Is it always this quiet around here?"

"It seems that way," Marlene replied.

"You say that as if you are a guest here as well." Shelby followed Marlene to a bench set in the back of the house. The landscape formed a beautiful natural garden surrounded by trees and tropical flowers.

Marlene looked at Shelby with eyes that said little. "It's obvious I am not a guest here, but I do not feel like it is my home either."

"Really? I would think after all these years you would be as attached to the place as Blaize."

"How can I be?" Marlene replied. "Until Blaize had left to find Cleophus' father, he had not left this island for sixteen years. I on the other hand had not set foot on this soil until a week before he left."

A shocked Shelby exclaimed, "What?"

"I can see my brother did not tell you." Marlene glanced down quickly. "Blaize saw Cleophus for the first time a month ago. This is the first time I have returned to Hummingbird Island since my parents' funeral. Cleophus and I lived in St. George."

"So you had the baby alone there?"

"Yes."

"But why didn't you return home?" Shelby pressed to understand.

"Perhaps that is something you should ask my brother."

Shelby could feel a tiny pain growing in her chest. What if Blaize hated Cleophus because he was illegitimate? Shelby hoped the unkind image of Blaize that had crept into her consciousness was wrong. "You mean Blaize did not want you on Hummingbird Island because you had a child and you weren't married?"

"No." Marlene shook her head slowly. "I must confess Blaize is not that big of a prude. My not being married had nothing to do with it. I'm not saying he would not have been more than happy if I had been married, but my being a single mother played only a part in my staying away from Hummingbird Island." Marlene paused as she summoned up the past. "Had I come back, Blaize would have accepted Cleophus and me. As a matter of fact, I'm sure it would have saved him many hours of grief knowing we were here under his control, and not out depending on the charity of others. At least I would not have been defiling the family name."

Shelby wrestled with this newest discovery.

"I guess you're wondering why my brother did not tell you that I did not martyr myself along with him, by becoming a recluse on this island."

"The thought did cross my mind," Shelby replied.

"When you get the chance you should ask him.

I would be interested in knowing what he had to say." Marlene rose from the bench. "I think I'll start preparing dinner now. Listen, I don't want you thinking too badly about Blaize. After all, you are Cleophus' aunt. Our ancestors may turn over in their graves if I push them even the slightest bit further."

More than confused Shelby said the only thing she knew to say, "Do you want some help?"

"No, I believe I can manage," Marlene answered without turning around.

Shelby watched Marlene disappear into the house. She sat on the bench for a while longer, but she was antsy. Marlene's revelations renewed the distrust in Blaize Shelby had recently put to rest.

She watched the birds fly in and out of the canopy of trees that lay beyond the house. It reminded her of a woman's hat with flowers and birds perched on top as decoration. Although the forest was thick, Shelby could clearly see a path cutting through it. A walk would help calm her, she thought; the sights and sounds would serve as a distraction.

She advanced toward the pathway with her mind reeling. Why had Blaize lied? She was certain he had told her Marlene and Cleophus lived with him on Hummingbird Island during his sixteen years of seclusion. Or had he? Shelby stopped and bit down on her thumb knuckle. Perhaps he hadn't. He did not say they lived on the island, she surmised, but he did not tell her that they did not either. Had the omission been deliberate? She continued down the path, brushing aside the overzealous plants that blocked her way. Now Blaize's somewhat formal mannerisms toward Cleophus made sense. He barely knew the boy better than she did. Shelby let loose a short, exasperated laugh. But what could have made Marlene stay away for all those years, Shelby wondered as she walked further into the wild.

By the time Shelby got to the end of a long line of questions, she was deep inside the interior of Hummingbird Island. She stopped and looked around her. The air was filled with endless birdcalls and beneath them was a steady, continuous shushing sound. When Shelby decided that she should turn back, the path that had been so clearly defined from the safety of the bench was now awash with variegated greens. Although Shelby felt certain about the way that she had come, now, when she attempted to retrace her steps, there appeared to be two paths instead of one.

"I know I came from this direction." She advanced carefully, looking for a familiar bush or tree, of which there was none. "This is going to be a little tough," she told herself. "It's good it's still daylight or I might be in trouble." She looked up at the sky which was barely visible through the trees.

Walking with as much confidence as she could

muster, Shelby progressed back up the path, but the slushing sound got louder, something Shelby was certain should have been occurring in reverse if she was going in the right direction. As she advanced the sound became a mild roar. Shelby stopped. She was certain the source was to the left of where she stood. Carefully, she made her way through a thicket. And there it was. A waterfall cascading over a rocky cliff nearly twenty feet high. "I have never . . ." Shelby gushed as she gazed at the natural wonder.

The water ran, tumbled and frothed into a good-sized pond. "This is unbelievable. Oh my heavens, this is beautiful." Shelby continued in awe.

"I've got to stay here for a while. This is like a wonderland, and all I have to do to get back to the house is take the other path." She lay down with her feet near the edge of the crystal clear pond. Reverently, Shelby stretched out her hand to trail it across the water.

"What do you think you're doing?" Blaize demanded from the edge of the thicket.

His unexpected appearance shook Shelby and her hand dropped, splashing water into her face. She balanced herself on her forearms and looked back at him. "What does it look like?"

"I would advise you not to wander off like this alone without telling someone."

"Oh, I'm sorry," she replied, her voice too sweet. "I didn't realize we were supposed to inform each other of everything. That there should be such honesty between us."

"I would think common sense would have told you it is not a good idea to roam around a strange island."

"I would think common decency would have told you that you should have informed me that you had never seen Cleophus before a month ago."

A split second of discomfort flashed on Blaize's face before it disappeared. "I didn't think it was any of your business."

"None of my business." Shelby turned over and flopped onto her butt, her hands hitting the ground in an exaggerated manner. "You made me think you were this dear sweet uncle to Cleophus ever since he was a baby in your sister's arms." She made a rocking gesture. "And that I would be the wicked auntie from the west if I didn't jump on a plane and come help him. Now *I* find out that you have only known him for a month."

"What does that have to do with your helping Cleophus?" Blaize walked toward her.

"Nothing. But I thought we were developing some kind of relationship here." Shelby looked up at him, exasperated. "I don't mean anything romantic, but just as two adults who could speak the truth to one another."

"I told you the truth."

"Oh. So you just happen to omit that part?"

"I told you what was necessary," Blaize replied

in a deadpan voice. "All that you needed to know. I wasn't obligated to tell you more."

Shelby looked into his harsh features. Blaize's cold, standoffish remarks stung. Somewhere along the road she had come to believe there was trust between them. Something that had deepened because of the threat that had been made against her. A trust that she had broken when she demanded to see Cleophus. But the man that stood before her now was not the man she had come to trust.

Shelby scrambled to her feet. "That's right. You are not obligated. And how stupid of me to think we had any kind of relationship at all. Now, I wouldn't want one." She challenged him with her eyes, but the hurt showed underneath.

"Shelby." Her name was a harsh whisper before Blaize enfolded her in his arms. "Let's not argue," he said softly. "I don't want to argue."

They shared a tormented kiss. One that tempted . . . One of hunger . . . The energy between them spoke worlds. Blaize held Shelby so tightly that she could barely breathe, but still she returned the kiss with the same ferocity, her mouth having a mind of its own. Declaring her need.

"Do you see?" he whispered against her lips. "We do not need obligation to feel this." He kissed her again.

Once again Shelby responded, but a voice of reason sounded in the midst of passion. Struggling with her own desire she managed to turn her head away. "This is not right," Shelby said softly, pulling back. "I've got to get back." She turned and started up the first path she saw.

"Where are you going?" Blaize shouted from the edge of the pond.

"Back to the house." She glanced back at him.

"But you don't know your way back."

"I'll find it," Shelby replied. Afraid of getting lost. But more afraid of what might happen should she remain in the secluded place near the waterfall.

"Wait," Blaize called. "I'll show you the way." In a few strides he had overtaken Shelby, and was leading her back through the thicket.

Chapter 17

Shelby and Blaize walked toward the house in silence. There was a volatile, magnetic energy between them was palpable. It was difficult for Shelby to watch Blaize walking in front of her. She was aware of how he held his head; the way his locks lay against his massive back; the rise and fall of his backside as he made his way through the rain forest. Shelby was afraid that at any moment Blaize would turn around and take her in his arms. She knew if he did she would not have the power to resist. Then where would she be? Strung out on a man who wanted nothing more than her body when she had, and was willing to give, so much more.

But to Shelby's dismay and to her relief Blaize did not turn around. In single file they entered the house through the kitchen door. Marlene looked up from stirring a pot on the stove.

"So you found her?"

"Yes," Blaize replied, glancing at Shelby. But just that moment of eye contact was charged enough to alert Marlene that something was amiss. She eyed them suspiciously.

"I think perhaps, if Blaize hadn't come, I would have eventually found my way back." Shelby tumbled over her words in an attempt to sound natural. "But I'm grateful that he came to find me."

"It was my pleasure," Blaize responded.

An awkward silence followed.

"I guess times do change." Marlene sang the phrase. "I've never known you to be so gracious, my brother. So accommodating."

"Time does change things, Marlene. I'm glad that you are beginning to realize that," Blaize replied. But it was obvious he was not referring to his situation with Shelby.

Quickly, Marlene turned away and started stirring the pot again. "Dinner is almost ready. I didn't know who all would be eating, but there is plenty for everyone."

"Thank you," Blaize replied. "But I think I'm going to head over to the mainland. I've got some business to take care of. I'll do nothing but get in trouble if I remain here." He looked at Shelby one last time before he left the room.

"I think I know what kind of trouble he's talking about," Marlene said beneath her breath.

But Shelby barely heard her. She looked out the kitchen window. Already the descending sun had started to paint the sky in the fabulous colors of dusk. "Isn't it rather dangerous for him to take that ferry across the water after dark?"

Marlene glanced over her shoulder. "Don't tell me you are worried about Blaize. If you are, you are wasting your time." She clacked the wooden spoon against the metal. "He can take care of himself better than most. He's been crossing that water after dark ever since he was an eager teenager hot and heavy after the girls. I'm sure as a man he can manage without incident."

"Of course you're right," Shelby replied, the thought of a hot and heavy Blaize of any sort sending steam up her collar. "I forgot. I don't know what I was thinking about." She laughed self-consciously. "I'm the only one here who doesn't know their way around."

"There's something different about you." Marlene walked over to a counter and leaned against it. "You appear to be a bit out of sorts."

"Do I?" Shelby looked at Marlene, her eyes too wide. "Perhaps it's because I got myself lost."

"Perhaps." Marlene wiped her hand on a drying towel. She paused. "I hope I am not being too forward but I must ask, is there something going on between you and my brother?"

"Why no." Shelby placed her palm over her heart. "Not really."

"Not really. And what does that mean?"

Shelby could feel Marlene's eyes taking in her

every move. "That there really isn't anything going on between us." Shelby lifted her palms. "Of course I find your brother attractive. Most any woman would. But I try not to be swayed by every pretty face that comes my way."

"But Blaize is much more than a pretty face," Marlene replied. "I think we both know that. If you don't I am telling you so now. It is going to take a special kind of woman to deal with him. To understand the workings of his mind and heart. I have been gone for many years, but even as a young man he had more depth than most older men I know now." Marlene smiled a cynical smile. "Perhaps I was even a little jealous of the wisdom he possessed. He shined that much brighter in my parents' eyes because of it."

"You make Blaize sound very special." Shelby's voice was breathy as she looked down at her hands.

"He is. Make no mistake about that."

Silence hung between them.

"The food will be on the table in about ten minutes," Marlene announced. "I'm going to check on Cleophus. I don't think he feels well enough to come down to the table tonight, but tomorrow is another day." She started to exit the room, then changed her mind. "I'll be going on the mainland tomorrow to do some shopping. Would you like to come with me?"

"Sure I would." Shelby smiled. Marlene nodded and smiled back.

*   *   *

Shelby struggled with the lock on the French doors that led from her bedroom to the patio outside. She had tried to sleep but it proved to be impossible. Her thoughts vaulted from Cleophus lying ill in the bed on the floor above her to Blaize ferrying across the dark expanse of water with nothing but the moon to light his way. The threat that had been made at the hotel also surfaced, but it seemed of little consequence. The world and its problems felt a million miles away from Hummingbird Island.

How strange life was to have brought her to such a place. An island that could have been the setting for one of the old movies she loved. Its inhabitants as intriguing as the film stars of yesterday.

Shelby rattled the door handle one more time, but this time it finally gave way, and an intoxicating tropical breeze flowed into the bedroom. She tightened the belt of her short robe and stepped out with bare feet onto the tiles. Shelby closed her eyes and let the warm air embrace her, imagining it was Blaize's arms about her, his breath upon her face.

She couldn't believe how far gone she was on the man. All these years of having her head on right, then along came Raphael Blaize. Now she didn't know where her head was. She bit her bottom lip as she considered the irony of the situation. And it wasn't just because he was the most beautiful man she had ever seen. It was, as Marlene said, because whatever lay beneath the surface made him shine that much brighter.

The beautiful sound of a night bird floated on the breeze and Shelby placed her chin on her entwined hands and sighed. She turned to go back inside, but a noise sounded to the right of her. Shelby watched as the patio doors opened. A barechested Blaize in gauze pants emerged. The tropical breeze lifted his locks behind him like the fringes on a cape. She had been watching only a moment over the waist-high hedge when his head turned slowly in her direction. It seemed he had been aware that she was standing there all along.

"It is hard to ignore the call of the night, isn't it?" Blaize asked, looking up at the stars.

"Yes. It is," Shelby replied, wondering if his question held a double meaning like her answer.

"How long have you been out here?"

"Maybe five minutes. And you? When did you get back?"

"A couple of hours ago. But I couldn't sleep. I kept thinking about you lying in the bed in the room next to mine. I tried to imagine how you would lie when you slept. What you were wearing or if you wore nothing at all."

Shelby was glad Blaize was not looking at her when he spoke. If he had been he would have seen her melt under the heat of his words. "You didn't tell me that you would be sleeping next door." Shelby skirted the subject.

"If I had would it have made a difference?"

"No." She paused before she stated boldly, "As a matter of fact it is a pleasant surprise."

"Is it?" Blaize turned and faced her.

"Yes. I would be lying if I said otherwise. And I'm tired of lying to myself. This is really difficult for me, you know."

"What is difficult, Shelby?"

"Keeping you at bay. Telling myself making love to you is not the right thing to do. That it would just be an act of passion with no promises for tomorrow."

"But is tomorrow ever promised to us? Sometimes even what the stars have divined does not come true. So therefore what we may feel in our hearts today is true for that moment. It is best to live in the present, Shelby. Sometimes the future will disappoint you."

"Wisely spoken as usual." Her full lips turned in an ironic smile. "Still, I have held on to the belief that the next man I give myself to will be my partner for life. It is hard to let go of old fairy tales."

"Let go of them, Shelby." Blaize walked over to the hedge. "And we will create our own fairy tales . . . together."

Shelby looked into his eyes and felt herself falling under Blaize's spell. Then she took a deep breath. "I've waited too long, Blaize. And what is a woman without her fairy tale?" She reached out and touched his face. "It's a good thing this hedge is between us. Because in the time it takes you to enter my side of the patio I will have locked my doors, and if you knock, I promise I will not answer." She turned to walk away.

Blaize's voice followed her. "But just like your resistance, this hedge is an illusion." He popped a latch among the leaves and crossed over to Shelby's side. "Once that is accepted it vanishes with ease."

From the rear Blaize slid his arms around her. "I'm in the mood for a fairy tale tonight, Shelby. One that we will remember for a long, long time." He drew her back against his body. Like a swan Shelby's neck stretched to the side as she gave in to the gentleness of his touch.

"I can't believe this is happening," she said softly. "That these are your arms that I feel about me and not my imaginings from moments before."

"Believe it, my sweet. Because before this night is over, there will be no doubt in your mind that I am real, and the love that we have made is real as well."

With languid eyes Shelby looked up at the stars, and from his towering height Blaize leaned over and placed a lingering kiss on her lips. Before Shelby knew it she was facing him. Their bodies performed an intimate dance, Shelby pressing forward with Blaize surpassing her fervor. Their lips locked in a draining kiss.

When the contact turned into an excruciating

tease Blaize swept Shelby into his arms and an involuntary cry of surprise escaped her lips. They looked into each other's eyes and Blaize could see protest forming in Shelby's. "Don't stop me now, my sweet," he cajoled her. "Put that mind of yours to rest," he said, opening the French doors. "This is not a night for logic. This is a night for love." Blaize placed Shelby gently on the rumpled covers.

"Don't stop talking to me, Blaize," Shelby coaxed, and her heart beat with a fright-filled passion. "If you stop I can't promise what I might do."

"Is that all you need?" Blaize whispered in her ear. "Then I am more than willing to please."

He planted kisses on her mouth as he untied her housecoat. "Talk to you, Shelby. That I will." The silky object slid off her shoulders and lay beneath her. "Touch you." Blaize caressed her breasts beneath her gown before his hand wandered in an exploratory fashion, the satiny shirt rising almost to Shelby's waist. "Oh, how I have imagined."

His hand slipped between Shelby's legs and a gasp of pleasure rose from her throat, only to be greeted by another searing kiss. He fondled and touched her, arousing the seed of her pleasure until Shelby writhed on the bed. In her mounting desire her hands rubbed any part of him that she could reach. "It's been so long since I have felt such pleasure." Blaize spoke to her again. "If touching you can make me feel this way, then having you will be beyond anything I have ever imagined." He rolled to his side and discarded his pants.

"Oh, Blaize," Shelby exclaimed when she saw his nude body. Mesmerized, she reached out and touched him.

His neck stretched back as he bit his bottom lip. "Sweet day, my Shelby." He moaned as she manipulated him into stellar hardness. "You are a woman who is beautiful as well as talented," Blaize encouraged her.

Their mouths locked in a kiss, and Blaize and Shelby held one another with the passion of two people who have found the key of life. And when their moment of oneness approached, they came together easily. With an indescribable tenacity they strove for the prize. Minutes later, their bodies like human liquid, they churned until the most exquisite blend was in their reach.

"This is what fairy tales are made of, Shelby," Blaize rasped. "A tale only a man and a woman can know."

"A tale only the right man and woman may know," Shelby breathed as they quivered together.

Later Blaize and Shelby lay on their backs, looking out through the arched window above the French doors, breathing so heavily they could hardly speak; still the sight of a shower of shooting stars caused Blaize to bolt upright.

"What is it?" Shelby asked, startled.

"Did you see that?" Blaize continued to stare into the night sky.

"What?"

"The falling stars."

"Yes. I saw them and I quickly made a wish. I heard somewhere that's what you're suppose to do." The novelty of their lovemaking made Shelby feel like a child. She sat up and pulled the sheet over her breasts. "I have never seen so many shooting stars before."

"It is a sign," Blaize said, his tone disquieting.

Shelby looked at him. If he insisted on seeing something in the stars did it have to be foreboding? But Shelby still replied, softly, "A good one, I hope."

"I'm afraid we won't know the answer to that until the time comes," Blaize returned.

They looked into each other's eyes before Shelby turned her back to Blaize and closed her eyes. She didn't know what Blaize believed in, and at that moment she didn't want to know. Shelby simply wanted to savor the wonderful experience they had shared. To nuzzle into the covers that were still warm from the heat of their bodies. Still pulsating with the energy of their passion.

It was too soon for Shelby to think of what the future might bring. But it seemed Blaize was already looking for why they should not be together. Shelby turned just enough to see the stars. To her they appeared harmless and beautiful. She recalled the childlike wish she'd made: "I wish to be a part of a family."

Shelby sighed when Blaize finally lay down behind her. In a smooth movement his arm tugged at her waist and they came together, fitting like a petal on the bud of a flower.

"Blaize, when was the last time you made love to a woman?" Shelby was surprised at her own candor.

"Just a few moments ago," he replied.

"You know that's not what I meant."

"Let's suffice it to say it had been a long, long time. Long enough for me to relish every movement you made. Every breath you took. I don't have to remember the others, Shelby, when I have you."

Shelby closed her eyes again. "You should be a poet."

"And you the inspiration for my greatest poem," Blaize said softly into the dark.

Chapter 18

"I didn't know if getting up and coming to Sauteurs this early was going to be a bit much for you," Marlene said, carrying a basket of vegetables. "But you appear to be doing quite well."

"Yes, I'm fine." Shelby tried to subdue the smile that had been on her face from the moment she woke up and Blaize went back to his room. "I like getting out early. Although I didn't think you would be shopping for fruits and vegetables." She looked at the partially full basket hanging on Marlene's arm. "Didn't I see an extensive garden on Hummingbird Island?"

"Yes. But these are a few of my favorites that Blaize and Keith did not plant." She patted a large melon. "Besides, unlike my brother, I don't like being cooped up on the island. I thought I'd get up and out early, before Cleophus wakes up, and do my poking around."

"Do you think Cleophus will be up today?"

"I hope so," Marlene replied. "But his down days seem to be increasing as of late." A shadow crossed her face.

Shelby looked down. "Well, I hope my coming will change that."

Marlene did not reply. Shelby looked up and realized she was distracted by something or someone on the opposite side of the street.

"Yes. I hope it will," Marlene finally said in an absentminded manner. "Look, I've got some personal business to attend to. Do you think you'll be okay if I go—" She made a motion with her head.

"Sure," Shelby replied, a little surprised.

"I'll be back shortly, and we can get something to eat at Morne Fendue. It's an old plantation house about a mile and a half away." Marlene looked over her shoulder as if she was trying to keep someone in sight.

"You go ahead. I'll be fine," Shelby reassured her, although she felt a little uneasy about being left alone. "I'll just wander around the markets. How long will you be?"

"No more than twenty minutes," Marlene called, crossing the street. "You should go to Carib's Leap. It's a big tourist attraction."

"Where is it?" Shelby shouted.

"That way." Marlene motioned, her words blending with the sounds of the town.

Shelby walked in the direction which Marlene had indicated. Right away she saw a sign advertising the site. "Carib's Leap," she read aloud.

"Would you like to buy some spices?" A little boy held up a couple of lumpy sacks. "I've got nutmeg and cinnamon."

"I don't think so," Shelby replied.

"Sure you do. What good is it to come to Grenada if you are not going to buy spices?"

"How did you know I wasn't Grenadian?"

"You look like a tourist." He shrugged his shoulders.

Shelby looked down at her blue-jean shorts and T-shirt. "Since you know so much, what do you know about this Carib's Leap?"

"Plenty. If you are traveling alone you might want to hire me for your guide."

"I am alone, but the sign points right beyond that cemetery. Why would I need a guide to take me there?"

"Atmosphere. Local flavor," the boy replied, smiling.

"You are a slick one, aren't you?"

"Maybe," he sang. "But I'm also a good guide."

"Okay. You sold me. How much?"

"Two Eastern Caribbean dollars." The boy stuck his hand out.

"How about two American dollars?"

"Even better." His smile widened.

Shelby paid him.

"Now." He stepped out in front of her. "This town, Sauteurs, takes its name from the French word for jump. You know our history is full of French things."

"I've kind of gleaned that," Shelby said, walking beside the manly ten- or twelve-year-old. She wondered what Cleophus was like at that age.

"Gleaned?" He looked uncertain.

"Never mind," Shelby replied as they rounded a church labeled St. Patrick's Roman Catholic Church.

"The town was also named Sauteurs because of its place in history. It is the site where many, many years ago, in the sixteen hundreds, forty Carib warriors jumped to their deaths from the cliffs that you will see. They jumped to avoid being taken prisoner by French soldiers."

"Really." Shelby marveled as they approached the ledge. "They didn't want to be prisoners that bad."

"Yes. They were brave men. Part of my heritage." The boy seemed pleased with the impact his words were having. "I just thought of something." He stuck his index finger in the air, backing away. "Wait right here. I've got something for you."

Shelby watched as he ran off toward the church. He was a good guide, she thought, turning back toward the cliff. She was glad she had hired him.

Shelby looked over the ledge. There were fishing boats all along a village beach. She could also see Hummingbird Island and the surrounding islands. Shelby compared it to the others. "Let's see—"

"Yes. Let's see." A man who was standing far too close repeated.

"Oh. Where did you come from?" Shelby tried to turn and face him, but he made that impossible. When she attempted to step to the side he deliberately blocked her way.

"The question is what are you and your friend planning on Hummingbird Island?"

"What?" Shelby was even more aware of how close she stood to the edge of the cliff.

"I understand there is to be a ritual in a few days."

"I don't know anything about that."

"But your friend, Raphael Blaize, does." He pressed closer.

A cold chill went up Shelby's spine as a small shower of pebbles tumbled over the edge. There was no doubt in her mind that the man was trying to frighten her, or even worse.

"Blaize was on the mainland yesterday evening, encouraging the locals to join him in a couple of days at a Rites of Passage. In other words, stirring up trouble."

Shelby tried to maneuver to get around him. But the man adeptly kept her locked in.

"We warned him what would happen if he didn't cancel his plans." He took hold of Shelby's arm. "But obviously he thought we were kidding." He paused. "But we—"

"That's the lady! That's her!" A voice cried from

behind them. "She didn't pay me all my money."

Shelby turned as much as she could in her awkward position. She could barely see the boy who had served as her guide. He was jumping up and down, pointing in their direction. His shrill voice had attracted the attention of some tourists.

The boy walked toward them. "I want my money, and I want it now." A crowd began to gather near the church.

Shelby could sense the man's indecision, then he reluctantly released her. She stepped away from him. He averted his face and kept his back turned as she started across the lot. "I'm sorry." Shelby's voice trembled uncontrollably. "I thought I paid you your entire fee."

She could barely speak when she dropped down to her knee in front of the child. His eyes were large when he asked, "Are you okay? You said you were alone. And then I saw the man standing so close to you over the cliff. There was something strange about it."

Shelby nodded. "I'm okay." She tried to calm the frightened boy who had converted from the man-child guide to the young child that he was.

Shelby thought of telling the crowd that had gathered by the church what had happened. But already they had started to move on. Shelby's next inclination was to get as far away from the man and Carib's Leap as possible. She grabbed the boy by the hand and got to her feet. Rapidly, they started for the street.

"What was going on?" the boy asked, looking back.

"Just come on," Shelby said, unsure of what to tell him. There was a chance she could put him in jeopardy as well. They stopped when they arrived in the market area.

"What's your name?" Shelby looked into the child's alert brown eyes.

"Eric."

"Now listen to me, Eric," Shelby said. "What happened back there is none of your concern."

"But the man, he looked like he was going to hurt you," Eric protested.

"But I'm not hurt, am I?" She dug in her wallet and pulled out a twenty-dollar bill. "Here take this. It doesn't come close to what I owe you, but it will have to do for now. Do you live near here?"

"Yes."

"If I were you, Eric, I would go home and stay there. You've done more than enough for one day." She put her hands on his shoulders. "Now go."

The boy ran off down the street and Shelby headed in search of Marlene. There was a chance she was in danger as well.

She followed the direction Marlene had taken once she crossed the street. Shelby got lucky at the third establishment she searched. It was a small restaurant with a counter and two tables. Marlene was sitting at one of them with a man. She was smiling amorously into his face. The man appeared to be enjoying himself until Shelby stepped inside. Surprise crossed his thick features, but he quickly masked it with a mechanical smile.

"Marlene." Shelby locked eyes with the man.

"Shelby." First Marlene was surprised, but that morphed into irritation. "What are you doing in here?"

"I'll tell you later. But I think we should go. Now."

"What?"

"Please, Marlene," Shelby pleaded, trying to maintain her composure.

Marlene looked at her friend, then back to Shelby before she replied. "All right."

"It's okay, darling. I'll catch up with you another time." The man leaned over and planted a lingering kiss on Marlene's lips.

Reluctantly, Marlene rose from the table and followed Shelby outside.

"You going to tell me what's going on?" she asked as they started up the street.

"I'll tell you once we are safely on the ferry and on our way back to Hummingbird Island," Shelby replied.

Chapter 19

Blaize entered the house minutes after Shelby and Marlene. He had been standing on a cliff near the chosen spot for the ritual when he saw them coming across the water. He had been on the lookout for their return. Shelby had been on his mind the entire morning.

From where Blaize stood, Shelby and Marlene appeared to be deep in a conversation that did not let up even after they reached land. Their movements were exaggerated, unnatural. Their steps hurried.

Blaize watched the woman he had made love to the night before with mixed emotions. What was he to do about her? he thought, wiping the sweat from his brow and closing his eyes. Blaize stood still as a rivulet of perspiration entered his eye and began to burn. Why was he asking himself such a question? Why did he have to do anything about her? They were two adults who had made love.

Why did there have to be more? Because a part of him wanted to give her more—the part that she had captured with her flashing eyes, her quick mind and her warm and tempting body.

But the other part of Blaize reminded him that theirs would be a difficult match. Even a Grenadian woman would find his world and his purpose challenging. *How can I expect Shelby, an American, to ever understand my ways? It would be nearly impossible.*

In three weeks Shelby would return to the United States to live the life she had become accustomed to, and he would remain on Hummingbird Island, devoted to the teachings of his parents and their ancestors. That was where they belonged.

Blaize tried to put the issue behind him as he descended the hill, but Shelby had stirred something deep within him, and it had begun long before their lovemaking. The way she protected the memory of her brother, and the courage Shelby had garnered to come to Grenada. She was a woman of strength. A woman of character.

Still, he had to confess that the night before had been the most satisfying night of love in his life. Memories of their morning together edged their way into his thoughts. When Shelby rose from the bed, Blaize had wanted to pull her back down by his side. Make love to her again. But she told him of her promise to Marlene to go shopping in Sauteurs. So instead of finding pleasure with her again,

Blaize allowed his fingers to trail over her velvety brown back, then molded his hands around her hips.

Blaize couldn't tell what Shelby was thinking. And although he wanted to know, he did not ask. Nor did she volunteer her thoughts. With a smile that touched his heart, Shelby looked back at him before she entered the adjoining bathroom and closed the door.

When Shelby reemerged, she was surprised to see him still in her room. "You're still here" were all the words that passed between them. He nodded, then watched her get ready for the day. The only noise in the room was the sound of Shelby's preparations. Their eyes met often. There was safety in that. No chance of saying too much or too little.

No sooner had Blaize closed the front door and started into the house than Marlene spoke from the drawing room. "You need to come in here, Blaize. Shelby claims some man was about to throw her over Carib's Leap." She stood stiffly by a collection of paintings.

Shelby saw Blaize's eyes narrow as he entered the room. His clothes were covered with dirt and chipped wood. She wanted to throw herself into his arms and feel his strength around her. But she hesitated because of Marlene, and because she really didn't know if, in the light of day, he would welcome it. Her hesitation pained her. *What have I done?* The realization caused a pang in Shelby's chest. What had she done? she thought, another vein of panic rising. She had made love to this man, was in love with him, and had no clue what he really felt about her. And now, because of him, someone was willing to threaten her life.

"Tell me what happened, Shelby." Blaize came and stood at her side.

She looked up into his eyes. Frightened for herself and for her uncertain feelings. "If the little boy I had hired to be my guide hadn't shown up, there's a possibility I could be at the bottom of that cliff with the bones of those Carib Indians."

"You hired a guide?" Blaize looked confused.

"Yes." Shelby swallowed hard. "To tell me about Carib's Leap. And when I was standing on the ledge a man came up."

"What did he look like?" Blaize took off his gloves.

"That's what I asked her." Marlene cut her eyes.

Shelby looked at Marlene. She could tell she was still upset over being called away from her tête-à-tête. "I didn't get a good look at his face," Shelby said, frustrated. "He stood so close to me I couldn't turn around. And then when I got away from him, he kept his face turned so no one could see it."

"And you are certain that you were in danger?" Blaize pressed for the truth.

Shelby relived the man's grip on her arm and the cold tone in his voice. "I've never been in danger like that before, but there is no doubt in my mind, my life was being threatened. He went so far as to mention your name." She looked at Blaize again. "And to repeat the threat that was made if you insisted on going forward with the ritual."

"What threat?" It was Marlene's turn to be confused.

Blaize's silky voice was charged with a restrained anger. "A threat was made against anyone close to me if I held the Rites of Passage."

"And you did not tell me this?" Marlene's mouth remained open.

"Since you've come back to this island, you haven't remained in a room with me long enough for me to tell you anything," Blaize replied.

Marlene looked down, then up again. "You still should have told me." She walked over to an ornate chair and turned her back. "But that is totally bizarre. Who would make such a threat?"

"I don't know." Blaize gazed out the window, then turned his head slowly. "Shelby said she hired a guide. Where were you when all of this was taking place?"

Guilt crept up Marlene's face. "I had some personal business to attend to."

"What kind of business? A man?" Blaize dropped the singular question.

"I'm a grown woman," Marlene flared. "And it's none of your business what I do or who I do it with."

"It is my business when it puts you or others that

are a part of this family in jeopardy," Blaize retorted.

"Are we talking about today, or sixteen years ago?" Marlene squeezed her arms in front of her.

An explosive silence erupted before Blaize replied. "I am talking about today." He pointed. "I am talking about Shelby. If the circumstance is similar to another, I guess it's simply coincidence. Or maybe it is a warning for you to mend your ways."

"Mend my ways." Marlene laughed sarcastically. "I believe if it were up to you I would still be a virgin. That's the only kind of woman that you believe is good enough to be a Blaize, isn't it?" Her eyes flashed. "Well, I'm not a virgin, and I am a Blaize, and there is nothing you can do about it."

Blaize looked down and let go of a tremulous breath. "You are a Blaize, Marlene, and you are my sister. I would never want it any other way." He extended an olive branch, but Marlene wasn't taking it.

"How was I to know your plans to hold a Rites of Passage was causing such trouble? It's because of it that they're threatening everyone. But you're doing what you always do. Blame me for everything." She shouted.

"What's the matter, Mama?" Cleophus appeared under the archway.

They turned and looked at the boy. He was dressed, but his clothes hung on his thin frame.

"Nothing is wrong, Cleophus." Marlene swiped away a tear that threatened to fall from the corner of her eye.

Cleophus looked at the tense faces around him. "I'm not a child, Mama. I may be sick, but I'm not a baby anymore. So tell me what is going on here."

Marlene looked uncomfortable as she crossed the room to his side. "There's nothing you can do about it, Cleophus."

"But how do you know unless you tell me." His thin body stiffened. "I feel useless enough around here. Maybe this is something where I can make a difference."

Marlene looked at Blaize. "I don't know where to start. I never told you a lot about my parents." Marlene stumbled. "Your grandparents. Because—" She looked at her son but nothing more came out.

"It's okay, Mama. I know you never told me a lot about them, but I know about them anyway."

"You do?" Marlene covered her mouth.

"Yes. People were always talking about them." He looked sheepish. "Like they were some kind of legend. I know Grandmother and Grandfather died during the massacre on Bloody Wednesday. They're a part of our Grenadian history."

"Yes, but . . ." Marlene's tone implied there was more. Her shoulders slumped with an unspoken burden.

"But that's not all they were known for, Cleophus," Blaize said. "Your grandparents made sure certain ancestral rituals were remembered and practiced. Rituals that were brought over to this land by our African ancestors. But turned into a blend of African and Indian ancestry when some of our ancestors married Carib Indians."

"And these were rituals that my grandfather headed up?" Cleophus' eyes widened.

"Yes," Blaize replied. "They were unique to our family, but the benefits were shared with anyone who wanted them. One thing your grandfather always said he desired was for the rituals to never be forgotten. That they be passed down from generation to generation. That your mother and I raise our children in the way of our ancestors."

Cleophus looked uncomfortable so Marlene picked up the baton.

"You know you haven't been well for years, Cleophus, but it's only been recently, since you turned sixteen, that things have gotten much worse."

Cleophus nodded. "And because I have a rare blood type, I have not been able to receive the treatment I need in order to get better."

"That's right. And that's why your Aunt Shelby has come." Marlene looked at Shelby. "She has the same blood type that you have."

Cleophus looked at Shelby. A slight smile touched his lips. "That's very kind of you, Shelby." He extended his hand.

Shelby looked at his hand, but she couldn't contain herself. Instead of taking it she wrapped Cleophus in her arms. "You're more than welcome, Cleophus." She forced herself to let go.

"But aren't you here to represent my father's side in the ritual?" Cleophus asked with steady eyes.

"Say what?" Marlene looked stunned. "How do you know about that? I never told you anything about the rituals. I remember so little myself."

Cleophus looked down for a moment before he visibly fortified himself and said, "Grandfather told me."

Marlene sounded sick. "What are you saying?"

Shelby held her breath. Blaize's eyes turned hooded.

"It's the truth, Mama." Cleophus walked over to her and pulled her hands down from her face. "He did tell me. Through my dreams. Ever since I turned sixteen Grandfather has been coming to me in my dreams."

"Is it possible?" Distraught, Marlene held her fist in her hand. "Is Father trying to make me pay for what I have done by haunting my child?"

"Oh no, these haven't been scary dreams, Mama," Cleophus assured her. "I think he has been coming to me to prepare me for something."

"To prepare you for the Rites of Passage," Blaize said softly.

"Yes. That's what he called it. But he said representatives from both sides of my family would come to support me." Cleophus looked at Shelby. "My father could not physically come, so you have come in his place."

"Yes. I have," Shelby replied, nearly choking on the words.

"But I want you to know my father will be there. He will be with us in spirit. Grandfather has been in communication with him and he assured me of that." Cleophus turned a sad smile on her. "He told me I resembled my father."

"Cleophus—I mean, your father has been mentioned in your dreams?" Shelby was shocked.

"Yes, Grandfather talked of him. He told me my father is doing work in other realms, but that he will join us for the ceremony. And that he thanks you and sends you his love."

Shelby nodded and swallowed. She had never encountered anything like this before, but the sincerity in Cleophus' eyes convinced her that he believed what he said was true. "I'll be there for you, Cleophus," Shelby assured him again. "However you may need me, I will be there."

Blaize and Shelby locked gazes. She thought of the threats and the man at Carib's Leap, but the pride and love she felt for her nephew, Cleophus, gave Shelby the strength to challenge anyone who might stand in her way.

Chapter 20

"What the hell happened?" Keegan whirled around, his good-looking face distorted by anger. "I expected Shelby Russau to be shaking in her boots, and instead here she comes into the restaurant where I'm sitting with Blaize's sister, giving out commands."

"I didn't expect the boy to pop up like that," Alphonso Jacobs tried to explain. "I saw her pay him some money. So when he left, I thought he was gone for good. How was I to know the woman had shorted the kid?"

"So there you were standing with the woman." Keegan shoved him, and although Alphonso was much bigger than Keegan, he took an obligatory step back. "Did anyone see your face?"

"No. I made sure I kept my back turned," Alphonso spoke quickly.

"And you think you did something by doing that, don't you?"

"Why no, Keegan. I just—"

"You just blew the whole thing." Keegan's arms went up in the air. "I should have sent Dennis in your place. At least he gets what he goes after. But I thought this was a man-sized job, and it would take a man to handle it. Obviously, size doesn't have anything to do with manhood." Keegan looked from the burly Alphonso to the pint-sized Dennis.

"I can handle it, Keegan," Alphonso defended himself. "Like I said, I didn't know the woman had stolen from the boy."

"That doesn't make sense to me," Keegan replied. "Why would a woman Blaize goes for do a thing like that? Are you sure the boy didn't suspect something?"

"I don't think he did." Alphonso looked at the ceiling. "By the time I felt comfortable enough to go back to the main street, he was nowhere in sight."

Keegan flopped down into a chair. "Maybe it's not as bad as it looks. Maybe this incident scared Miss Russau enough that she'll be able to convince Blaize to back off of the ritual." Keegan wrapped and unwrapped his fingers.

"You might have something there, Keegan. I can tell you she was scared," Alphonso declared. "Scared real bad."

"It's possible she was frightened," Dennis jumped in, "but that's the extent of it. About an hour ago some folks, including Francis Whyte, headed over to Hummingbird Island to help set up the site for the ritual. They were quite excited about it. Said many others plan to head over there during the next couple of days."

"Those backwoods idiots," Keegan erupted. "If they blow my deal, I swear, more people than Blaize are going to pay." He struck a table with his fist. "Don't they know people are into technological progress nowadays? This ritual mess is going to scare off the folks I'm negotiating the business deal with. If they think we don't have a pool of educated people to choose from as a workforce, it's over."

"There are educated people here in Grenada." Dennis tried to quell his anger.

"I know that, but these folks are accustomed to the way things are done in America. You know what I mean. You were just there. Things are different."

"Don't mean it's better," Dennis mumbled.

Keegan lost his patience. "Are you on my side here or not?"

"I'm on your side but . . . I'm a Grenadian. A full-blooded Grenadian. And there's nothing wrong with how we live." Dennis stuck his chin out. "Maybe you don't understand that, being born in America and all."

Keegan knew he had to back down. He needed Dennis and Alphonso. He couldn't do what had to be done alone. He didn't want to. "I understand, Dennis. My father is Grenadian. Remember? I know our worth." He rallied. "But it's all about image these days. And if those people read in some paper that we are still holding ancient rituals to solve our problems, it's going to be hard for me to get them to sign on the dotted line. And that means I don't make the kind of money I want to make off of selling my land. And you two don't get paid the money I'm promising you at the end of the deal."

Dennis shrugged. "We can always go to the ritual. They won't know everyone who's going to come. We can get over there, pretend like we're supporting what's going on, and cause all sorts of problems instead."

Keegan looked at Dennis. A slow smile spread across his face. "That's why I like you. You're always thinking." Keegan got up and walked around the room. "And I can find out exactly where everybody's going to be and what's being planned from Marlene. She's got the hots for me. I've made sure of that. This will just be my opportunity to take further advantage of a situation that I've already cultivated." Keegan slid down in his chair with a satisfied smile.

"I hope I'm not interrupting anything." Keith looked at the group gathered in the drawing room. "But some folks just arrived on the island. The men have some tools, and the women are carrying baskets that look like they're loaded down with something," he explained.

"I bet it's Francis Whyte," Blaize replied. "Last night when I was on the mainland he said he might get some folks together today and come over. They want to help set up for the Rites of Passage." He gazed around the room. "I better go out and meet them."

"It might have been Francis," Keith responded. "But I can't see that far anymore. As a matter of fact I thought I saw another boat heading across the water."

"Well, we'll see," Blaize said. "The best thing for us to do now is meet them halfway. See if we can help carry some of the provisions they've brought with them."

"I want to come," Cleophus said.

Blaize walked over and put his hands around the boy's thin shoulders. Shelby noted the difference between Blaize's muscular body and Cleophus' frail one. "After we get things set up a little better, perhaps you can come over and lend a hand. But right now it's going to be a little chaotic. We're going to continue the digging I've already started. We've got to dig out the place for the ceremonial pit so the ritual can be held within the body of Mother Earth," Blaize explained in a tone that indicated he had found a kindred soul in his nephew. "We'll have to cut down a few trees because we'll need logs to put around the sides of the pit. They'll border it, and make seats around the edges. It's going to be heavy work, Cleophus. And I don't think you're quite ready for that."

Reluctantly, Cleophus showed he agreed. "OK ... then I want to help out around here anyway I can."

"We're going to need it, aren't we Marlene?" Blaize looked at his sister, who had a sort of tortured look of pride on her face.

"We've got to prepare lots of food," Marlene replied in a lost manner.

"And some of our parents' ceremonial items are still stored away," Blaize added. "Perhaps you can have Cleophus find them."

"That's a good idea." Marlene accepted Blaize's verbal efforts to bond them together as a family unit.

Blaize started for the door behind Keith. Shelby watched him from the corner of her eye as she headed toward her bedroom.

"Shelby," Blaize called.

"Yes." She turned with her heart pounding. Was he about to make her feel wanted? A part of the family?

"I'm sorry about what happened in Sauteurs."

"I know that." Shelby looked down. It took all the effort she had for her shoulders not to droop with disappointment. When Shelby looked at Blaize again her chin was held high. "But now, you're not the only one who wants the Rites of

Passage. I can't say I understand and believe everything Cleophus said, but I have this feeling this entire thing is bigger than you and me. Even bigger than Cleophus. And I'll be proud to do my part."

Blaize showed the first hint of a real smile she had ever seen on his face. "You're something else, Shelby Russau."

"I am that." She turned and walked down the hall, part of her heart heavy because Blaize had not reached out to her in a loving way, the other uplifted by the thought that Cleophus, her brother, might be doing his thing, although it was somewhere else.

Chapter 21

"What are you doing here?" Keith stopped pushing the half-full wheelbarrow. Francis Whyte looked up and another man waved.

"I told you I might come, Poppy." Danielle waved back, yelling, "*Oui foot.*"

"That is the truth," the man replied. "You're looking good."

Danielle smiled a beautiful smile before she hugged her grandfather. "You might not know it, but Grenada is full of talk of the Rites of Passage that Blaize is going to hold here. You don't need to be in the middle of all of this. Look at you, he's got you doing the heavy work of a young man. And with him no where around."

"So you and your mother decided you should come and drag me back to the mainland? Because that's the only way I'm going to come. Only if you force me, physically." Keith looked at his pretty granddaughter with grandfatherly pride.

"Don't be difficult, Poppy. You have been this man, Blaize's, servant long enough. And I'm going to tell him so," she declared, shimmying her hips.

"You've got something to say to me?" Blaize asked, watching the shapely young woman's antics.

"I sure do." She whirled around, ready to lash into him. But with one perusing gaze her anger was tempered by interest. "You're Raphael Blaize?"

"That's what I said."

"I expected . . ." Danielle searched for the right words.

"What did you expect?" Blaize probed.

"Someone . . . who looked older."

Blaize swung the shovel over his shoulder. His pecs danced, and his six-pack grew even more defined. "Sorry to disappoint you," he replied.

"Oh. I'm not disappointed at all." Danielle smiled sweetly. "As a matter of fact it's quite the opposite."

"I see." Blaize continued to look at her. "So you've come to take my right-hand man away?" He motioned toward Keith.

"I was thinking about it," Danielle replied. "But now I believe perhaps I should stick around and see for myself what goes on here before jumping to conclusions."

"I'll be damned," Keith said under his breath. "The old Blaize magic is alive and well."

"What did you say, Poppy?" Danielle looked at her grandfather.

"I said I think you'll do well at my place. There's plenty of room."

"Good," she replied, eyeing Blaize again.

"If you plan to stay, perhaps we can find something for you to do to help prepare for the ritual," Blaize suggested.

"Is that what you're doing?" Danielle pointedly examined him.

"Yes."

"I'll be eager to help you out in any way I can." She gave him a doe-eyed look.

"I don't mean out here," Blaize corrected her. "I mean at the house. The women are there. Planning the menu for the celebration that's going to take place afterwards."

"Do I have to go where the women are?" Danielle pouted just a little. "Can't you find something for me to do out here?"

"You don't look like the outdoor type," Blaize replied.

"You never know until you try me," Danielle said in a teasing tone.

"Well at the moment I can't think of a thing," Blaize rejoined.

"I'll take you over to the house, Danielle," her grandfather volunteered. "You might know some of the women. If not, I'll introduce you around."

"Don't bother, Poppy. I wouldn't want to interrupt your work." She patted her grandfather's forearm. "Blaize looks like he was going that way.

Would you walk me over?" Danielle went over to Blaize and looked directly into his eyes.

"I thought you were so concerned about my well-being." Keith was fed up with his granddaughter's blatant flirting.

"I am, Poppy." She looked back at him. "But you said the only way you'd leave Hummingbird Island is if I physically forced you. And that right there let me know how much you enjoy this place. I don't want to stand in the way of that."

"I'm sure you don't, Danielle." Keith shook his head.

She turned to Blaize. "So would you walk me over?"

"Why not?" Blaize replied. "I'll bring back some more gasoline for the saw."

"We could use it." Keith grabbed the handles of the wheelbarrow and pushed it toward a growing pile of rubbish.

Danielle followed Blaize into the forest. His steps were clear and purposeful. With Danielle's tight dress, keeping up was difficult.

"Hey, who you racing?" she called ahead.

"No one."

"Then give a girl a break. I don't want to break out into a massive sweat in this dress. At least not from walking, anyway."

Blaize slowed down but he kept moving.

"My, this is a beautiful island," Danielle exclaimed. "If I had known it was this wonderful I would have come before."

"It's kind of hard to see how beautiful it is through all these leaves, don't you think?" Blaize replied.

"Maybe. But a woman knows a beautiful thing when she sees it." She let her meaning sink in. "Why don't you have a woman to help you enjoy this beautiful place?"

"How do you know I don't?"

"Oh. Word gets around." Blaize looked back long enough to see Danielle patting her cleavage with a tissue. "You know you're an island celebrity. But I must say that recent picture in the paper didn't do you justice. And who was the woman in the picture with you?"

"Her name is Shelby," Blaize answered as they emerged from the forest.

Danielle ran to catch up to Blaize's side. "Now this is what I call a house." Her eyes gleamed as she examined the perfectly kept two-story building.

"Thank you."

"And you are what I'd call a real man." Danielle placed her arm through his as they approached the kitchen door.

"I've brought plenty of flour to make johnny-cakes. And I figured we'd fry some sweet-potato patties too," Jeanette Whyte announced.

"Sounds good," Sylvie replied. "I'm ready to do

whatever peeling or stirring that's required."

"That's the kind of spirit we need around here," Jeanette said, circling the kitchen as though it was her own.

"That's right. Make yourselves at home," Marlene offered as she looked around nervously. "We appreciate your coming to help out."

"Don't worry, I will," Jeanette replied, unloading her basket. "It's about time someone took up the banner in remembering our ancestors. I'm proud of your brother for having the guts to do it. Although it did take him a long time." She gave a look of consternation, then clapped her hands. "But it's never too late." Jeanette leaned forward and squinted toward the window. "Who's that coming across the yard?" she asked as Shelby entered the kitchen.

The women turned their attention to the edge of the forest.

"That's my brother, Blaize," Marlene replied. "I don't recognize the woman with him."

"I know that's your brother. And if you don't mind my saying so"—Jeanette lowered her voice— "and if no one will tell Francis, I'd recognize your brother with his shirt off or on any day."

Sylvie sniggled.

"We all know it's the truth," Jeanette continued. "He's a sight for sore eyes."

"Look a there." Sylvie placed her hand on her

hip. "But don't he have one humdinger ringer on his arm."

"What do you mean by that?" Jeanette asked.

"That's Danielle Albanie. And I can tell you now the woman is man crazy."

"Well, from what I can see from here—" Jeanette pursed her lips "—looks like she's laid claim to Blaize already."

Shelby moved to get a better view of the window. The woman called Danielle, who was walking arm and arm with Blaize, was pretty in an obvious way. She took advantage of what nature had given her with bright lips and exaggerated eye makeup. But Blaize appeared to be interested in her parasitical getup as she smiled, walked and talked at his side. Shelby thought that, at any second, her hips would bump into him they swiveled so much.

Shelby hoped she looked relaxed when Blaize and Danielle entered the kitchen. Blaize looked over at the doorway where she stood and acknowledged her with his eyes. Shelby wanted to return it with a casual smile, but feared the disinterested look she had placed on her face might crack.

"Hello, Sylvie," Danielle said with a smug smile.

"Hey, Danielle." She dragged out the last syllable of Danielle's name.

Danielle placed her hand on Blaize's arm. "I don't know anybody else, Blaize. Care to introduce me?"

Blaize glanced at the painted hand. "That's Francis' wife, Jeanette." He pointed.

"My sister, Marlene.

"And this is Shelby. A member of the family."

Before Shelby could speak Danielle said, "So that's why you were in that picture with Blaize. I thought perhaps you two had something special going. But I guess not." She smiled.

"It doesn't pay to assume, does it?" Shelby replied, pleased to see a streak of red on Danielle's teeth. But it didn't give her enough pleasure to mask her anger over Blaize's introduction.

"Danielle is from St. George. She came to Hummingbird Island to take her grandfather, Keith, back with her, but she decided to stay and help out with the preparations for the ritual. I told her I was sure you ladies could use her help in the kitchen."

"Sure. We don't turn down any help in here," Jeanette replied.

A lackluster ripple of agreement followed.

"Well, I'll leave you to it," Blaize said. "I've got to get some gasoline out of the shed before I head back."

"Maybe we can have a good meal and a pre-celebration tonight. To get things going," Jeanette said, turning to Marlene. "That is, if it's all right with you?"

"As a matter of fact we had considered that." Marlene warmed to Jeanette's stroking. "We can set up in the back of the house. Blaize, do you think you can put together a couple of tables for to-night?"

"That won't be a problem," he replied.

"And we can have a *jump ups*," Sylvie enjoined.

Jeanette waved her hand at her before she smiled. "You're always ready to drink and dance."

"Some of us like that"—Sylvie shimmied—"some of us not."

"How about you, Shelby?" Blaize asked with his hand on the doorknob. "Do you think you will be up to some precelebrating?"

"I'm still new around here, but I'm beginning to get the hang of things." She gave a syrupy smile. "If the way I feel at the moment is any indication, I'm up for just about anything."

"Well, I'll look forward to that." Blaize paused before he added "ladies" and walked out of the door.

"One of the first things we need to do is get you an apron," Jeanette said to Danielle. "That dress you wearing isn't quite the dress for preparing food."

"I don't want to do anything messy anyway." Danielle sat on a stool.

Sylvie rolled her eyes at Jeanette.

"There's not too many things you can do in a kitchen that's not messy." Jeanette's forthright personality pushed through. "I thought I heard you say you were interested in helping out."

"I am interested in helping out. I'm interested in

a lot of things on Hummingbird Island."

"Anybody who hangs around here has got to do something." Jeanette put her foot down. "You got an extra apron, Marlene?"

"There's one hanging behind Shelby near the door," Marlene replied.

Danielle wriggled off the stool and crossed the floor. "If you insist." Shelby stepped aside so she could reach the apron. "How are you related to Blaize?" Danielle asked.

Shelby was not in a mood for explaining. "It's rather complicated," she replied.

"Complicated?" Danielle looked her up and down while eyebrows went up all around the kitchen.

"Shelby," Marlene called.

"Yes." She focused across the room.

"Why don't you help Cleophus find the ceremonial objects we talked about earlier? It will give you an opportunity to share some time with him alone."

There was a moment of silence. Shelby knew Marlene was attempting to keep the peace, and it would be the perfect opportunity to talk with Cleophus.

"Where is he?"

"In the bedroom at the far end of the west hall."

"I'll go see if I can find him." Shelby gave Danielle one last look before she walked out.

Chapter 22

"Having any luck?" Shelby asked when she saw Cleophus struggling with the lid of a huge, old trunk.

"Not yet." He smiled, although he was nearly panting. "I just managed to get this old thing open. And boy, it was heavier than I thought."

Shelby crossed the room as quickly as she could without looking like she was rushing. She didn't want to dash water on the obvious pleasure Cleophus was deriving from being busy. "These old trunks are heavy, aren't they?" She grabbed the lid and let it slip back as far as the hinges would allow. "They're heavy without anything in them. So you can imagine how heavy they are to carry when they are packed to the brim like this one."

"People say, in the old days we were in better shape." Cleophus removed an old book from the top of a pile. "I guess that went for everybody. Many of the older people on the mainland feel us younger folks have gotten lazy. They say we don't have nearly as much to do, but we can't even get that done."

"That must be a universal complaint," Shelby replied.

"You think so?"

"I'm sure. You'd hear that no matter where you are." Shelby got down on her knees. "Can I help?"

"Sure." Cleophus glanced at her but he was obviously more enthralled with the treasure hunt. "Blaize told me the articles would be in this trunk." Cleophus continued to remove things.

"Do you know what we're looking for?" Shelby surveyed the hodgepodge of items.

"Mm-hmm," he replied. "Blaize described them to me. But he didn't have to. I had already seen them in my dreams."

"Oh." Shelby removed a cigar box full of buttons. She wasn't quite comfortable with the spiritual aspects Cleophus accepted so easily. "Care to tell me about them?"

"What the dreams?"

"No, I was actually talking about the ceremonial items. But if you'd like to tell me about your dreams I'm open to hearing them."

"Maybe some other time," Cleophus replied.

"That's fine with me." Shelby was somewhat relieved.

"One of them is called the Ancestors Talking Stick," Cleophus dove in. "It's a stick that's dec-

orated with shells, paint, string. And other things.
It's carved and it's real old. My Grandfather used
it many times in ceremonies. He said some of the
decorations came from the Ancestor Stick his father owned. That stick was very, very old, and got
broke somehow."

Shelby found herself staring at Cleophus. His
voice was so much like her brother's, and he
looked like him as well. But Shelby couldn't imagine her Cleophus chatting about dreams and spirits
so easily. "The Ancestor Stick sounds fascinating,"
she responded.

"I think so." He tilted his head to the side. "But
it is also powerful. All the energy, from all the
people who have ever touched the stick and the
objects on it, is present during every ceremony in
which it is used. That's why it is an important part
of the ritual."

"I see," Shelby replied.

"There's also the Libation Cup. It is elaborately
decorated as well. But I don't know how old it is.
Grandfather said he did not know." Cleophus
stopped his rummaging. "Do you think one day I
will be as strong as Blaize?"

Cleophus' abrupt change in subject matter threw
Shelby. "Of course you will," was her glib reply.

"No, I mean seriously." He looked at her with
large eyes that held a duality. In some ways he was
so much the child, in others he was older than she
was. "Considering my illness and all."

Shelby put down the bundle of letters she held in her hand. "I believe you will, one day. Once you've had the blood transfusion, and any other medication or treatments your doctor recommends."

Cleophus threw his head back and made a face. "And of course, to complicate things, I had to have AB- blood. The ra—"

"The rarest blood type there is," Shelby finished the sentence for him. "Welcome to the club."

"Thanks." He managed to smile.

"So I guess you're worried about getting well and gaining your strength back," Shelby said.

Cleophus looked at her with steady eyes. "Oh no. I know I'm going to get better. Grandfather told me I would."

"But you just asked me if I thought you would ever be as strong as Blaize," Shelby replied.

"But that's because I wonder if we have the same body type. I have my father's family's blood type. And I'm told I have his face. So I wondered if I had enough of my mother's genes to have a body like Blaize."

"Got ya." Shelby blew a breath, then put her hand on his shoulder. "You probably do have enough, but even if you don't, your father was a big, strong man as well. So you have genes on both sides of the family working for you."

"My father was a strong man?" Cleophus looked surprised.

"Yes, he was," Shelby replied with conviction. "He had muscles galore and height as well. Your mother never told you about him?"

"I tried to ask questions when I was younger, but she would give short answers that didn't tell me very much. Eventually, I stopped asking." He looked at the contents in the trunk. "So my father was strong. I thought he was"—Cleophus paused—"sickly like me."

"I don't recall your father ever being really sick, that is until he returned from Grenada. I guess that's why it surprised everybody so when he died." Shelby got quiet, then she looked deep into Cleophus' eyes. "Your father was a strong, intelligent man, Cleophus. Someone you could be proud of, and who would have loved you immensely had he lived."

Cleophus started pulling things out of the trunk again. Shelby could see a few tears running down his cheeks, but she didn't mention them.

Shelby returned her focus to rummaging. Minutes later she came across a long handmade wooden box. "I think I've found something interesting here." She raised up on her knees and pulled it out.

Cleophus, with a dry face, focused on Shelby's find. "I bet that's it," he said, settling in to see what was inside.

"You do?"

He nodded enthusiastically.

"Well, why don't you open it?" Shelby suggested. "You're the person with the inside track."

"The inside track?" Cleophus questioned.

"You've been given all the important information about the objects. So if this is the real thing, you should be the one to open it," she reiterated, pushing the box toward him.

Cleophus lifted the lid and there were two wrapped objects inside. "I think we were right," he said, picking up the longest one. Carefully, he laid the object on the floor and unwrapped the colorful cloth that bound it. Cleophus and Shelby were not disappointed. Lying inside was the Ancestor Stick.

"This is it!" Cleophus exclaimed. "Isn't it beautiful?" He examined the carved wood decorated with semiprecious stones, shells, paint and cloth.

"It is beautiful," Shelby replied. "I never thought it would be such a work of art."

"Let's unwrap the other one," Cleophus said, quickly reaching inside for the other bundle. Soon the Libation Cup lay beside the Ancestor Stick. The decorations were more simplistic, but the cup was stunning as well. "I can't wait to tell Uncle Blaize that we've found them. He'll be proud to use these during the ritual. Grandfather says the energy from these objects will help him with his divining."

Shelby realized it was the first time she had heard Cleophus refer to Blaize as Uncle Blaize. But it was something else that Cleophus said that held her attention. "Did you say divining?"

"Yes. Reading of the stars."

Shelby sat back on her heels. "I don't think I understand."

"Grandfather taught Blaize the art of foretelling the future by reading the position of the stars. Uncle Blaize is a Stargazer," Cleophus announced proudly.

Shelby didn't know why she began to smile, but Cleophus didn't take her amused reaction too well.

"This is serious, Shelby," he admonished her.

"It is?" Shelby thought about how Blaize had bolted upright when they saw the shooting stars the night before.

"Yes. Very. For generations families depended on my family's ancestors to read the stars for them. They would help them with personal crises, as well as help prepare them for what was in store for them as a group. A family. Or a neighborhood."

"And Blaize can do that?" Shelby didn't know how she felt about the things Cleophus was telling her.

"He was taught to do it. But Grandfather says for years he did not use it. It was only after my grandparents died, when Uncle Blaize secluded himself on Hummingbird Island, that he started practicing. Grandfather said it was a good thing that they died when they did. If not, Blaize never would have accepted his part in our family's destiny."

"But is it ever a good thing when people die?" Shelby couldn't conceal her disbelief.

"Of course it is," Cleophus said matter-of-factly. "If we never died, when would we have time to assess all the lessons we've learned in each lifetime?"

With everything else that Cleophus had revealed, this answer was too heavy for Shelby. "Let's pick up. And when the time presents itself you can show the Ancestor Stick and the Libation Cup to Blaize."

"Aunt Shelby." Cleophus pinned her again with his wide-eyed stare.

"Yes." Her heart was in her throat. Cleophus had called her aunt for the first time.

"What were my mother and Uncle Blaize arguing about in the drawing room?"

Shelby paused. "I don't think it's my place to tell you that, Cleophus."

"Did it have something to do with how my grandparents died?"

Shelby thought for a second. "To be honest with you, I'm not sure."

"I think it did." He looked down. "And maybe once the ritual reunites all the people spiritually, it will reunite my mother and Uncle Blaize as well."

"That's a lot to expect from one ritual, Cleophus." Shelby didn't want him to get his hopes up too high.

"Not really. Grandfather says a small number of

people can affect many, many others, if what they are doing is out of love. And if this Rites of Passage does all that, Aunt Shelby, my being sick is a small price to pay."

Chapter 23

"Don't worry about me," Cleophus said, lying across his bed. "I'm just going to take a nap. But by the way the two of you are acting, it feels like you're giving me this grand send-off." He looked at his mother and Shelby.

"All right, we're going," Marlene replied. "But I'll check on you later."

"That won't be necessary, Mama. I'm going to get up real soon."

Shelby waved as she walked toward the bedroom door with Marlene in tow. Cleophus returned it with a comical smile as if to say, "Why are you waving good-bye?"

Shelby and Marlene stepped out into the hall. They could hear laughter coming from the kitchen.

"I'm amazed that a *whole set* of people have already come over to the island." Marlene said. "I hear they are pitching tents with the intention of staying through the Rites of Passage."

"Quiet Hummingbird Island isn't so quiet any-more." Shelby contemplated all the changes that had taken place within the last twenty-four hours. "This is turning into quite an event," she remarked. "And it sure makes me wonder about the part I'm going to play."

"I can't help you there," Marlene replied. "Mama and Papa performed so many ceremonies, but for me as a child, they all ran together. I guess I just didn't understand back then."

"But what child does?" Shelby quipped.

"Cleophus," Marlene said softly. "He's changed an awful lot during the last few months. That's one of the reasons I came back. He'd say things in his sleep that frightened me. And sometimes he'd ask me questions that I couldn't answer. And all the while he seemed to be getting sicker and sicker." Her eyes widened with fear. "I had to come back to Hummingbird Island. Despite our relationship, I knew that Blaize would know what to do."

"Cleophus is a very special young man," Shelby began. "While we were together he asked me about his father, and then he asked about you and Blaize." She glanced at Marlene. "He seems to think there's this big rift between you." They stopped at the top of the stairs. "And he's wonder-ing what caused it."

"What happened between Blaize and me doesn't have anything to do with you or Cleophus," Mar-lene replied defensively.

"And I told him that," Shelby jumped in. "That I wasn't the person to ask."

Marlene started down the stairs. Shelby followed her with a change in subject. "So what are you planning to wear to the gathering tonight?"

"I hadn't thought about it." Marlene continued her downward track.

"All I brought with me is a white dress that I plan to wear at the ceremony." Shelby paused before she continued. "Blaize bought me a dress, but I've already worn it. And I wouldn't want to wear it again considering Miss Danielle's behavior." The last comment slipped out before she knew.

Marlene stopped and wagged her finger. "I knew you and my brother had something going."

"At this point 'some thing' is probably the right term for it," Shelby confessed.

A pleased smile spread Marlene's lips. "I've got something that will make him say 'Shelby *have on a nice dan-dan.*' All the other men will be saying that too."

"*Dan-dan?* Sounds a little too spicy for me," Shelby replied.

"Well what are you going to do, wear a T-shirt and blue jeans?" Marlene put one hand on her hip.

Shelby looked down at her baggy T-shirt and the oversized jeans. "Perhaps I can use a little spicing up," she replied.

"Good." Marlene's eyes sparked fire. "And I've got just the thing to do it."

* * *

"How is that woman related to Blaize and Marlene?" Danielle artistically sliced the breadfruit.

"I don't know," Jeanette replied. "But if you concentrated on cutting up those vegetables rather than on what's going on in this house, that pile of breadfruit would be going down much faster."

Danielle ignored Jeanette's remark. "She seemed to get an attitude when I mentioned there was no other kind of relationship between she and Blaize." Danielle tapped the knife against the counter. "I'm just wondering what's on the woman's mind."

"We know what's on yours," Sylvie retorted.

"I can't help it if I noticed that Raphael Blaize has *money by the grab*, and is the most eligible bachelor on the island. You'd notice too if you thought you had a chance to get him," Danielle added.

"I'm not the kind of woman who is always at the center of *mo-vay-lang*. Scandal follows you every where because you chase every thing in pants that might, and I mean might, have a few coins in his pocket," Sylvie retorted.

"This is more than I can take." Jeannette jumped in. "We're here to celebrate our ancestors. To have a good time."

Sylvie mumbled. "I *not like Danielle's head.* Never have."

"It doesn't matter if you don't like me," Danielle said in a syrupy voice. "Most women don't. But I tell you what. You better keep that man of yours' eyes off of me tonight. Or it might be me that he's thinking about when he lay down with you."

Sylvie turned toward Danielle with a butcher knife in her hand.

"Don't you know that woman is messing with you? And you just letting her." Jeanette put her hand on Sylvie's arm. "Any woman who thinks every man wants her, just let her think that. It's only her that's going to be embarrassed when she realize some men don't want a woman like that. And if I am right"—Jeanette nodded her head and chewed on her lip—"and normally I am, I think Raphael Blaize is one of those men."

"Embarrassed? Don't no man embarrass me," Danielle declared.

"Well, if you want that to remain true, I think you better get your sights off of Raphael Blaize. Because it seems to me his interest lies elsewhere." Jeanette opened up the cassava flour and started dipping it out with a cup.

"I guess she been told," Sylvie said, sucking her teeth.

Danielle put down the knife and placed both her hands on her ample hips. "If you mean that so-called relative of his"—she looked at the women— "she's no competition for me."

Chapter 24

Shelby tugged at the *pareo* that in her words "showed more than any woman was ever supposed to show outside the bedroom." She had shared that philosophy with Marlene, who just laughed before she went on her way. Shelby headed for the party outside.

In truth, the wrap skirt wasn't that bad, although Shelby felt like it was. She had never worn anything that accented her hips in such a way. And the semi-midriff top that played up her curvaceous waist also aroused her sense of modesty.

"It's either now or never," she said as she stepped outside, where the music was the first thing to hit her.

It was obvious the people there had come to have a good time. And there were more Grenadians than Shelby had expected. She could tell partying was a natural state of affairs, and they had come prepared for one of their favorite pastimes.

A band consisting of drums, shakers and an elongated wind instrument played a bolero rhythm, while the guests talked and laughed loudly. Food and drink were also flowing as the people mingled and socialized.

Shelby looked the crowd over. She didn't see Blaize. As a matter of fact she didn't see anyone she knew and her inhibitions grew.

"What am I doing out here like this?" she said to herself under her breath. "Trying to impress Blaize? Well, he's not even here." She looked around and decided to go back inside to wait for Marlene.

"You must be the woman from America."

Shelby focused on the slim, light-skinned man who had spoken. His shirt was open to the waist, revealing a hairless, wiry chest. "That's me," she replied

"What's your name?"

"Shelby Russau."

"Mine is Robert."

Shelby nodded her greeting.

"You want to *fire one*?" Robert asked, pointing toward one of the tables.

"I beg your pardon?" Shelby looked from the man to the area where food and drink were being served.

"You want some Planters punch or *mauby*?"

"Maybe not just yet." Shelby looked around

again for Blaize. "Do both of the drinks contain alcohol?"

"No-o." The man made a smooth motion with his body. "The Planters punch is made of fruit juice and rum. *Mauby* is a bittersweet drink made from the mauby tree. It's good, but for a night like this"—he spread his arms—"the Planters punch is better."

"Okay," Shelby acquiesced. "You convinced me."

"You want some?" The man's eyes brightened and his smile widened.

"I think so," Shelby said, wary of his enthusiastic reaction.

"Come with me and I'll get it for you."

Shelby accompanied Robert over to the table. She could feel heads turning as they went by. Then she saw Robert make a gesture which was quite expressive.

"Do you always do that?" she asked.

"What, this?" Robert fanned his fingers rapidly just below his chin.

"Yes. That."

"Only when the woman have on a nice *dan-dan*. And she's looking good in it."

"Well, I've heard that phrase before."

"You have?" Robert put on a most animated face. "And whoever told you this, he did not get you to come with him like I did?"

"It was a woman who told me," Shelby replied.

" Oh-oh." Robert threw his palms up as if to say, "I won't touch that." Then he reached over and passed Shelby a paper cup full of Planters punch.

She took a sip. The fruity drink was heavily laced with rum.

"You like it?" Robert asked.

"It's good." Shelby turned and looked the crowd over again. This time she was in luck. She spotted Blaize. He was in his customary gauze pants. But this time he had topped them off with a short-sleeved matching shirt. Shelby tried to catch his eye through the crowd, but it wasn't easy. As he made his way everyone wanted to talk to him, and Blaize wasn't turning a single individual down.

"Do you like Grenada?" Robert invaded her thoughts.

"Yes. I think I like it, from the little that I've seen." Shelby stepped back to give another couple who had started to dance more room.

"Maybe you should let me show you around, so you can see more of it."

"I'll keep that in mind," Shelby said, looking in Blaize's direction. She took another sip of punch and, to her surprise, Marlene emerged with the man she had been with at the restaurant. Shelby smiled because Marlene looked so happy and satisfied.

"What's making you light up like that?" Robert followed her plane of view. "O-oh, the happy couple, eh?"

"It's good to see two people enjoying one another's company. Maybe they're in love. And that makes me smile."

"So you like this love thing," Robert said. "Well, she may be in love, but the boy don't love nobody but himself."

"You know him?" Shelby scrutinized the man Marlene was with.

"I have seen him around, and from what I know, I would not trust him with any thing of mine."

"What's his name?"

"George Keegan. He thinks he's big stuff because he was born in America. He always wants to talk about how backwards the people here in Grenada are. He should go back to America if the Isle of Spice is not good enough for him." Robert stuck his nose in the air. "You see there?"

"What?" Shelby asked.

"He is with one woman but his eyes are glued to another. I'm not that kind of man. If I am with you, I am your man."

Shelby tried to see what woman had captured Keegan's attention. It wasn't long before Robert told her.

"Look. He can't take his eyes off of Danielle."

Danielle made her way through the crowd, dancing every other step. Hitting one man on the head. Inching her shoulder up toward another. At first it appeared she was moving around at random. But soon it was clear, she was keeping Blaize in sight, and hoping he was doing the same with her.

"What do you call the kind of music that's playing?" Shelby asked, draining her cup.

"It's *zouk*. Sounds good, eh?"

"Yes, sounds real good," Shelby replied as Danielle accidentally bumped into Blaize. "How blatant," Shelby observed.

"Say what?" Robert asked.

"Do you want to dance?" Shelby extended the invitation as her head began to buzz pleasantly.

"Come. Come." Robert backed away from the table. "You've got the dancing man here."

Before Shelby knew it every part of Robert was moving, and with the help of the Planters punch she decided to imitate his style. Moments later they had drawn a small crowd. Some of Robert's friends teased him, saying things like, "You gone let her show you up." and "*Ah Fus* that American woman is doing your dance better than you."

Shelby had always had a knack for dancing. She laughed at the remarks and threw herself into the music even more. It was fun letting go. A kind of fun she hadn't enjoyed in a long, long time. And this time it was for a good cause, the Planters punch assured her, showing Danielle that she wasn't the only woman with womanly wiles.

Several couples joined them on the grass and Shelby was certain by now that Blaize had spotted her, he was so close. She was right, but to her dismay so had Danielle, and she wasn't about to let Shelby steal the show.

"One dance is not going to hurt you." She dragged Blaize forward, pulling his arm with both hands.

The crowd parted as Danielle and Blaize progressed. Danielle was definitely causing a scene, and from the expression on Blaize's face he wasn't too pleased about it.

"Maybe later," Blaize replied, but Danielle wasn't taking no for an answer.

"Just one dance with me," she cooed.

Danielle's antics had captured the attention of everyone around them.

"It's your celebration, mon," one man chimed in. "Go ahead and dance with the girl."

A masked look descended on Blaize's face before he said, "All right. One dance."

Danielle squealed and kicked off her shoes as she led Blaize within yards of Shelby and Robert. Once there she planted her feet firmly in the grass and started rotating her hips. With a tempting look on her face she focused on Blaize.

Shelby didn't know if it was the abandonment of the dance, the Planters punch or just boiling jealousy that made her want to call out, "Hussy." But she was glad she had enough restraint not to follow every whim that hit her.

For a moment Shelby felt a touch of revenge when Blaize looked her way and nodded. But she didn't want him to know how she really felt, so she returned his greeting with a quick nod of her own.

Shelby pretended to be more interested in her dance partner than she was in what was transpiring between Blaize and Danielle.

Soon the crowd had turned the dance into a competition. They rooted loudly whenever one of the dancers made an extravagant move. Secretly, Shelby was pleased that she and Robert were receiving the majority of the shouts. Blaize appeared barely interested in what he was doing. Danielle, on the other hand, was putting forth enough effort for the two of them.

Drops of perspiration raced between Shelby's breasts as she swiveled and swayed her hips, her arms raised high above her. The music was almost hypnotic, and with her eyes closed Shelby became lost in it, along with her memories of the night with Blaize. Once, when she opened her eyes, Blaize was looking directly at her, and she felt he knew what had been on her mind. That's when he became her partner. Robert and Danielle did not exist.

The chemistry between Shelby and Blaize was not lost on the crowd. It was only after someone shouted, "Looks like the wrong people are dancing together. Am I right, Blaize?" that Shelby was able to tear her eyes away from him. Laughter erupted. And Robert rejoined, "I'm not happy about it but I think you are right."

Danielle looked from Blaize to Shelby, her face blazing with scorn and embarrassment. "You can't see me?" Danielle spoke loudly for the crowd's benefit. "I can *day-may-lay* myself, and give you something to look at."

"I'm sure you can," Blaize replied.

"What does that mean?" Shelby asked Robert.

"Although I should not tell you"—he feigned injury—"it means she can handle the situation."

Shelby's brows knitted together as she looked back at Danielle, but they got an aerobic workout as she continued to watch Danielle inch up to Blaize, so close that the tips of her large breasts touched his semibare chest. Then, without pause, she pulled her dress up to the top of her thighs, and with her knees pointing outward with everything between them on display, she started undulating her hips as she descended to the ground.

Some of the women standing on the sidelines began to whisper to one another, while the men hooted and yelled. One shout rang louder than the others. "Wonder who's going to have him tonight? I wish I was you, Raphael Blaize, and it wouldn't be the first time."

Shelby was mortified. Not even the Planter's punch could soften the blow. *What is going on here? What am I doing? Competing for Blaize like a dog in heat? Making my raging hormones the business of all of Grenada?* She looked at the faces in the crowd. They were all focused on her. The men's faces were laced with anticipation, whereas the women looked disdainful but a bit curious as well. *Oh no, this is not me*, Shelby thought. *I can't believe I'm out here making a spectacle of myself in front of these people.* She looked at Danielle, whose butt was nearly touching the ground. *Danielle can do whatever she wants, but I'm not turning myself into a circus for anyone.*

Shelby continued to dance to prompts and encouragement from the crowd, but the enjoyment had gone out of it. She wondered how much longer the number would go on. This time she was out of her league, and glad to be so. No man was worth compromising her dignity.

"That Danielle has no shame," Marlene said, holding Keegan's arm.

"It looks that way," he replied, his lips tight.

"Is there something wrong?" Marlene studied his face.

Keegan flashed a smile, but he couldn't hold it. "No, nothing's wrong. I just can't stand to see a woman degrade herself for a man."

Satisfied with his answer Marlene snuggled closer. "She's been after Blaize ever since she arrived on the island, and she doesn't care who knows it."

"And how long has that been?" Keegan inquired.

"Since this morning. Why do you ask?"

"I was trying to get an idea when most of the people started arriving." His eyes shifted as he spoke. "There is quite a crowd here. The ceremony is going to be a big one."

"It is. I believe the participation is more than even Blaize expected."

"Does he have anything else special planned before tomorrow night?"

"He's planning a prayer at dawn. It's going to be near the water. It is his way of thanking the day, as he says, 'that will give its life for the ceremony.'"

"What kind of talk is that?" Keegan asked harshly.

Confused by his response Marlene shrugged her shoulders and replied, "It means the end of the day will be the beginning of the Rites of Passage."

"Oh." Keegan looked down and composed himself. "I understand."

Chapter 25

The enthusiastic beat of a steel drum ended the *zouk* tune, and the crowd erupted into applause. Danielle fell toward Blaize in a display of exhaustion. He raised his arms and caught her. It was the last straw for Shelby.

"Thanks," she said to Robert. She turned to walk away.

"Where you going?" He grabbed her arm. "I'm just getting started."

"You and everybody else it appears." Shelby glanced at Danielle and Blaize. "But I've had more than enough."

It was obvious the crowd had been bolstered by the dance performances, and they were primed and ready for more. There was no doubt in Shelby's mind, Danielle was ready to give them any and every thing they desired.

"*Ay* Blaize," a guest shouted. "You ready to go another round?"

Shelby waited for Blaize's answer.

"Of course, he is." Danielle rubbed her hand against his chest. "From the look and feel of him I think—no, let's say, I hope, he can go all night."

Guffaws and gales of laughter took over.

Blaize stepped away from Danielle. "No, I am not tired, but I've got important things to do at daybreak. You can join me if you like." He addressed the crowd. "I'm holding a prayer at dawn. Down on the main beach. Just a little something to honor the day on which we'll be reopening our hearts to the essence of who we are."

"I feel plenty open already," a man shouted. "But I think it's the rum punch. Maybe if I *fire a grog* I'll open a little further."

Some laughter followed but it quickly died away.

"As with everything here, you are to do what you feel called to do," Blaize announced. "You're not breaking any laws by not participating. Your joining me tomorrow morning or tomorrow night is totally up to you," he said as he walked toward the musicians. "But I didn't intend to put a damper on the celebration. This is your night." He took a shaker and made it sound rhythmically. "Continue *work up*. But I hope to see you in the morning."

Once again Shelby watched Blaize get swallowed by a group of enthusiastic islanders. Danielle didn't look too pleased over how Blaize had subtly dumped her, and now he appeared to have forgotten all about her as his eyes searched the crowd. Blaize's wandering gaze stopped when he spotted Shelby. This time he did not placate the crowd. He excused himself and made his way to her side.

She was ready to give him a mouthful, but before she could Blaize took her hand. "Come on. Let's go." He led her toward the forest.

"Where are we going?" Shelby looked back at the crowd. Many of the islanders, including Danielle, watched as they slipped into the trees.

"Into the rain forest," Blaize replied.

"That's obvious," Shelby said, walking as close to Blaize as she could. "But it's almost pitch black in here."

"Don't you trust me?" His voice came from the darkness in front of her.

"After your performance with Danielle, you'd be better off asking don't I trust your eyesight."

Blaize stopped and Shelby bumped into him. "Don't put words in my mouth, Shelby. I said exactly what I wanted to say," he said huskily.

Shelby looked up, attempting to see his face, and she was met by the soft moistness of Blaize's mouth. Her body melted against his as his tongue sweetly explored hers. When Blaize released her, Shelby replied, "If you think that is going to get you off the hook, you just might be right."

Blaize took her hand again and started forward.

"Seriously. How can you see where you're going?" Shelby asked.

"I was born on this island, and for sixteen years I never set foot off of it. I know this land like no other. It would be difficult for anyone else to go where we are going, but Hummingbird Island and I are one. It is my heart. I feel what the island feels."

Blaize's voice held such conviction and passion. Shelby knew he believed every word he said, and it was clear to Shelby that there was a part of Blaize that she would never understand. "So you would never leave this island, would you?" Shelby held her breath as she waited for the answer.

"Never," was his adamant reply.

Blaize's answer struck home, and it struck hard. Shelby didn't know what she had envisioned, but somehow she believed there was a possible future with Blaize. She could see them sharing an evening at The Pier in St. Petersburg, or dining with Linda and James. St. Pete was the only home Shelby had known. There were no family ties there, but the roots she had established were stable. Comfortable. And Shelby believed that for an orphan, any kind of roots were golden.

She closed her eyes momentarily and she thought about the beauty Grenada possessed. It was more than the landscape. It was also the warm camaraderie the islanders shared, but somehow Shelby felt excluded from that. There was no way around it. For some she was a stranger to be targeted and scorned. Hummingbird Island was not her home and, from the way Shelby felt now, it could never be.

"This is what I wanted to show you," Blaize announced as he led Shelby into the clearing. "You didn't know you had stumbled on a very special place yesterday morning. A place that for years had given me refuge. Comforted me in times of sorrow. Allowed me to laugh at my weakness when my sanity was being strained. That's what you had found, Shelby. You had found the center of my heart."

Deep in thought, Shelby had blocked out the soft roar of the waterfall. But now, as they stood together at the edge of the pool, a chill worked its way through her as the water rushed down in a cascade of moonlit silver. It looked like an animated painting with a star-sprinkled sky illuminated by the magical glow of lunar light.

"This is where I would go when I wanted to look upon beauty like no other," Blaize began, "but now I can look at you and all this beauty is surpassed by far." He touched her cheek.

"Don't say that," Shelby replied. "I'm not beautiful. I never have been. I do okay, but beautiful . . . only in your wildest dreams." She gazed into his dark eyes.

"Then don't wake me, Shelby." Blaize got closer

to her. "If you are a dream, then I am the master dreamer. Because in you I see perfection." He traced his middle finger around the curve of her jaw then down the front of her neck.

Not being able to stop herself, Shelby leaned her head back and gave him full reign. "Talk to me, Blaize. When you talk to me I can't think of anything else. I'm not plagued by my fears. You keep me in the moment. Where I want to be. I don't want to think about the future. I want to focus on now. Only now."

"I'll do more than talk to keep you here." Blaize descended to the grass, then balanced on one knee. "I'll take you away to the perpetual moment. An instant in time and space that is consumed with nothing but pleasure." Slowly, he pulled Shelby down beside him.

"That is what an orgasm is, my Shelby. Death to anything but pleasure."

He kissed her, and Shelby came to him with everything she had. She didn't want to think that someday hundreds of miles of water would lie between them. She didn't want to acknowledge that as deeply as Blaize believed the teachings of his ancestors, with the same amount of conviction she chose not to believe anything. Shelby refused to accept that they were so far apart in the way they approached life, that it would take more than a master builder to construct a bridge between them that would hold. Right now the touch of Blaize's lips was enough to make her forget. The feel of his body against her was all the reality she needed . . . for right now.

Feeling a sense of urgency Shelby reached for Blaize's shirt and pulled. Buttons flew into the dark green grass around them. "I want you, Blaize. I want to remember this night of making love next to a cascading waterfall. I want to remember making love with the moon shining down on me, as naked as the day I was born."

Shelby didn't have to utter another word. Blaize covered her with his kisses and soon they were both naked with the tropical breeze caressing their bodies as eagerly as their hands.

Blaize entered Shelby and they both inhaled from the sheer pleasure of the joining. Shelby could barely speak, but her mind churned with so many thoughts she could not hold back. She had to say what was on her mind and in her heart. "What are we doing here, Blaize? People are back there celebrating the ceremony that you will lead tomorrow, and here we are—"

"Celebrating, my *doo doo*." Blaize kissed her lips and spoke again as he moved within her. "Celebrating in the oldest way known to woman and man."

Shelby's insides quivered in sync with the vibratory quality of his voice. It was powerful, intoxicating, but it did not quiet the unease Shelby felt. Although she did not believe the things Blaize and Cleophus espoused, she wanted to believe that Blaize believed in them, and to Shelby making love in the forest now was sheer hypocrisy. "But if you believe so strongly in the things you say, how can you be here with me like this tonight?" She held tightly to him, her mind in turmoil, her body striving not to miss a single stroke.

Blaize rose above Shelby and stared deep into her eyes. "Do you think what we do now is anything less than sacred?"

Shelby heard herself say, "I don't know," as her heart and body responded to the passion he aroused. Never in her life had lovemaking been so good, until even Shelby thought, *Can this be other than a gift from God?*

Without Shelby saying it Blaize seemed to become aware of her surrender, and he pleasured her until Shelby's mouth formed a silent scream. When Blaize spoke again his lips were against her ear. "There is no contradiction here, my Shelby. If I took you for the sake of taking you, with no feeling, no heart, then we would have broken a sacred law. But to have you with my heart as full as my body, we honor each other and those who have come before us."

Shelby thought she had known the ultimate pleasure minutes before, but it was proving not to be true as Blaize seemed to derive stamina and prowess from the very ground beneath them. Shelby could do no more than hold on, and with her holding gave Blaize, as well as received, what was theirs for the taking.

Chapter 26

"You can come with me, Keegan," Marlene coaxed.

"No, that's okay. I'll wait here." He didn't bother to look at her.

"But it won't take but a few minutes. Cleophus is probably asleep. I just want to make sure he's feeling okay. I think he may have overdone it earlier."

"I'll let you handle that," Keegan replied. "I'll be here when you come back."

"But you've never met Cleophus. This could be the perfect opportunity," Marlene insisted.

"I told you. I'll be here when you get back." Keegan's patience was wearing thin.

His reply hurt, but Marlene tried not to show it.

"Now go on." Keegan gave her a smack on the lips. "I'll be waiting for you."

Reluctantly, Marlene walked away, but before

she went into the house she turned to look at Keegan. He had already disappeared.

Danielle turned up the paper cup with one jerk of her head. The colorful liquid spilled on her dress when Keegan grabbed her hand and snatched the cup away.

"What do you think you're doing?" she squealed, then looked surprised to see Keegan standing beside her. "You've ruined my dress."

"What did you think you were doing with Blaize a little while ago?" he retorted.

"You don't know the *wine* when you see it?" Danielle snapped.

"Is that what you call the *wine*? I've been seeing that kind of dancing for years at Carnival, but the only time I see a woman act the way you were acting was in a bedroom."

"I don't have to listen to that kind of talk," Danielle replied, attempting to walk away.

"And I don't know what's got into you." Keegan squeezed her arm. "But you better get it out."

"You're hurting me," Danielle accused.

"I'm going to do more than that if you don't behave yourself."

She looked at him and fumed. "What are you doing here anyway? I thought you were against the Rites of Passage ceremony," Danielle accused in a loud voice.

"Obviously, I changed my mind." Keegan's eyes

threatened her to contradict him. "And if you know what is good for you, you will change yours."

Danielle looked down. When she spoke again her tone was considerably lower. "What am I supposed to do when you are giving your attention to Blaize's sister? Just play dead?"

"That is business. I've told you that before."

"Well, maybe my interest in Blaize is strictly business too." She tossed her head haughtily.

"You just make sure it is." Keegan spaced each word. "Because if I find out you have had him in your bed, you won't be having another man. I'll guarantee it."

Danielle looked Keegan up and down. "I'll *study* on that a while," she replied before she walked away.

Keegan stood alone and watched the crowd. He didn't like the way the cards were stacking up. First the foiled attempt in Sauteurs, and now Danielle was acting like a loose cannon. Things would have been so much easier if Blaize had remained on Hummingbird Island. The deal would have gone off without a hitch and he, Keegan, would have had big money in his pocket and Danielle to go along with it. But the men said the deal would be off if the "rumored barbaric ceremony" took place. That they didn't want their forward-thinking company attached to a place that was "back in the Stone Age. It wouldn't be good for their image." So he had to stop the ceremony from taking place. He had no choice.

"Looks like Danielle is giving you some trouble," Dennis remarked from behind him.

"Don't you worry about Danielle. I can handle her."

"Are you sure?" Dennis pressed. "She's got her sights on Blaize. And you know how Danielle can be when she targets a man. She might do or say anything. Even tell him about our plans."

"Don't get too pushy, Dennis." Keegan looked at him with a deadly glint. "I'm still in charge here. And like I said, Danielle is my business. Causing some problems around here is yours."

"I'm working on it," Dennis boasted. "I thought I'd have a little fun with it. Did you hear me tell Blaize the rum had already opened me up?" Dennis snickered. "Implying I didn't need no ceremony."

"Is that the best you can do?" Keegan retorted. "It's going to take more than that to derail the ceremony. So you just use that brainpower of yours to come up with something that's going to really work."

"It's in the works," Dennis replied. "I've got something planned for the morning. By then Alphonso will be here and—"

"Don't tell me about it. Just do it," Keegan said angrily as he watched Danielle work the crowd.

* * *

Marlene kneeled down and rubbed her hand over Cleophus' head. She noticed how peaceful his face looked with his eyes closed. You would think he didn't have a trouble in the world.

Her lips turned in a sad smile for him and for herself. Through the years Marlene wished he could have had a father to guide him, to help him know his worth as a man. But it never worked out, no matter how much she tried with one man after another. In the process she had garnered quite a reputation. Not as a loose woman, but as a desperate one. A woman desperately trying to create a family in the wake of losing another. A situation, Marlene believed, created by her selfishness.

"If only I hadn't insisted on going to St. George that day. Mama and Papa would still be alive." With tears in her eyes she stared at her son's face. "You would have grown up on Hummingbird Island like Blaize and me. Healthy and strong. Surrounded by a loving family. I wish I had done better by you, Cleophus."

Marlene could feel the tears flowing down her face. She cried for the past, the present and the possible future.

Keegan's face surfaced in her mind. She liked Keegan. He appeared to be a man who was about something. A man with a plan; someone who could provide a home for her and Cleophus. It didn't take Marlene long to realize she was thinking the same old thoughts, and that her motive for being in a relationship, ever since the birth of Cleophus, had not changed. It was unsettling to say the least. Yet, when Marlene faced the truth, she knew time was growing short. Cleophus would soon be a man on his own, or even worse, her biggest fear would come true. He wouldn't be around at all.

Marlene's hand went up and covered her mouth, stifling a soft sob. *So what good was pursuing this thing with Keegan?*

In the back of her mind Marlene knew Hummingbird Island would always be her home, and that Blaize would never, had never, turned her away. But it was her own guilt that made Marlene feel unworthy of staying. She felt responsible for making it a place of death and sadness. A place where she would never see the smiling faces of her parents again.

So what else is there to do but find another place, another home, Marlene rationalized. And right now Keegan was her only possible ticket. Still, judging the way he was acting tonight, Marlene wasn't so sure. He was preoccupied and distant. And that old thing called female intuition told her he had more than a passing interest in Danielle, no matter how he denied it.

Cleophus opened his eyes when one of his mother's tears landed softly on his face. Sleepily, he looked at her. "What's wrong, Mama?"

"Nothing." Marlene dried her tears. "I decided

to check on you because you didn't show up down-stairs."

"I'm still tired," Cleophus said groggily. "And I wanted to make sure I was at my best tomorrow, so I decided to turn in."

"That sounds smart," Marlene replied, touching his cheek. "As long as you are all right."

"I'm fine, Mama."

Marlene planted a kiss on Cleophus' cheek and stood up. She watched him adjust his head on the pillow, turning his face away from her. She turned to walk away.

"And Mama."

"Yes," she replied softly.

"Some things are going to happen. In the begin-ning you won't be very happy about it, but in the long run you will come to find out they were for the best. Promise me, you won't be too sad."

The hair stood up on the back of Marlene's neck. She didn't like it when Cleophus talked this way. As of late it was happening quite often. Uncertain as to what he was referring to, Marlene replied, "What are you talking about?"

"Just promise me, Mama. You'll know soon enough." Cleophus rose up. His eyes reached out to her. "Don't be afraid."

"I'm not." She searched for the strength to make her answer true.

"And so I have your promise?" Cleophus coaxed.

"Yes. You have my promise." Marlene didn't feel like fighting the forces that were working in her son's life any further.

"Good," Cleophus lay down again. "I will see you in the morning."

"Good night, son," Marlene said as she closed the door behind her.

Chapter 27

The crowd thinned considerably as the islanders made their way to an area filled with makeshift tents, blankets and sleeping bags. Shelby could see the glow of several fires sprinkled throughout. She watched from the shelter of some trees as Blaize bid the guests who were settling down good night. He had invited her to come with him, but she knew the blush of fresh lovemaking was written all over her, and she wanted to keep it from prying eyes. At least for now.

When Blaize joined her again they walked in silence back to the house. A few people remained in the yard, including Keith, Marlene, who was standing next to Keegan, and Jeanette, who was busy giving orders on how the food, pots and other kitchen articles should be put away. Most of the stragglers paid little attention to Shelby and Blaize as they walked by. But the same couldn't be said for Danielle, who eyed them with the evilest eye she could muster.

"Where you been?" she called, putting her hands on her hips. "The celebration is all but over."

"I hope you had a good time, Danielle," Blaize replied, reaching out to guide Shelby by placing his hand in the middle of her back.

"Early on I was having a good time." She swayed a bit. "But that changed all too quickly. I thought you said she was a relative of yours. If so, what kind of funny business are you playing?"

Before Blaize could answer Keith approached his granddaughter. "I think it's time for us to go to my place. We've got an important day tomorrow."

"Important day." Danielle let go a skeptical laugh. "I don't know if I want to participate in a ceremony that Blaize is going to lead. If this is the kind of example he is setting for all of us. Going off like that with a relative. It is dirty. Unspeakable," she announced.

"Danielle, you don't know what you're talking about." Keith tried to put his arm around her, but she shook it off.

"I'm the only one who is not afraid to talk," she insisted.

"Your grandfather is right," Marlene spoke up. "You don't know what you're talking about. You've had too much to drink. And once again you're making a spectacle of yourself."

"Me? You're a fine one to talk," Danielle retorted as her grandfather pulled her away. "At least when I go after men I do it for the fun of it. The pleasure. Not out of desperation. And when they show interest in me"—she poked her chest with her index finger—"it's because of me, and not because of who my family is, and what they might be able to get out of me. Am I right, Keegan?" she yelled as her grandfather pulled her over the hill.

Everyone looked at Keegan.

"What did she mean by that?" Marlene turned her attention to the man beside her.

"Yes, Keegan. What did Danielle mean?" Blaize stopped before he and Shelby were about to enter the house.

"How am I supposed to know?" he replied. "Drunk people say many things."

"Yes, they do." Blaize eyed him. "But I must admit I am surprised to see you here on Hummingbird Island. I know people can change, but I never expected you would be involved with something like a Rites of Passage ceremony." He paused meaningfully. "If my memory serves me right, you were very much against that sort of thing. Your interests lie in things, how do I say it, in things that are questionable."

Keegan put on a nonchalant face, although the corner of his eye quivered.. "You said it yourself, Blaize. People *can* change. Our viewpoints on life, love." He put his arm around Marlene. "I just hope that *we all* can believe that," he concluded with a pat smile.

"I can't guarantee you anything." Blaize looked from Keegan to Marlene. "But I will try." He and Shelby entered the foyer.

"I get the feeling you don't like Marlene's boy-friend," Shelby said.

"I don't know if Keegan is her boyfriend," Blaize replied. "This is the first time I've seen them together. As a matter of fact, this is the first time I've seen him in years."

"I saw him yesterday."

"You did?" Blaize's brow furrowed.

"Yes. When we went to the mainland. I found Marlene sitting with him in a restaurant after the incident at Carib's Leap."

Blaize's eyes became hooded. "I think we better keep our eyes on Keegan. From what I recall, he would have had to change an awful lot to be a halfway good guy. I don't know how Marlene picks these men. Ever since Cleophus was born Keith would bring me reports about the men she attached herself to. I guess she was trying to make a home for the boy."

"Why didn't you tell her to come back to Hum-mingbird Island?" Shelby looked puzzled. "To come back home?"

Blaize hesitated before he spoke. "At the time I couldn't find it in my heart to do it. I was angry with her. Angry with the world, and I just wanted to shut them all out."

"So you're telling me, if Marlene had returned here with a newborn baby you would have turned her away?" Shelby couldn't believe what she was hearing.

"I didn't say that, Shelby," Blaize refuted. "I said I couldn't find it within my heart to *ask* her to come back. If she had come, I would have welcomed her. This house and Hummingbird Island are as much her home as they are mine."

"But I don't understand." Shelby shook her head. "You knew she had a baby, your nephew. Our nephew. But you were so angry you allowed them to live any way they could without *offering* your help?"

"It's not as simple as it sounds." Blaize's jaw tightened.

"It's very simple," Shelby disagreed. "They're your family, Blaize. Do you realize how important that is?" She spoke from the pain of old wounds.

"I think I have a greater sense of what that really means than you ever can." His tone was cold. "Here in the islands we value family in a way that you in America have never understood. So don't preach to me about family, Shelby. My coming to America to bring you here was about family. The ceremony tomorrow and the risks that are being taken are about family."

"Really?" Shelby took a step back. She had to

put distance between them. He had hurt her and she wanted to hurt him back. "So we're back to that, are we? The Grenadians and the Americans. You're so stuck in your own little world, you might as well have never left Hummingbird Island."

Shelby could barely look at him she was so upset. "I don't know what family means. At least I *want* to know. I think part of the satisfaction you got out of bringing me here, and what you will get tomorrow from conducting that ritual, is how much it makes you appear that you are dedicated to family. But let me tell you something, Blaize, you don't have to *do* all that to show how important family is to you." Shelby struck her palm. "Love is about family. Being there in a time of need is about family. You think your running around and making this grand show is about family?" She made a comical expression. "That's about your assuaging your guilt for all the years you did not reach out to Marlene and Cleophus." She folded her arms across her solar plexus. "And one more thing, Raphael Blaize. Don't tell me that here in the islands you understand family in a way that we Americans never can. Maybe we've had our problems. And maybe we can't give a blow-by-blow tracing of our ancestry back to the Stone Age, but it doesn't mean we can't love as deeply and maybe even deeper than you will ever be able to do."

A thick barrier had been raised between them

and, at this point, neither Shelby nor Blaize was willing to cross it.

"I think I'll spend the night outside with the others," Blaize remarked.

"You do whatever you feel you need to," Shelby said.

She watched as Blaize headed down the hall in front of her, then entered his bedroom without a second glance. Her progress down the corridor was much slower. Her mind was going a million miles a minute. *What happened? How did we get from lovemaking to an irreparable argument?*

Shelby didn't know. But she was certain the things they had said had been lurking beneath the surface all along. Hurtful things that would have been said or shown sooner or later. Shelby knew sooner was better. At least her mind knew it, but it didn't stop the pain in her heart.

"Your brother doesn't seem too pleased to see me," Keegan said, flicking a fruit seed from his pants. "It's been a long time since we tangled. But from the way he's acting it could have been yesterday."

"My brother is very protective of our family and what it stands for." Marlene lifted her chin proudly. "Of me." She paused. "Maybe he doesn't understand why you're here. Maybe you should have made your intentions toward me plain, and he would have known there was something other than the ritual that brought you here."

"He's so protective, is he?" Keegan's jaw worked spasmodically. "Then where was he that night your old boyfriend put you and your son out on the street? Where was that protective brother of yours then?"

"Blaize didn't know anything about that. How could he have known?" Marlene was shocked by the viciousness of Keegan's tone. "But if I had turned to him, he would have opened his arms and his heart to Cleophus and me right away."

"That's right." Keegan nodded placatingly. "But you didn't feel worthy of his acceptance, so you came looking for me only two days after I gave you the slightest indication that I might be interested in you. So don't play that highhanded Blaize family attitude with me. You don't feel worthy of being a Blaize, but you can talk so high and mighty about the family standards." His look was full of disdain.

"I *know* what you are willing to do, Marlene, to keep a roof over your son's head. So you can pretend all you want when you're around that eccentric brother of yours, but I know the real scoop on you. And don't you forget it." Keegan got up and walked away before Marlene hurried inside.

Chapter 28

Cleophus watched the activities in the yard from behind his bedroom curtain. He was still very sleepy, but something had awakened him and urged him to go to the window. Cleophus watched as the man stormed away from his mother. And just as he was about to head over the hill two men stepped from behind a bush. Their sizes were comically opposing. One was big and hulking like a wrestler, the other extremely small. He reminded Cleophus of himself. Moments later, looking around suspiciously, all three men disappeared into the trees together. Cleophus could no longer see them, but he knew these men were dangerous. Dangerous for his family and to its legacy.

Quietly, he made his way across the room and placed his ear to the door that separated his mother's room from his own. He could hear her moving around inside. Cleophus listened for the familiar sound of crying, but the oak door was too thick, and there was none. Still there was no doubt in his mind that she was crying. He had heard her cry more than he cared to remember. He'd heard her cry over him. Over men. Over the circumstances in which they found themselves.

The first time Cleophus realized they were a part of the legendary Blaize family his schoolmates and their parents talked about, he was shocked. How could that be, he asked himself, when they were living hand-to-mouth? He was a little boy then, but not so young that he didn't realize their lives were less than ideal.

The men his mother latched onto always made it plain that he was not their child. That he was the son of a foreigner and sickly to boot. When he asked his mother about his father and his grandparents, she had told him as little as possible. That his grandparents had died on Bloody Wednesday, and that she had a brother, Raphael, who still lived on Hummingbird Island, but they never saw one another. They were estranged.

Cleophus decided his mother and her brother were estranged because this brother had done something despicable. Despicable enough that his mother preferred to live off the charity of others than to ask him for what was rightfully hers. It was only after Cleophus became so sick and his mother felt she had no other recourse that she returned to Hummingbird Island, and Cleophus set foot there for the very first time.

When Cleophus met his Uncle Blaize he was determined to dislike him, and at first that wasn't very hard to do. They had only been on the island one week before he left for the States. Cleophus had not been told where Blaize had gone or why. At least not by his mother or Keith. His grandfather had told him in his dreams.

During the upcoming weeks, Cleophus had been shown and told many things. He also came to understand his Uncle Blaize's plight. He was a man who had decided to divorce himself from the world after the brutal death of his parents—kind people who had shown compassion and love to anyone who was willing to receive it. Cleophus also knew it was his grandfather who had awakened him to see the men gathered at the edge of the forest.

Slowly, he walked back to his bed. He did not know exactly what was in store for tomorrow, but he knew he would need all the strength he could muster.

"We've got everything we need, Keegan, to bring this show to a halt," Dennis said in a self-satisfied tone. "We've hidden it near the ceremonial site."

"Like I told you earlier," Keegan remarked, "don't tell me. Show me."

"We'll show you and everybody else. The sun won't be the only light lighting the horizon. They're going to be down on the beach praying, and we'll be at the ceremonial site burning their little altar and their arena to the ground. All the work they did today will be nothing but a pile of ashes. And they will have to work like *la-jab-bless,* the she-devil herself, to rebuild if they want to have things ready for tomorrow night."

"Now you're talking." Keegan looked in the direction of the temporary settlement. "They've made makeshift tables and everything else around there. Burning that place down should take some of the wind out of Blaize's sails and more than dampen the others' spirits. Most of the idiots will probably think it's a sign or something telling them to leave that mumbo jumbo alone. Permanently." He laughed.

Dennis took a deep breath. "I don't know about all that. But I'm hoping it will shut down everything tomorrow. I can't say what might come of it later. You know how people from the Isle of Spice are. It is hard to keep us down. I would not even consider trying if it wasn't for the money. I need it to go back to school."

"You act like these people got so much heart. So much resiliency." Keegan made a face. "They don't. Look at them. They are satisfied with a garden with a few vegetables and a few coins in their pockets. I don't understand it. They're all just like Blaize and his sister, full of words and no substance."

Dennis looked upside Keegan's head like he

could smack him. "What do you mean by 'these people'? These people are you and me. And they have more spirit than anybody I know. What else would you call it? Being able to come together and love one another like family after Bloody Wednesday? It shows what we Grenadians are made of."

"Yeah." Keegan turned his head in dismissal. "You just make sure you burn that area. And you burn it good." Keegan walked away.

Dennis stood and stared into the darkness where Keegan had disappeared. "I'm beginning not to like Keegan's *head*. Somehow he thinks he's better than the rest of us. I'm going to have to prove to him that he's not."

"What are you going to do, Dennis?" Alphonso pressed.

"It's what I'm not going to do," Dennis replied.

Blaize headed for the area where the others were camping out. He tried to put his mind on tomorrow and not on the hurtful words with Shelby. He would find refuge with the people who truly believed in what he was doing, not with some foreigner who did not and could not understand his island heart.

Shelby had lain down with him moments before, only to place a cruel flashlight on the one area of his life that he had guarded so carefully. He had been right to think he should keep his distance from her. It was only weakness that made him give in to her beguiling eyes and soft frame. That was all he had wanted, Blaize tried to reassure himself. The companionship of a woman. Something he had chosen to do without.

Blaize had stayed away from women for a long time to strengthen his mind and body. Prepare himself for the time when he would pick up the baton that his father left. Blaize had waited for the sign that would beckon him from his cocoon, Hummingbird Island. The sign that would preface the work his father had always wanted him to do. Marlene coming home with Cleophus had been that sign, and Blaize had latched on to his duty with a tenacity that he had never known before. That was why he went to America to find Cleophus' father. That was why he was holding the Rites of Passage Ceremony, no matter what Shelby believed. He wanted to uphold and protect his family. Maybe he was trying to make up for lost time, but his motive was pure.

Blaize could see the fires flickering nearby. These people had willingly come to support him. Unlike Shelby, who had distrusted him every step of the way. They could relate to the heartache that had gripped his life for years. They too had lost people they knew and loved on Bloody Wednesday. It was the worst day in the recent history of his country. Yes, they had managed to mend their lives, but for Blaize the rip was too jagged to be repaired with a simple stitch of time. His family had been torn asunder. Distrust and enmity had been planted between him and Marlene. They both had suffered months and years of self-doubt because of it. And now they were being given an opportunity to heal those wounds. And Blaize would not let anyone, *anyone,* make him doubt himself.

A tropical breeze blew against Blaize's face, stirring up a familiar fragrance. It was Shelby's scent. The one that floated in her clothes, her hair, on her body. The smell brought back the feelings and sensations they had shared no more than an hour before. An electrical charge sparked in Blaize's belly as he remembered. He hated himself for having fallen so deeply under her spell.

Who was Shelby to say what he should have done after his parents' death? How could she ever know the pain of losing the two people in your life that meant so much? It was impossible for her to understand unless she had been through it. Blaize's mental tirade came to an abrupt halt. How was Shelby to know? The question echoed in his head. Because as a child she lost not two but three of the most important people in her life. Three. Her mother. Her father. And her brother, Cleophus. Yes, Shelby Russau knew loss perhaps in a way that Blaize would never understand.

His shoulders drooped as if a heavy object had been placed on them. And there was no doubt in Blaize's mind that Shelby did know how it felt. If he, as an adult, faced such a battle over the death of his parents, how deep were the scars of someone who suffered the same loss as a child?

Blaize stepped back into the shadow of the trees. So maybe Shelby was right about the other things as well. He could feel his body tensing. Maybe all of his motives had been selfish ones. Maybe he was trying to camouflage his shortcomings with a flamboyant performance of loyalty. *Maybe I am not worthy of taking the baton from my father, who operated from a stance of pure love.*

Blaize gazed at the people settling in for the night. All of a sudden he realized he could not join them. How could he, now that he was so unsure? He retraced his steps and took the path that led deeper into the island. He would camp at the site where the Rites of Passage ceremony would be held. Perhaps in that place, that was built to honor his ancestors, he would find clarity and settle the fight in his head and in his heart.

Shelby climbed into bed and pulled the sheet up around her. She could see the palm trees outside the window bending at the whim of the warm tropical breeze. How strange that the bed would feel so cold. Last night it had been warm, inviting, even hot. But Blaize had been there. Traces of the scent of the oils he used were imprinted on the sheets. Sheets they had made love on for the first time. That seemed so long ago. How could two people come together and fall apart in such a short period of time?

Shelby started to shiver. Her body shook until her teeth clattered. She drew her knees up and lay on her side. Maybe this would make it stop.

Shelby assessed how she felt. Instantly ill. That was what it was. Like her heart was being forced to stop beating. Could you actually fall in love with someone so deeply, so fast? The answer was yes. She was proof of it.

Her mind raced over the words that had passed between her and Blaize in the foyer. *Why couldn't I just be quiet? I knew I was treading in dangerous water, but I couldn't stop. I couldn't stop because I couldn't believe the Blaize I had come to know could be so cold and unforgiving. But maybe the truth is . . . I don't know Raphael Blaize. I had only fooled myself into believing I did. All the profound attributes I had given him were for my own benefit. So that I could dabble in the fantasy world of girl goes to island, falls in love and lives happily ever after with handsome stranger. But this is real life. This is no fairy tale.*

The words that Blaize had whispered in her ear as they lay on the grass next to the waterfall emerged. "We will make our own fairy tale," he had said. Well, this surely wasn't it. Fairy tales always had a happy ending.

Chapter 29

Shelby sat beside Cleophus and Marlene on the sand. She had never witnessed a sunrise. The colors were so very different from the sunsets she had seen time and time again in St. Petersburg. The shades of yellow, orange and red that were peeping over the horizon were pure announcements of a beginning.

Shelby looked around again. She attempted to be low key with her search, but the result was the same. No Blaize.

"Where do you think Blaize could be?" Marlene's silky brows furrowed. "I would think he'd be the first one on the beach." She looked at the sizable crowd that had gathered.

"I don't know," Shelby said, glad to be able to speak her thoughts aloud.

"Something is wrong," Cleophus said softly.

"What?" Marlene looked at her son.

Shelby listened with a sour feeling in the pit of her stomach.

"Something is wrong," Cleophus repeated in a strong voice. He looked toward the interior of the island. "Blaize is in trouble," he announced as if he were hearing the information for the first time.

Shelby's fists balled up at her sides. She had been patient with the strange things that had been happening ever since she arrived in the island country. But by now her nerves were frayed from a restless night. She knew Cleophus meant well, and that he was a very ill child, but Shelby had taken as much as she could in opening up to the possibility of believing anything that she could not see or touch. Cleophus saying that Blaize was in danger was just too much to believe. "Cleophus, I know you mean well—"

"I see smoke." Francis Whyte pointed over their heads.

Shelby, along with everyone else, turned and looked.

"I see it!" another man shouted.

"But it's too far to the west to be any of the structures." Marlene was on her feet.

"It's not the house," Cleophus corrected them. "It is the place where the ceremony will take place tonight. Someone has set it on fire."

They all looked at Cleophus. Some of the women started to whisper before another man said,

"It makes no sense. Many of us left ceremonial objects there from our own Rites of Passage." The man shook his head. "And after we've worked so hard. Who would set the ceremonial site on fire?"

"Not only that but the fire could spread," Francis Whyte said. "And we could all be in danger."

"I assure you." Cleophus looked at them with clear eyes. "It is the truth. There are people here who do not want the ceremonies." The group looked around suspiciously as Cleophus turned to Shelby. "That's where Uncle Blaize is. He slept at the ceremonial site. You will find him near the altar. He is in danger because of the fire."

Francis Whyte broke into a run.

"I'll show you a quick way to get there," Keith yelled from the edge of the trees. Several of the men followed Francis. Before Shelby knew it she was on her feet, racing behind them.

"What do you plan to do?" Marlene called after her.

"I don't know. But I can't stay here knowing Blaize may be in trouble."

Some of the others started in behind Shelby, but Cleophus spoke up and stopped them. "There is nothing we can do there." His voice was strong and sure. "They will do whatever is humanly possible. It is our duty to pray for help. We must go through with the prayer ceremony that Blaize had intended for this morning. We must call out to the Universe and let it know that we know and honor its power." Cleophus paused and looked around before he spoke again. "I have been given the knowledge of how to call upon the elements. I volunteer my services to lead this prayer."

Some of the women looked skeptical, even frightened. The older men who stayed behind grumbled and shook their heads in disbelief. It was Marlene who came to her son's defense. Marlene who encouraged them to listen to Cleophus.

"I can imagine what you must be thinking right now, but I implore you to listen to my son. I have finally come to accept that he has been given an extraordinary gift. I believe he has been given this gift through the trial of his life-threatening illness. He says my father, his grandfather, Eric Blaize, has been coming to him in his dreams." She waited until the denials stopped. "At first it was difficult for me to believe it, but as time passed I could not ignore the truth. Cleophus has spoken of things, known things, that he could not have known if my father had not told him."

"This is crazy, Marlene. He is nothing but a child," Sylvie said.

"Until recently, he was just my little boy." Her voice cracked with emotion before Marlene visibly pulled herself together. "And now I tell you as my friends and my neighbors that he is a child who has been granted the privilege of communicating with those who have passed over. I too was afraid when I first considered it. But I was afraid for another reason. A selfish reason. I thought my father had chosen to haunt me, punish me for being the cause behind my parents' death." Cleophus stepped up and held his mother's hand. "But now I realize Cleophus' gift is far from a punishment. It is a blessing, and proof that I must throw away my guilt, and forgive myself as my parents have most obviously forgiven me." Marlene enfolded Cleophus in her arms and wept.

Despite his diminutive size Cleophus stood strong and tall under her weight. He was the pillar of strength that his mother needed.

The crowd gathered near them and watched. Several of the people bowed their heads. Others nodded in agreement. There were still a few who looked about uneasily.

"You say you will lead the prayer?" Jeannette spoke out.

"Yes. My grandfather showed me a special prayer for this morning. One that will appeal to the Universe to bring the elements. I didn't realize it then, but he must have known there would be trouble this morning." The crowd reacted with loud skepticism, but Cleophus remained undaunted. "All I ask is that you remain here on the beach with me. You do not have to say a word if you don't want. But I will need your concentrated attention. The power of prayer is always that much more powerful when two or more are gathered together," Cleophus appealed to them.

"What do you have to lose?" Marlene asked. "We can at least give him the opportunity to try."

"I agree," an older gentleman said. "I remember Eric Blaize, and he always said we have no future if we cannot trust our young."

Mumbled agreements circled through the group. Soon everyone was quiet and all eyes were on Cleophus. In silence he walked to the edge of the water and faced the rising sun.

"You wait until I get my hands on that Dennis." Keegan spoke through the handkerchief he held up to his face. "Damn him."

"Sorry, Keegan." Alphonso blinked against the smoke. "But I couldn't do it by myself. It would take too long. I was afraid somebody might come up here before I lit all of them." He tried to ignite another rag damp with kerosene.

"You didn't use enough kerosene, you idiot."

"I wasn't supposed to do this part. Dennis was supposed to take care of that. I guess this is what Dennis was talking about last night."

"What?" Keegan uncovered his face. He started to cough immediately.

"He said something about what he wasn't going to do. So I guess this is it," Alphonso replied, squinting through air filled with smoke. He was about to light another rag when someone coughed nearby. "Did you hear that?"

"Shh. Of course I heard it."

"Somebody's up here," Alphonso continued. "Sounds like they're somewhere in the middle of this thing. I didn't come here to murder nobody. We've got to stop lighting these rags. They might die in the fire," Alphonso declared.

"It's too late for that now," Keegan said gruffly. "The best we can do is try to get a real fire going instead of these smoke bombs, and get out of here. That way there won't be any evidence. Whoever that is might have heard us, and might be able to identify us. But if there is a big fire, we won't have to worry about that."

The coughing was continuous and hard.

"But we can't leave—" Alphonso began.

"Who's there?" Blaize managed through haggard coughs.

Silence and more smoke filled the air.

"Who's there, I said." His anger was clear.

"Do what I said," Keegan barked.

"Is that you, Keegan?" Blaize gave in to a fit of coughing.

Shelby's heart beat frantically as she made her way into the interior of the island. Over and over again her mind said, *Not again. Not again.* Shelby realized it was the first time she had opened her life and her heart to a man. Yes, there had been a few others, but the feelings had been shallow streams. Outside of the relationship she had with Linda there was no one that she truly cared about. And now there was a possibility that Blaize would be taken away from her.

Trees and bushes brushed an oblivious Shelby's face. They were just like everything else that had happened since Cleophus foretold the impending danger. There was a part of Shelby that was watching herself as she had watched the old movies she loved so well. Distance was her lifeline to sanity as she crashed through the Grenadian rain forest.

With little effort Shelby kept up with the men. She had never been a runner or any kind of athlete, but her love for Blaize strengthened her. Her fear of losing him made her legs go faster. What would she do when she arrived on the scene? She had no clue, but Shelby actually prayed to whoever might be listening to give her the strength and the know-how to do what was needed.

The nearer Shelby and the others got to the area, the thicker the smoke became. Once they reached the ceremonial ground it was hard for Shelby to see her hand in front of her face. "Blaize." Her shrill voice rose above the other calls. "Blaize. Can you hear me?"

Shelby walked in the smoke like a blind person unfamiliar with the territory. Holding the bottom of her T-shirt over her nose, she reached into the milky whiteness. "Blaize. Answer me, Blaize. Please, answer me."

She was rewarded with a sound of coughing coming from the side. Shelby knew it could not be the others, for they continued to call Blaize's name from somewhere ahead. Frantically, she ran toward the sound. "Blaize!" She called again before she tripped and fell over a spasmodically coughing body that lay on the ground.

"Blaize." With her eyes stinging from smoke Shelby could barely say the name. She maneuvered herself toward the body. Shelby was relieved to discover it was easier to breathe near the ground because the smoke hovered just above it. "Blaize." She reached out to touch him. "It's me. Shelby."

To Shelby's horror and surprise a hand clasped over her mouth. It smelled of matches and kerosene. She struggled to pull away, but the person rolled on top of her and she found herself looking straight into George Keegan's watering eyes.

Chapter 30

Cleophus held his arms out toward the sky and, in a voice that carried across the beach, he said, "Good morning, Mother Earth. Sister Sky. Brother Wind. Sister Water. Brother Fire. Mother Goddess. Father Spirit. All of you who are here with us in love and light. All That Is. We Love You God."

The words echoed on the wind and Cleophus, who was usually soft-spoken, could feel the amazement of the people behind him. He knew they had heard his every word. He knew this, too, was a new gift.

"We have come here to honor you today," he continued. "To open our hearts, and to accept how little we know of the workings of the Universe. We stand before you this morning, ready and willing to carry forth our lives in a way fitting for those who understand and rejoice in its oneness. We thank you for this day that reaches into our past, shines on our present and illuminates our future. All Is One. So be it."

Then Cleophus began to raise his voice in a melodious song that was as sweet and comforting as the breath of a freshly nursed babe. His slender figure swayed with his tune and the very breeze appeared to accompany him. "Where I stand is holy, holy is the ground. Forest, mountain, river, listen to the sound. Great Spirit circles all around us."

Soon he could hear individuals joining in. First his mother's voice, and then another. And another. Before long the beach was filled with the voices of the islanders. Their arms raised toward the sun, repeating the phrase in a seraphic fashion.

With his eyes closed Cleophus listened as their beautiful voices blended with his own and the whirring breeze. Soon their volume gained in strength and so did the wind, until it turned forceful, blowing spray from the water into the air and into their faces. With their clothes damp and flailing like handkerchiefs in the wind, the Grenadians continued to raise their voices in song.

A frightened Shelby stared into Keegan's triumphant eyes. "No, it isn't your precious, Blaize," Keegan said, with his hot breath on Shelby's face. "Why do all you women find him so attractive? Attractive enough to degrade yourselves, like Danielle did last night. Or to put yourself in jeopardy as you have done this morning. If you hadn't come up here you wouldn't be smack-dab in the middle of this. You should have had enough from the incident on Carib's Leap." He paused momentarily, and continued after recognition surfaced in Shelby's eyes. "But it's too late to do anything about that now. You're here. And you've seen me. I can't afford to let you go."

Shelby struggled beneath him. She shook her head until Keegan's hand loosened its grip on her mouth. It was all the opportunity Shelby needed. She sank her teeth into the mound of flesh beneath his index finger. Keegan yelled and reared up. His black shirt caught the strengthening breeze, and flapped like the wings of a giant black bird. Once again Shelby tried to turn opportunity to her favor, but her aggressiveness had only made Keegan angrier. He reached down and placed his hands around her throat.

"You shouldn't have done that," Keegan said, his eyes fanatical.

"And you shouldn't have done that." Blaize reached down and grabbed Keegan from behind.

Blaize's voice was like heaven to Shelby's ears. Straining to see through the smoke, Shelby watched in shock as the wind picked up in strength.

"This is the last time you get between me and something I'm doing." Keegan's eyes widened as he reached back, clutching at Blaize's eyes. But with one powerful motion Blaize threw him to the ground.

Keegan roared like an animal. "You think you can walk in and out of people's lives whenever you want? It doesn't matter how it affects them, as long as it is convenient for you. Well, I'm here to tell you that's not acceptable. And when I'm done you won't be able to pull that shit again." Keegan lunged for Blaize.

"You might have a bone to pick with me." Blaize dodged the attack and once again Keegan ended on the ground. "But this is not about me. This is about our people. Honoring our heritage. Why destroy the ceremonial site that your friends and neighbors have labored to build? It makes no sense," Blaize appealed to Keegan's sense of reason.

"No sense." Keegan struggled to his feet as the smoke thinned around them. "You're trying to bring back these senseless ways. Make us the laughingstock of the world, and you say it makes no sense. What decent technological society is going to take us seriously if we are still offering herbs to the gods and performing rituals around altars?"

"Any society that acknowledges Buddhism or Catholicism," Blaize quipped. Then he was on Keegan before Keegan knew it. Blaize pressed his knee into Keegan's back and pinned his arms down to his sides.

By then the wind was whirling. Shelby watched in amazement as the smoke lifted up and away, resembling a curtain on opening night. Blaize and Keegan were on center stage several feet away from the altar. The other men who had come to put out the fire stood holding Alphonso. He looked as meek as a child.

"Don't you speak of Catholicism in the same breath as that low-life circus you plan to perform tonight," Keegan fumed with his mouth in the grass.

Blaize looked at Keegan for a prolonged moment before he coughed again, then heaved a great sigh. "This day wasn't meant for fighting and dissension, Keegan. I'm truly sorry that you see what we plan to do here tonight so negatively. But ceremonies like this have been performed for ages. And I'm sure they will continue to be performed long after all of our deaths." Blaize paused and looked around him. "Now, I'm going to let you up. You need to be grateful that you didn't do more damage than you did. I might not have been so generous."

Blaize walked over and put his arm around Shelby. "Are you okay?"

Shelby nodded, but she kept her eyes on Keegan.

Blaize turned and addressed Keith, Francis Whyte and the others. "Let's escort Keegan and his counterpart down to the beach where the others are waiting. I'm sure they will be interested to know what took place up here."

Chapter 31

Shelby could hear the singing before they reached the beach. Blaize glanced at her over his shoulder. Curiosity was written in his eyes.

They emerged on the sand. Shelby saw Cleophus and the others with their backs turned and their arms lifted to the heavens. The silky blue sheet of water stretched out before them as their clothes waved in the wind like flags.

As Shelby drew closer their singing clarified into words. Words with meaning. Soft. Embracing. Expansive.

Maybe Shelby's reaction was the result of the heart-wrenching experience she had just gone through, but somehow the beauty of what she heard and saw caused tears to roll down her face. The contrast of what had occurred in the interior of the island to the uplifting scene before her opened an understanding. Life was not good or bad. One or the other. It was an endless flow of both. *Because* of the contradictions Shelby could celebrate the differences.

As if by magic, when Shelby's group joined Cleophus and the others, the wind settled down into a gentle tropical breeze. One after another, looks of surprise crossed the singers' faces as they took in the disheveled appearance of Blaize, Shelby and Keegan.

"What happened?" Marlene was the first to speak. "Keegan. What went on up there? Is everyone safe?"

Keegan glanced at Marlene, then looked away.

"Yes, everyone is okay," Blaize replied. "The ceremonial site is still intact as well. There was lots of smoke and some charring, but overall, little harm was done."

"So why do you look like you've been in a fight?" Marlene said, puzzled.

When neither Blaize nor Shelby spoke, Francis Whyte did the honors. "Keegan and his friend here"—he pointed to Alphonso—"tried to burn up the ceremonial pit."

"What?" Marlene responded with disbelief.

"That's right. And I think he attacked Shelby," Keith added. "At first there was so much smoke it was hard to tell. Then this whirling wind came and lifted the smoke right out of there. It was a sight."

Some of the islanders looked at Cleophus, but Marlene was intent on getting to the bottom of the situation. "You can't say something like that if you're not sure," she defended Keegan.

"He's got it right," Blaize replied, eyeing his sister with apprehension. "Keegan attacked Shelby. I had to pull him off of her while the others cornered his friend."

Shelby gave Alphonso a good hard look for the first time and recognition dawned. "You look like the man who threatened me at Carib's Leap." Shelby walked toward Alphonso.

Alphonso looked at the ground.

"He probably was," Blaize said. "It seemed like too much of a coincidence that Marlene was being distracted by Keegan while that was happening to you. They probably planned it that way."

"Keegan, is this true?" Marlene went and stood in front of him.

He looked at her with emotionless eyes.

"It is true." Marlene's voice was breathy. "Why? Why would you do something like that?"

"Because of a business deal," Dennis said as he emerged from the forest. Several others islanders followed. Yards behind, Danielle brought up the rear.

"You son of a bi—" Keegan started for Dennis but was stopped by Whyte.

"How do you know that?" Blaize asked.

"I'm ashamed of it now." Dennis looked down. "But I was in on it," he confessed. "Keegan said a big technological contract was on the table, but they weren't going to sign if our country didn't appear to be moving in the right direction. Meaning a progressive image. Ready for advancement." He looked at Keegan, who pinned him with a deadly glare. "He said the Rites of Passage ceremony was going to make us look like we were back in the Stone Age. He promised Alphonso and me money if we could help him keep the ceremony from taking place."

"You telling everything on them," Jeanette called out. "What changed your mind?"

"I realize he does not believe in who we are." Dennis patted his heart. "People of great resiliency. A people who have the ability to embrace one another with all our hearts despite an occurrence like Bloody Wednesday. This is the kind of spirit it takes to change a neighborhood. A country. The world. We are not a backwards people. We may not play a major role in the technological world race, but with spirits like ours, we can teach others how to heal their wounds. Wounds between people."

There were nods of agreement and comments full of pride.

"If we are a people with such big hearts"—Danielle sauntered toward the middle of the crowd—"why are we surrounding Keegan and Alphonso like they are criminals?" She walked past Marlene and put her arm around Keegan. "He has a right to do as he believes, just like we all do."

An ashen look appeared under Marlene's skin.

"Surprised are you?" Danielle donned a smug look. "He never wanted you for anything but information. My Keegan is an aggressive man. He makes things happen. And I stand behind him all the way." She gave him a lingering kiss on the corner of his mouth.

"He has a right to follow through with what he believes in, but not if it is against the law and affects other people and their property," Blaize replied.

"You so busy saying what other people should and should not do. I think you better take a look in your own house. Last I heard a man messing around with his own kin is not one who should be setting rules for anybody." Danielle gave Shelby a meaningful look. "As far as I am concerned you can't control yourself. So don't try to control my man."

"It is not good to try to find fault in innocent people just to spite them," Cleophus' mellow voice advised. "I'm nothing but a child, who will become a man tonight, but even I know that. And I am sure, being a part of Keith's family, you are aware of that, as well." Danielle looked uncomfortable under Cleophus' clear stare. "My Uncle Blaize went to America and brought my Aunt Shelby back to help me. She is my father's sister. And I am proud to claim her, and that part of myself that she will represent tonight."

Marlene stepped closer to Keegan and Danielle.

"And now that has been cleared up, since you say you stand behind Keegan no matter what, Danielle, you can stand behind him when you take the ferry back to the mainland." She held her head high although her voice broke. "I just want the two of you off of Hummingbird Island."

"It'll be my pleasure," Danielle quipped. "I've got things to do, and I've had my fill of plants and bugs."

"We'll make sure they get on the ferry with no problem," Francis volunteered.

"Are we going to send him with them?" A woman pointed toward Dennis.

"He's not riding anyplace with me," Keegan said through clenched teeth.

"I think you've called enough shots, Keegan." Blaize looked at Dennis. "We need your kind of spirit at the ceremony tonight. If you want to stay, you are welcome."

"I want to stay," Dennis proclaimed. "Thank you for your acceptance."

"It's settled then. I'm sorry I wasn't here to start the day as we had planned," Blaize said to the crowd.

"It worked out very fine," Jeannette said. "From all I can tell, I think things worked out just as they should have." She turned to Cleophus. "And I'll be more than proud to participate in your Rites of Passage ceremony tonight."

Chapter 32

Shelby stood waiting, uncertain as to what she should do. She watched Marlene hurry away from the beach, not even waiting for Cleophus, who was surrounded by a group of islanders. Everything had happened so quickly after they spotted the smoke that this was the first clear-thinking moment Shelby had.

When she had raced behind the men toward the smoke, all Shelby could think about was that Blaize's life might be in danger. She had felt compelled to act. Shelby had no idea what she would do once she arrived. All she knew was she loved Blaize and she didn't want to lose him over a quarrel about family or anything else.

Her heart felt at peace with the clarification of her feelings. Shelby closed her eyes. It moved her so, and she wanted to share her conclusion with Blaize. She had to clear the air from the night before. She knew he cared about Marlene and Cleophus. His family. She also realized her accusations originated with her own fears over being abandoned, intentionally or not, as a child. Shelby wanted to put salve on the hurtful things that she said, and to let Blaize know how much she cared.

"We're heading back to the ceremonial site," Francis Whyte announced, looking at Blaize. "Keegan created a little cleanup for us, but we can take care of that in short order."

"I'll join you in a moment," Blaize replied, glancing at Shelby.

"That won't be necessary," another man said as they walked away. "We know you've got things to take care of. We can handle this."

"I know," Blaize called after them. "But I'd like to be a part of it."

The man looked at Shelby. "It's up to you," he replied and continued on.

Shelby looked down. Confused. It was obvious they thought Blaize might want to spend some time alone with her, but that didn't appear to be very important to Blaize.

"Shelby," he said.

Her name on his lips reminded Shelby of the first time she heard him say it. But the tone was very different. Shelby wasn't sure how, but she was certain she had never heard him use this tone before.

"Let's walk."

She fell in beside him as he walked further down

the beach. All of Shelby's senses appeared to be heightened. Colors were brighter. The smells of the water and forest claimed their own space within Shelby's awareness. And although Blaize walked at least three. feet away from her, Shelby felt the heat coming from his body. It was interesting how a life-threatening situation made things so perfectly clear. What was important and what was not. Love was important. The things that sustained life were important.

They progressed in silence until Blaize said, "You remember the shower of shooting stars we saw after we made love the first time?"

Startled by his question, Shelby looked at him. His profile was strong. Set. She had expected to look into Blaize's eyes, but his profile was all he offered. "Of course I remember."

"Now I will tell you what they meant. The shower of stars symbolized the giving of everything. That one or both of us would do exactly what the heavens had done, give everything for the other." He spoke, looking straight ahead. "Even risk his or her life."

Shelby listened to the musical words. Everyone here was so accepting of predictions, spirits, dreams. Although Shelby had seen what some would consider to be evidence of them on Hummingbird Island, to her they were still foreign, amorphous. "So you believe that prediction was fulfilled this morning?"

"Yes, I do."

Shelby didn't know what to say. Blaize answered her with such finality. What if the prediction was filled? Yes, she had risked her life for him, but wasn't that a good thing? Why did she have this funny feeling in the pit of her stomach as if all hell was about to break loose? "Then I guess it was," she replied lamely.

"Now, for certain, I must come to terms with some of the thoughts that kept me awake deep into the night," Blaize said in solemn tones, then paused. "I did a lot of thinking after we parted."

"So did I," Shelby replied. "And now after this morning—that's one of—"

Blaize stopped her. "Please, Shelby. Let me finish."

"All right." She folded her hands in front of her as she walked. Shelby knew she didn't want Blaize to finish. She wanted to tell him all the wonderful understandings she'd come to. Lighten the heavy feeling that was growing inside her.

"That night I didn't tell you what the stars meant because, quite frankly, it shook me up to see it," Blaize went on. "Not only the prospect that one or both of our lives would be in jeopardy, but that so large of an emotional investment would be made between us." He paused. "To be honest, that was almost more daunting than the thought of my life being threatened. You have to remember, Shelby, I chose to stay secluded on Hummingbird Island for sixteen years. No one forced me to do that. I did it because I didn't want to be connected. I understood no connections meant no emotional risks."

He continued in a steely tone. "After my parents were killed, it was as if I could feel every pain there ever was, and I wanted to be free of that. I had never felt so helpless before. I never dreamed I could. So last night, when you asked me why I didn't ask Marlene and Cleophus to come and live on Hummingbird Island, I didn't want to face the answer, which was, I couldn't ask. I was so raw emotionally that any tipping of the scale would have sent me over the edge, and to me that meant I was weak. I was not strong. And a man needs to be strong, Shelby." He looked at her, but his eyes appeared far away.

"So it was only after last night that I admitted that truth to myself. And it made me realize how little I knew myself. Or should I say, how little I allowed myself to admit."

"But that's not necessarily bad, Blaize," Shelby said, hoping to lighten his mood. "It could be a place for new beginnings. A new, more expansive way of looking at life."

"I came to that same conclusion," Blaize agreed. "So, I am ready to start over. I realize if I can't trust myself to be honest about who I am, and what I am about, how can I trust any deep emotional involvement with another human being."

Blaize looked out over the water, as Shelby

waited for him to say in plain language what all of this meant. Her heart knew, but her mind would not let him off that easily.

"What are you saying, Blaize?"

"I am saying things have happened between us so quickly, under the most unusual circumstances, that we need to allow ourselves room to see who we are in the midst of all of this."

"I know who I am," Shelby said firmly.

"Maybe you do," Blaize agreed. "But I am not so sure about who I am when it comes to you." He was totally present when he looked into her eyes this time. "And right now there are things that we must concentrate on that have nothing to do with us. Mainly, Cleophus. He is the reason I brought you here. He is the reason behind the ceremony tonight."

Shelby nodded. "I understand. Too much, too fast, huh?"

"I don't know if it could be summed up so simply or not," Blaize replied.

"You don't know if it's that simple?" Shelby's face scrunched up. "But of course we've got all the time in the world to figure this out since I live right next door."

"I know where you live, Shelby," Blaize said stoically.

"Well, I'm glad you know something, since all of a sudden you don't know who I am, who you are, or what you feel. I would say this is pretty bad timing, especially after what happened no more than an hour ago."

"But it's because of what happened that things are so clear to me now," Blaize told her.

"Yeah. Well, you've lost your sense of who you are and I've totally gained mine. And right now my senses are telling me to do this." She turned and left Blaize standing on the beach alone.

Chapter 33

Shelby was thankful she didn't encounter anyone on her walk back to the house. Her anger-fueled adrenaline lasted until she arrived inside, and then the hurt set in. Shelby could barely see for the tears she refused to let fall. *How could two people who claimed to care about each other be so far apart?* It was emotional overload, and in her confusion she walked past her bedroom and accidentally opened the wrong door. She looked into a closet that had been transformed into a tiny room. A swollen-faced Marlene sat on the twin-size mattress that nearly covered the floor.

"I'm sorry," Shelby apologized. "I'm so messed up I opened the wrong door." She pressed her hands against the sides of her face.

Marlene turned aside to wipe away her tears.

"There's no need to do that," Shelby remarked. "I guess birds of a feather flock together."

"Say what?" Marlene looked puzzled.

"You and me, dear. We're in the same boat."

"And what boat is that?" Marlene was still confused.

"Our men done dumped us," Shelby announced with a slapstick expression on her face.

They looked at each other and broke out laughing. Shelby plopped down beside Marlene and they laughed until they cried, spilling out the sorrow that was the root of it all.

"Girl, what's wrong with them?" Shelby asked, crying but starting to laugh again. "I don't get it. Why are things so much simpler for us?" She slapped her thigh. "You care for me or you don't. And if you don't, don't make me think you do," Shelby proclaimed.

"Right," Marlene agreed. "Keegan and the rest of them that I've known, they have you thinking you're on the right track, that you're going to build something together and then boom—"

"He's not sure anymore," they said in unison and began to laugh again.

"But the truth is"—Marlene's face lit up with a conspiratorial glow—"I'm happy the one named Jonas wasn't sure. What a mistake that would have been." Gales of laughter rolled again before it died away and silence filled the room.

"Oh-h. What a day," Marlene said. "Why does God pack so much into twenty-four hours?" She looked at the ceiling. "It was the same thing the day our parents were killed. The night before they forbade me from seeing Henry, the first boy I ever really liked." She donned a sorrowful smile. "He was modern. He didn't think much of tradition. Henry said Mama and Papa were old-fashioned and I would be too if I kept listening to them." Marlene looked down at her hands. "Blaize sided with them. He said he knew Henry and that he was no good. That I should stay away from him." Marlene paused. "I always thought he was Mama and Papa's favorite, but up until then he had always been on my side. That night I felt he jumped ship just to impress them. To secure his position. I felt like an outsider. So to lash out I told them I didn't need them. That I was old enough to make my own decisions. I was eighteen years at the time.

"Early that next day, without permission, I took the ferry to the mainland. The only way Mama and Papa knew I was headed for St. George was a friend of theirs was getting off the bus as I got on." They sat in silence before Marlene continued. "Papa knew something major was going to happen. He had warned a lot of folks about it, but I gave that stuff little attention. He was my Papa. Not a diviner or visionary. Just my Papa." She paused. "He must have felt I might be in danger. And I know Mama. She wouldn't let him go to look for me without her." Marlene closed her eyes. "When I saw my parents, I was marching with the other young people. I joined the group after they freed Prime Minister Maurice Bishop. We were marching toward Fort George with him in our midst. I could see my Mama and Papa's frightened eyes as they tried to push through the crowd toward me. I guess they had seen the armed soldiers. Around forty people were killed that day."

"Goodness," Shelby said softly.

"Goodness?" Marlene repeated, surprised.

"It's just an expression to say how awful that must have been. I guess it does sound rather confusing."

Marlene looked down, then continued. "Blaize and I held our relationship together long enough to pull the funeral off, but now, when I think about it, I guess like me he was in a state of shock. I took the money Mama and I had been saving for me to take a trip abroad, and left. I rented a small place near St. George. I never came back to Hummingbird Island until four weeks ago." Marlene sighed. "It was during Operation Urgent Fury, the rescue mission for the American medical students, that I met your brother, Cleophus. He came at a time in my life when I needed him most. I don't know if I could have made it without the tenderness and the caring he showed me." Marlene's eyes filled with tears again. "He was the first man I ever loved, Shelby."

"And I believe he loved you too." Shelby touched Marlene's arm.

Marlene nodded. "My life just tumbled on from there. Cleophus left. He wouldn't take me with him. He said I needed to repair my relationship with Blaize first. That he was blood. Family. And that family was most important. I never told Cleophus why my parents were in St. George on Bloody Wednesday. I know now it was because I felt responsible for their deaths and I didn't want Cleophus to see me in that light."

Shelby continued to listen.

"It was only after Cleophus left that I found out I was pregnant. I tried to contact him, but I moved and I never knew if he tried to write me back. I always believed if he really wanted to, he could have found me, come back for me. But he didn't. And I held it against him all these years until you stood in Cleophus' room and said he was dead. That never occurred to me. His abandoning me was far preferable to that." Marlene sniffed and took a deep breath. "After I found out I was pregnant I knew I wasn't going back to Hummingbird Island then. I had the baby, named him Cleophus, and I've been depending on one man after another ever since."

"It doesn't have to be that way," Shelby said softly.

"Of course it doesn't. It never did," Marlene replied with clear eyes. "Those were the choices that I made, that shaped my life."

Marlene went quiet.

"I think it's time for some new choices," Shelby said slowly. "Don't you?"

"Definitely. But how do I start?"

"By making up your mind and your heart. Your heart is what will keep your mind on track." Shelby stopped. "Your brother has really made an impression on me."

"He tends to have that kind of effect on people," Marlene rejoined.

"That's why I can't believe he stood there and told me he didn't know who *he* was." Shelby leaned forward to get a good look at Marlene's face.

"Blaize said that?"

"Yes, he did."

"You have really shaken him up," Marlene said.

"You think so?" Shelby looked uncertain.

"What else could it be? He's afraid."

"I don't know," Shelby replied. "We women tend to use that excuse every time a man doesn't want to deepen a relationship or commit to us."

"Yes, we use it a lot, but a lot of times it is true. I know that wasn't the situation with Keegan." Marlene crossed her arms abruptly. "He just wanted to use me. It's hard to admit it, but it's true."

"One day he's going to regret that," Shelby foretold.

"You think so?" Marlene looked hopeful.

"You're a great-looking, classy woman with plenty to offer."

"Thank you, Shelby. Sometimes you need to hear it."

"You're welcome. But on top of that"—Shelby wagged her finger—"you're going to make history tonight. That son of yours is a very special person, and I'm sure this Rites of Passage will be another story that's talked about many a warm, tropical night."

Marlene smiled, then said, "What do you mean, you? *We're* going to make history tonight. And you've got a special role in this too." Marlene's tone turned serious. "I never thanked you, Shelby, for coming to Grenada, sight unseen, to help Cleophus. It was a brave, loving thing to do."

"I'd do it again, Marlene. To help my brother's son, I'd do it again."

"You want to know something?"

"What?"

"I had made up my mind to dislike you. I thought you'd come here and try to convince Cleophus that America was so much better than Grenada. That Cleophus' part of him was superior to mine," Marlene confessed.

"Why did you think that?"

"Because most Americans, even though they don't intend to act that way, give that impression.

That they are doing us a big favor in coming to our island countries. But they don't realize we are a people with a rich heritage, and there is no money that can buy that, no technology that can better it. That's why my brother was so determined about bringing back the Rites of Passage ceremony."

"And I get to be a part of it," Shelby said.

"Yes." Marlene brightened. "As far as I know you are the first American to participate."

"For Cleophus' sake I hope I'm up for it," Shelby said, hanging her head, thinking about the conversation she and Blaize had on the beach.

"You will be," Marlene assured her. "It's like you told me earlier, it's all a matter of choice. You can go in feeling down. Feeling bad about Blaize's uncertainty. Or"—she opened her eyes wide—"you can feel proud and privileged to witness the passage of your one and only nephew into manhood."

"There's no choice in that, is there?" Shelby asked, knowing the answer.

"I don't think so," Marlene said.

"I know my big brother wouldn't think so either." Shelby's eyes softened. "And so I will be dressed in my favorite white dress this evening."

"That is the spirit. And I don't know if you brought anything that has a special significance to you, or perhaps something of Cleophus'."

"I thought something like that might be needed. I brought Cleophus' favorite watch and his favorite cap. It has pins all over it from events that he attended, and places that he traveled."

"That would be very special." Marlene's eyes softened again.

Chapter 34

Blaize paused, then tapped firmly on the bedroom door.

"Come in," Cleophus called.

"I thought we should talk before the ceremony tonight," Blaize explained as he entered the room. He didn't know why he felt awkward in front of the boy, but he did. He hoped his body language didn't show it.

"I'd like that," Cleophus replied, moving over to one of the chairs that sat beside a small table. "Would you like to sit here?" He offered the opposite seat.

"This is good," Blaize replied. Cleophus' gentle voice and small frame reminded Blaize of his frail physical condition. But even in the simple shirt and pants he wore there was something almost regal about him.

"I brought you this." Blaize placed a large package wrapped in paper on the table. "It's the outfit

that I wore during my Rites of Passage ceremony."
A hooded expression descended over his features.
"I'd be honored if you wore it tonight."

"You'd be honored." Cleophus' eyes lit up like
any child being given a gift. Hurriedly, he unwrapped the paper. Inside was a white linen top
and pants. The neck of the tunic and the hem of
the pants were embroidered with stars, moons and
suns. Cleophus traced the objects lovingly with his
hand.

"Your grandfather did the needlework. I remember my mother was going to do it, but Father insisted on learning how so he could do it himself."
Blaize spoke hesitantly.

Before Blaize knew what he intended, Cleophus
got out of his chair, came over to Blaize and
hugged him. "Thank you, Uncle Blaize. This is the
best gift anyone has ever given me."

Slowly Blaize's arms went up around the boy.
He closed his eyes and held him tight. It was the
first time Blaize had hugged his nephew, and from
the fullness in his heart it was far from the last.
"You are more than welcome, Cleophus." They
held on to each other, dissolving the years they had
been apart. Finally, Blaize moved Cleophus to
arm's length so he could study his face. "You
know, no matter what everyone says, you've got
the eyes of a Blaize." They both laughed as Blaize
rubbed Cleophus' head like that of an affectionate
puppy.

Cleophus turned and touched the pants set. "So you actually wore this at your ceremony."

"Yes. I did." Blaize knew Cleophus was playing up to him and he found it endearing. "I hope it makes you feel as powerful as I felt, but from what I heard happened on the beach this morning, you don't need any help in that arena."

"It was amazing, Uncle Blaize. Grandfather said when the time came I would know what to say and what to do. And it happened just as he had told me in my dream the night before," Cleophus explained with childlike wonder. "I know I give the impression of being comfortable with all of this, but that's because I didn't know how people would take it. Take me. It all happened so fast, Uncle Blaize." Cleophus' awe was written in his eyes. "I was getting sicker and sicker, and had to be in the bed more and more, and then the dreams started to come." He paused. "It feels good to really be able to talk to someone about it. Someone who has had similar experiences."

"Similar is right." Blaize realized his nephew had been walking a lonely road. "Because I can't tell you the kinds of things that are happening to you have happened to me. I can say, I believe what you have been telling us. I have never doubted it."

A wide smile lit Cleophus' face.

"Now for tonight," Blaize began. "Or have your dreams told you what to expect?"

"No," Cleophus said with a twinkle in his eye.

"I think Grandfather intentionally left that for you."

"You're playing with me now." Blaize lifted one eyebrow. "But the Rites of Passage ceremony is no joke." His tone turned serious.

"I know it isn't, Uncle Blaize." Cleophus looked repentant.

"But it is a very special time. A time when you will be officially recognized as a man." Blaize smiled and Cleophus smiled too. "In many cultures the male rites of passage can be quite daunting, dangerous even. They are set up to test a young man's strength. To see if he is strong enough, wise enough, to be considered a man.

"Perhaps if you had been living on Hummingbird Island when you first turned sixteen we would have held the ceremony then. But from what I understand, you have been having health problems for quite a long time."

Cleophus sanctioned Blaize's assessment with a nod.

"I believe, as your grandfather believed, that all diseases begin in the spiritual realm before they become physical. I don't think yours is any different."

"But why would Spirit want me to be sick, Uncle Blaize?" This time it was Cleophus who was seeking answers.

"It's not that Spirit wants you to be sick, Cleophus. Sometimes things that appear to be bad serve as the springboard for positive changes. Without the deep urge to make a change, a lot of us wouldn't."

"But I was only a little boy when I first got sick. What kind of changes should I have made?"

"Sometimes it is the innocent ones like you, Cleophus, that serve as the springboard for others to make changes. Others like your mother and me."

"Now I understand," Cleophus said sitting down in the chair. "Aunt Shelby and I had a similar discussion yesterday."

"You did?" Blaize could feel his body stiffen.

"Yes. I told her, if my being sick could bring many people together and make a positive difference in their lives, being sick was worth it."

"And what did Shelby say?"

"She went quiet. I think she accepted it, but didn't know how she really felt about it." Cleophus looked at Blaize. "If all of this is foreign to me, poor Aunt Shelby must be having a very difficult time. Our culture is full of supernatural things. *Obeah. La-jab-bless.* And some of us still believe individual spirits are responsible for everything that happens in nature. I don't think Aunt Shelby grew up with any of that. So this stuff could be quite frightening for someone like her." Cleophus appeared to contemplate what he had said. "But she hasn't held back one bit, has she? She came here not knowing what to expect, and she's been given plenty." He settled back in his chair. "Me and my dreams. Being threatened physically. Being called on to participate in the ceremony tonight, and soon she will literally give blood to me, someone she never met before three days ago. I think Aunt Shelby is a very brave and special woman," Cleophus concluded.

"Yes, she is," Blaize agreed softly. Shelby had been through a lot since he met her. Maybe it was the way Cleophus put it, but suddenly Blaize really realized how much Shelby had given, and was willing to give, to people who had been strangers no more than a month earlier. What kind of woman—what kind of human being—would be so charitable? Obviously, charity had not been his forte, or he would not have locked himself away for sixteen years.

"I hope Aunt Shelby has a special part in the ceremony tonight." Cleophus interrupted Blaize's thoughts.

"She has a very important part of the ceremony because she represents your father's family."

"Good. So will I have to do anything dangerous?" Cleophus changed focus.

"No. No, not really." Blaize tried to keep up, although his mind wanted to remain on Shelby. How had he been so selfish at a time like this? Shelby had been through hell and all he could do was think of himself. In a sense, he was doing the same thing he had done when he secluded himself on Hummingbird Island. He shut himself off because he was afraid of what he might feel. What he might do. Blaize forced himself to address Cleophus' question. "The only danger you will have to face is symbolic. Your health had to be taken into consideration. And this ceremony is being done on such short notice that many things have been condensed. When Father held the Rites of Passage, there were days of singing and dancing before the actual ritual. It was a kind of buildup."

"So last night was a mini-buildup," Cleophus said.

"You could say that," Blaize concurred.

"So when do I face the symbolic danger?" Cleophus asked.

"In the beginning, during a cleansing with sage and cedar. After that there will be an honoring of our ancestors. Then members of the family will give you gifts that we feel will symbolically help you make your transition from boyhood to manhood."

"More gifts." Cleophus lit up again. "Too bad a boy only turns into a man once."

Blaize couldn't help but smile.

"Then what happens, Uncle Blaize?"

"Once that is done the singing and dancing will begin again. This time as a celebration of your new identity."

"I think I can do that," Cleophus said.

"Good," Blaize replied. "I will be the one to escort you to the ceremonial pit. Everyone else will already be there waiting. They will have started an hour or an hour and a half before."

"Singing is very powerful, isn't it?"

"Yes, it is."

"I wonder why," Cleophus contemplated.

"It opens the way for the heavens to receive our prayers," Blaize told him.

"That sounds beautiful."

"It is beautiful and true," Blaize replied. "Our voices vibrate out into the universe, and it can't help but respond because everything vibrates. Beautiful music creates a wave of reactions that vibrate on the same level. Prayers being sent up on a song vibrate much more because of the powerful intent."

Cleophus sat back in his chair, looking down. Blaize watched his shoulders slope and his chin lower.

"What is it, Cleophus?"

"I don't want this to be the last time that we talk like this," he said softly. "After tonight the ceremony will be over and I will be a man. There won't be another reason for you and me to sit and chat."

Blaize got up and put his hand on Cleophus' shoulder. "There will always be a reason, Cleophus. We are family, and there is no greater reason than that."

Chapter 35

The chorus had been sung so many times Shelby now knew all the words. She sang as loudly as everyone else. When she had arrived at the ceremonial site the forest already vibrated with the voices of the participants, and it continued to do so moment after moment. No sooner did one song end when another began, increasing the vibration until Shelby could feel the music in her chest.

She and Marlene sat at the head of the round, ceremonial pit. They sat alone on opposite sides. The pit was defined by logs that had been cut in half, and stacked to create seats. The other attendees filled in the space across from them. All dressed in white, their bodies formed a semicircle that highlighted the myriad natural colors of the surrounding forest.

Keith was the busiest of all. He was the orchestrator, and it was obvious he did it with pride. Shelby watched as Keith straightened a handmade quilt, covered with images of people and constellations, that was draped over the altar. Carefully, he arranged the ceremonial objects on top of it, moving them back and forth until he felt they were situated perfectly. The Libation Cup gleamed in the middle of a large shell containing herbs. There was also a huge colorful feather, a bowl, and a smaller seashell. Countless blossoms were strewn on the altar and around its base.

Shelby felt anxious. She scanned a few of the familiar faces. Everyone seemed so intense. They sang with their eyes closed, their bodies swaying with a motion that was primitive and deep. Shelby sang, but she found herself looking around, wondering what the others were thinking, feeling, for it was obvious the music and the moment had sparked something rich within them.

She beckoned for Keith. She needed to talk to someone to relax the nervous energy that was building inside her.

"I hope I'm not doing anything wrong by calling you over here."

"No, it's okay." Keith reassured her. "I'm just making sure everything is right before the ceremony begins."

"The altar is really beautiful. Did you help Marlene and Blaize's parents with the ceremonies in the past?"

"All the time," Keith replied, holding his head abnormally straight. "I was helping them before

Blaize and Marlene was born. Back then the group that gathered here was no more than seven, maybe ten, people. Then over the years more and more people began to come. There may have been a birth or a marriage, and they would hold the traditional ceremony here on Hummingbird Island. On one or two occasions we may have had as many as a hundred people gathered round like they are tonight."

"This is my first time doing something like this. Is there anything I should know before we start?" Shelby hoped her question sounded calmer than she felt.

"Blaize will tell you what to do," Keith informed her.

"So he has conducted ceremonies like this before?"

"He assisted his father in a few of them, but he has attended them all of his life. It should be as natural as breathing."

Shelby looked at the people sitting directly in front of her. "Everyone seems so—"

Keith put up his hand, motioning for Shelby to be quiet. "We're about to begin," he said quickly, then lifted his arm, instructing everyone to stand.

Shelby stood too as the singing and the music took on the sound of a march. Everyone's attention focused on the path that led from the forest. Shelby's gaze darted from the path to the people around her, until Blaize, all dressed in white, stepped onto the ceremonial site.

Majestic was the word that came to Shelby's mind when she saw him. Blaize's loose locks framed his angular face above a buttonless linen coat that came to his feet. Glimpses of his bare chest could be seen beneath it, along with billowing matching pants. Before him, he carried the Talking Stick in both hands

Pulled up to his fullest height, Cleophus followed. His eyes focused on the back of Blaize's head as if nothing else in the world existed. Shelby watched him with his chin tilted ever so slightly and her heart constricted. To her he looked like an angel marching toward heaven.

When they reached the altar one more round of the chorus was sung before the music stopped and Blaize began to speak.

"We are here tonight to watch Cleophus Blaize cross the river from boyhood to manhood. We are here to celebrate the tradition that is the vehicle for that honor. We are here to proclaim our belief in the ancient ways, and to bring them the glory they deserve in the present."

"But our son." Blaize looked at Marlene. "Nephew." His eyes focused on Shelby. "Friend and neighbor." He glanced around the crowd. "Cleophus Blaize, cannot make the journey without preparation, and so we offer him the cleansing smoke of cedar and sage."

Blaize stepped toward Cleophus and lit the herbs inside the shell. The dry branches caught flame and in seconds the blaze grew higher and higher, until Shelby thought Cleophus' clothes might take flame. But Cleophus did not budge. He stood with confidence, without fear, until Blaize extinguished the fire with a smaller shell. The fragrant smoke ballooned upward, and Blaize fanned it in several directions with the feather from the altar.

"May you always be as brave as you were in that moment of purification," Blaize said, looking into Cleophus' eyes. "No matter how challenging the situation may be, may you stand fast and true."

Using the feather, Blaize dusted the smoke up one side of Cleophus' body, then down the other, before he asked Cleophus to present the palms of his hands and the soles of his feet.

"And now, Cleophus Blaize, would you take the Libation Cup and offer a drink to your ancestors, who have traversed this globe in all directions."

Cleophus nodded. In the four directions, north, east, south and west, he poured a drink of water onto the rich soil from the cup, before handing it back to Blaize.

"Who is here from your mother's side of the family to help you with your transition?" Blaize asked.

Cleophus looked at him as if he was about to call his name, but Blaize indicated Marlene with his eyes.

"My mother, Marlene," Cleophus said clearly.

"Then bring her forward and offer her the Talking Stick so we may know what aids you on your journey."

Cleophus brought Marlene near the altar and passed her the Talking Stick.

Marlene looked into her son's eyes before she began to speak. "I give you the journal that I kept for years as a child living here on Hummingbird Island, in hopes that it will help you see this island that is truly your home through a child's eyes, because I never afforded you that privilege. May you come to know the family that has always been yours through these pages. May these writings serve as a foundation in your life as a man."

Marlene gave Cleophus the worn journal and he clasped it to his heart and mouthed "Thank you" before she returned to her seat.

"Who is here from your father's side to help you with your transition?" Blaize asked.

"My aunt, Shelby Russau, who has come all the way from the United States of America."

"Then bring her forward and offer her the Talking Stick so we may know what aids you on your journey."

Cleophus brought Shelby forward and offered her the Talking Stick. Her hands shook as she took it, and suddenly the object that she and Cleophus had dug out of the trunk the day before held so much meaning. It marked this moment in which she openly acknowledged Cleophus, her brother's son, the only living relative that Shelby had.

Shelby didn't know if she would be able to speak she was so moved. But Cleophus looked into her eyes imploringly, so Shelby dug deep to express how she felt.

"I came here ready to give you your father's watch and his favorite cap. Small memories of a man with a big smile and an even bigger heart. The watch symbolizes time. Know that you have time to fulfill all your dreams. The cap is a symbol of the travels your father made and longed to make. May you travel far and wide, sharing the gift you are with the world.

"I do not mean to trivialize the worth of the objects I present, but as I stand here during this important moment in both our lives, the greatest thing I can give you for your journey into manhood is something that all children need, the knowledge that you are loved by your family, by your friends. Remember that. For love is the key to knowing how to live life."

Cleophus and Shelby looked into each other's eyes.

"I will remember," he said softly, before she handed him the watch and the cap and returned to her place.

"Now that you are armed with the support of your family from both lines, are you ready to make the crossing?" Blaize inquired.

"Yes," Cleophus replied.

Blaize gazed at the stars above him. "It is evident

in the stars that from this moment on your life will be a flowing river of proof of the power of the universe. Your days will be full of miracles for the people to behold and believe. You are a gift Cleophus Blaize, as a boy, and will be an inspiration as a man."

Cleophus clasped his hands in front him as Blaize spoke, as if his body was being infused with the very essence of the powerful words. As Cleophus watched, Blaize picked up a handful of blossoms from the altar and lifted them up to the heavens. "With the grace of the earth and the blessings of the heavens I open the way for the boy, Cleophus Blaize, to become the man."

Blaize strew a line of petals across the ground, stepped back and allowed Cleophus to step forward. When he did the crowd gave a great cheer.

"Welcome Cleophus Blaize, the man," Blaize shouted.

Cleophus grabbed Blaize and gave him a mighty hug. Moments later Marlene had her arms around the two of them while Shelby stood to the side and watched. It was their moment. A Blaize family moment, and although Shelby felt a longing to be a part of the group embrace, she was able to celebrate their joy. It was Cleophus who finally broke away and called her over as the music started again.

"Come here, Aunt Shelby." He motioned energetically.

When Cleophus called her name Blaize's gaze

found hers. He looked as if he wanted to say something but the exuberant crowd had rushed inside the ceremonial pit, and nothing could be heard besides singing, and the lively tune the band had begun to play.

"Let's dance, Aunt Shelby." Cleophus grabbed Shelby's hand after he made his way through a barrage of congratulatory pats and kisses. "I feel like celebrating."

Before Shelby could say a word Cleophus had her spinning around, reminding her of the days when she played as a child. But this was a spin with a calypso beat. And Cleophus moved his slim hips and torso as well as any islander.

"Welcome to Grenada, Aunt Shelby," Cleophus shouted above the music as the crowd pressed in on them.

Shelby was just about to shout back when she knew something was dreadfully wrong. Cleophus' eyes had taken on a glazed look and his mouth hung open as if he was on the verge of speaking. The very next moment he was on the ground.

"Cleophus," Shelby shouted, dropping to her knees. "Cleophus, what's wrong?"

At first no one but Shelby was aware of what had happened. The crowd continued to jump and dance as Shelby pulled an unconscious Cleophus into her arms.

It felt like an eternity but it must have been only

moments before Blaize and Marlene were at their side.

"What happened?" Marlene screeched.

"I don't know. One moment he was dancing and celebrating." Shelby looked at her, her eyes wide with fright. "The next moment he collapsed."

"Cleophus." Marlene clutched at her son and called his name.

"We've got to get him to the hospital," Shelby shouted. Her last words exploded into the night air because the music had dribbled to a halt.

"Oh no . . . no," Marlene cried, rocking back and forth on her haunches.

"Cleophus." Blaize pulled the inert body into his arms. "Cleophus can you hear me?"

"He can't hear you, Blaize," Shelby cried.

Blaize placed his ear to Cleophus' chest. "His heart is still beating." He looked into Shelby's eyes. "Perhaps he has been overwhelmed by the power of what he has just experienced. The energy . . . the spirit that can be created can be indescribable," he began to explain.

"I can't believe you're saying this and Cleophus is lying there unconscious." Shelby's eyes beamed. "This is not the time for your beliefs, Blaize. Cleophus needs to go to the hospital and he needs to go now," Shelby insisted.

It was a look that lasted no more than a split second, but Shelby knew she had killed any possible future between them. The world of rituals and beliefs was Blaize's world. And although she had stepped into it for a moment in time, it appeared it had never really entered Shelby's heart.

Blaize rose to his feet with Cleophus in his arms. "Dr. Minor was expected to arrive on the mainland tonight. We will take Cleophus to St. George's General Hospital. Maybe we can contact Dr. Minor from there."

He did not look at Shelby when he gave in to her demand. But they both knew something had been severed between them as the silent islanders parted to let Blaize and Cleophus through.

"We should get some things from the house in case Cleophus has to spend the night at the hospital," Marlene said in a shaky voice.

"That's a good idea," Shelby said stiffly, watching Blaize's back.

"I'll come with you," Jeannette offered. "It'll make things go faster. Plus, everyone is in a little bit of shock right now. You'll need a steady hand and head."

Marlene simply nodded before she hurried toward the house.

"They will meet you at the ferry," Jeannette shouted to Blaize, her ample hips rolling with her rapid gait. "Come on, child," she advised Shelby. "You can't turn back the hands of time now. You've got to get down to that ferry and you got to get down there quick."

Chapter 36

The lights on the mainland edged closer and closer. Shelby held tightly to the rails of the ferry. Not because the water was rough, but because of the uneasiness in her heart. Cleophus remained in a kind of deep sleep as they crossed the water in an eerie cocoon of watery sounds, including Marlene's crying. The multitude of stars was so close they seemed to press down on Shelby's head, punishing her for her disbelief. Blaize stood at the helm. His white coat rose every so often with the breeze. But he never turned around to look at Shelby. Not once.

When they reached the shore Blaize stepped out into the water and pulled the ferry onto the sand. "I'm going to find some transportation," he said, anchoring the craft. "I'll be back as soon as I can." He took a long look at Cleophus' motionless face.

"But where are you going to find a ride, Blaize?" Hysteria was just beneath Marlene's question as she reached out toward her brother.

"I'll find one." He placed a comforting hand on her arm. "Everything's going to be all right, Marlene. Cleophus is going to be fine. I promise."

Shelby wanted to say, "I believe you, Blaize," in hopes that it might lessen the divide between them. But she watched him leave in silence, the unspoken words stuck like rocks in her throat.

Marlene nodded nervously and settled down beside an unconscious Cleophus. She stroked his face and began to rock again.

"Where are we?" Shelby surveyed the empty beach and eroded cliffs.

Marlene looked up as if she didn't realize Shelby was speaking to her. "This is Bathways Beach. I think Blaize is headed toward the road that leads here from River Sallee. It's well traveled and maybe he'll get lucky."

Maybe, Shelby thought. She could feel panic rising, but she looked at the tears spilling down Marlene's face and she knew one of them had to remain calm. "He'll find transportation," she claimed as convincingly as she could.

"I don't know." Marlene surveyed the empty beach. "It's nighttime and most people come here during the day. Tourists come to see the speckled coral sands and visit a rock shelf that creates a natural swimming pool. I don't believe many people come here at night. Bathways Beach hasn't been developed like some of the others."

"It doesn't matter." Shelby swallowed. "We've

got to believe that Blaize will come back quickly with a ride."

"Believe." Marlene's face turned grotesque. "Do you believe Cleophus is lying here, lifeless like this? Believe." Marlene shook her head until her hair came loose from its style. "I'm where you were back on Hummingbird Island. Don't talk to me about belief right now, Shelby." Marlene wiped her tears with the back of her hand.

Shelby stood up and looked at the heavens. She knew how hopeless Marlene felt and it made her want to scream. But Shelby was afraid her scream would be so loud the sky would shake and the stars would fall.

She glanced into the darkness where Blaize had disappeared and she felt helpless. As helpless as she felt as a child when she realized she was alone in the world. It was clear to her now. It was at that precise moment that her belief died. There could be no belief, because there could be no Power who would allow all of her family to be taken away.

Shelby looked at Cleophus, then at Marlene who was struggling on the brink. *What if Cleophus died?* The question that she had been trying not to hear rang in Shelby's head. *What if, once again, her only relative in the world was taken away?*

Shelby closed her eyes and squeezed her fists. "It's not going to happen," she said softly. "It's not going to happen." This time it was louder. "I won't believe that it will happen again," she said so loudly her throat burned and her entire body vibrated with the words. Then all of a sudden the strain drained away, and it was replaced with a sense of calm.

When Shelby opened her eyes she felt as if something heavy had been lifted from her heart. She looked at Marlene, who was staring at her as if she had taken leave of her senses. Finally, Shelby said with a sense of wonder, "That's what belief is for, Marlene."

"What?" Marlene replied apprehensively.

"That's what believing is for." Shelby knelt back down and placed her hands on Cleophus. "When you have nothing else, you can believe and it will sustain you. When you have all you think you could dream of, believing will bring you more than your wildest dreams. To believe is not a privilege, it is a gift," Shelby proclaimed. "I finally understand, Marlene. After all these years it has finally come back to me."

Marlene remained silent. She looked at Shelby apprehensively.

"Don't worry," Shelby told her. "I'm okay. It's just for the first time I understand that if you and I had truly believed our lives would be full of love despite the deaths in our families, they would have been." Shelby looked deep into Marlene's eyes. "We could have accepted that gift. It was our choice."

Shelby started when she felt movement beneath her hands. Cleophus had stirred.

"Cleophus," Marlene called her son's name. "Can you hear me, baby?"

Cleophus did not respond, but Shelby and Marlene grabbed hands across his slender body.

"He is going to be all right," Marlene said, her eyes glistening.

"Yes, he is," Shelby declared with a tremulous smile.

No sooner had the words passed Shelby's lips than Blaize yelled from the distance, "I've got a taxi."

In record time he crossed the sand, and before he could reach them Marlene yelled, "Blaize! Cleophus moved. Not a lot, but he moved."

Shelby saw Blaize take a deep breath, then let it out slowly. "I told you he's going to be okay." He gave Marlene a hug before he pulled Cleophus into his arms.

Shelby wanted Blaize to hug her. She wanted him to hold her as she said, "I believe Cleophus will be fine. I think I understand how someone can believe in something just on faith and trust alone." But Shelby remained silent. Blaize had given no indication that she was in his thoughts. It seemed it was he, Marlene and Cleophus now. They were the family.

The cab was a short distance away. In minutes it headed for St. George's General Hospital with

Blaize and the driver in the front seat. Shelby sat with Marlene, who cradled Cleophus' head in the rear.

In less than an hour, they arrived at the hospital. Shelby looked around the nearly empty waiting area. By American standards it was a small, modest facility. She watched as a man with complicated injuries was wheeled outside on a gurney. He would be flown to Miami, Florida, where the latest medical technology would be at his avail.

Marlene had accompanied a groggy but conscious Cleophus to the back. Blaize was on a telephone at the check-in desk. Shelby tried to keep her gaze from straying in his direction, but the bright fluorescent lights of the medical facility put everything on display like jewelry in a sales case. Blaize was a startlingly handsome man when Shelby met him, and even more so now that she knew the kind of man that he was.

Shelby thought about how Marlene had given all power and jurisdiction over Cleophus to Blaize once they arrived at the hospital. She appeared overwhelmed by a couple of nurses and a doctor who insisted from that point on they were in charge of Cleophus' health. Blaize had stepped in and made it clear they could examine Cleophus, but no one but Dr. Minor would be allowed to treat him. When asked who would be accompanying Cleophus into the emergency room, without looking back Marlene indicated herself and Blaize. Shelby felt a pang from the oversight, but she was sure Marlene meant no harm. It was just at that moment Marlene was clear on who her support system was, who was family.

Shelby watched Blaize hang up the telephone. He started toward the emergency room, then stopped, turned, and walked over to her.

He stood above her. "I just thought I'd let you know that Dr. Minor is on his way."

"Thank you." Shelby was glad their silence had been broken. "Is he a friend?"

"I've known him for a long time. We were friends before he became a doctor. Then through the years he gained quite a reputation, especially with diseases of the blood like sickle cell and leukemia. He's been abroad for two months, primarily in Ghana, where sickle cell has been a problem."

"It's comforting to know Cleophus will have a specialist working with him," Shelby said before silence loomed between them. She searched for something to say. "And as far as you know Cleophus suffers from—"

"Sickle cell anemia," Blaize completed the sentence.

"Of course, I knew that." Shelby wished she didn't feel so restrained. "We talked about it at the Heritage House in St. Petersburg."

"Yes. The day you came to my hotel room,"

Blaize replied, his tone shifting ever so slightly. It was the first time they had touched.

Shelby's eyes widened, before she quickly looked away. "So there's a possibility this Dr. Minor might want to do the transfusion tonight."

"Anything's possible," Blaize said, wondering if she was remembering that first meeting as well. He had caught her at his door eavesdropping, and shocked her when he invited her inside. Up until that point she had not trusted him and the truth was, it wasn't until she actually met Cleophus that Shelby began to believe. Only a little.

Blaize turned toward the emergency room. Once again he changed his mind. "I want you to know something."

"Yes." Shelby held her breath.

"If I don't get to say it again, I really appreciate your coming to Grenada to help Cleophus. It was a brave thing to do. A giving thing."

"Thank you," Shelby said softly, feeling more like an outsider than ever. "I'm glad I came. Finding Cleophus has been one of the best things in my life."

Once again silence stood between them before Blaize nodded and went into the emergency room.

Shelby sat there a second before she realized she and Blaize had performed their good-bye speeches. There was nothing else to call it. From this point on, whatever happened, there would be no relationship between them. Cleophus would be the only link. And when her work was done, she would go back to St. Petersburg, and these days and nights in Grenada would be no more than a memory.

Shelby's mind focused on the words "her work." That's how Blaize seemed to see it. Not that Cleophus was her nephew, her one and only brother's son, but some stranger that she had lent a helping hand.

Shelby felt empty. She had experienced so much only to be left with a feeling of being used. Just someone who had come to Grenada for the convenience of, and to be used by, others.

"Miss Shelby," someone called from behind her.

Shelby looked behind her. Keith, Jeannette and Francis were standing just inside the waiting room door.

"We couldn't stay on Hummingbird Island knowing what you all were going through here," Keith said, fingering a hat.

"That's very considerate," Shelby replied.

"It's not just us. Almost everybody who was at the ceremony is gathered out front. We intend to pray for Cleophus until we get some good news."

Shelby got up and walked to the door. People were sitting and standing everywhere, their eyes focused on the hospital. "I don't know what to say."

"You don't need to say anything, Shelby," Jeannette advised her. "Cleophus is a very special young man. We all saw proof of that this morning.

We care about him and we want him to get better. This is a way for us to show our support. You'll let Blaize and Marlene know that we are here, won't you?"

"Certainly," Shelby replied.

"By the way, how is Cleophus?" Francis Whyte inquired.

"He's conscious, and they're running some tests. We're waiting for a specialist that Blaize has chosen. He's the one who will make the diagnosis and determine what kind of treatment Cleophus will need."

"Well, we'll be here when he gets here," Keith declared.

"Thank you," Shelby replied. "I'm sure your support will mean an awful lot to Blaize and Marlene."

Chapter 37

"Are you Cleophus' aunt?" Dr. Minor stood holding the door open with his back.

"Yes, I am," Shelby replied.

"Would you come with me, please? Blaize asked that I bring you back."

Sleepy and tired, Shelby got up from the cramped emergency room chair and followed the doctor. The first time she had seen him was an hour ago when he whizzed through the waiting area heading straight for the emergency room.

She slipped past Dr. Minor into the area where the patients were being cared for. There were a handful of people lying on gurneys as they passed through. Cleophus was one of them.

"May I?" Shelby pointed toward Cleophus.

"You haven't had an opportunity to see him since he arrived?" Dr. Minor stuck his hands in his pockets.

"No."

"Go ahead. Normally, they don't allow but two people per patient back here, but since Blaize and Marlene are in the consultation room, I don't see any problem with it. Just come straight back here when you're done."

"Okay." Shelby replied, then walked over and stood beside Cleophus' bed.

His eyes were closed. He had a clear liquid running through an intravenous tube and a bandage with a dark spot in the crease of his opposite arm. Shelby placed her hand on his hand. Cleophus held on to it before he opened his eyes.

"I'm sorry. I didn't mean to wake you up," Shelby said softly.

"It's okay. I wasn't really asleep," he replied, his voice a whisper.

"How do you feel?"

"Kind of funny. Not bad." A tinge of the old spark lit his groggy eyes. "Just funny."

"So you're not in pain or anything?" Shelby's brow knitted with concern.

"No. I'm just tired. And I've got this taste in my mouth as if I've just recovered from a very high fever. Do you know what I'm talking about?" His thin eyebrows lifted a bit. "It's a funny taste you get after a fever has broken."

"I think so," Shelby replied.

Cleophus closed his eyes.

"Well, I don't want to wear you out," Shelby told him.

Cleophus opened his eyes a bit and gave a hint of a smile.

"I'm about to go where your mother and Uncle Blaize are to hear what the doctor has to say about you. So you go ahead and rest." Shelby leaned forward and kissed him on his cheek. She was about to leave when Cleophus put pressure on her hand.

"Aunt Shelby, you won't forget me, will you?"

Shelby could barely hear him, but she was surprised by the question.

"Of course not. We're going to literally be bound by blood. You'll be impossible to forget," Shelby said jokingly. "Plus I'll have to hang around until you're up and on your feet."

Cleophus' eyes were completely closed as he spoke. "Don't forget me, Aunt Shelby. And know that people can be born in the same family and not feel like family. People have to want to be family. It is a heart-bound unit of love."

Cleophus' grip loosened on her hand as his breathing became long and even. Shelby stood and watched him for a moment before she headed to the consultation area, his last words fresh in her mind.

Moments later Shelby sat down in a chair brought in from another room. She wondered if she looked as tired as Marlene. Blaize, on the other hand, looked as fresh as Dr. Minor.

"We've got an interesting situation on our hands," Dr. Minor began. "I'm going to tell you now I don't know quite what to make of it. But I will present the information as it is."

"I see where you"—Dr. Minor nodded toward Marlene—"brought Cleophus in here about a month ago." He scanned the medical file folder on the desk.

"Yes, I did. He didn't seem to be able to get out of bed that day. His heart was beating very fast, and he appeared to be out of breath. So I brought him here."

"He doesn't have a private physician?" Dr. Minor looked over the rim of his glasses.

"No." Marlene looked at her hands. "He never has."

"I see." He sat back in his seat. "Well, they did some tests on him back then, and I think you were informed that he was suffering from chronic anemia."

"No one ever told me that." Marlene shook her head, then looked at Blaize.

"They didn't?" Dr. Minor looked at the medical information again.

"No," Marlene reiterated.

"What about sickle cell anemia?" Dr. Minor said.

"Yes, that's what they said Cleophus had. Sickle cell anemia."

"And they were right." Dr. Minor sat back again. "Sickle cell anemia occurs when the blood cells sickle. They don't keep their normal round, pliable shape as they move through the system. Cleophus' blood type is the rarest there is, AB-negative. Something like one person out of a hundred and sixty people have it."

"They told me in order for Cleophus to get better he would need a blood transfusion," Marlene explained, "and that they didn't have any of his blood type on hand. They said AB-negative was very rare and it would probably have to be gotten from a family member if it was to be found."

"And that's where you come in, Ms. Russau?" Dr. Minor looked at Shelby.

"Yes. I have AB-negative blood."

"I heard you brought her here all the way from St. Petersburg, Florida, Blaize."

"Yes. I did. I didn't want to take any chances with my nephew's health, so just as I hired you because you are the best physician I know to handle the kind of problem Cleophus is facing, I did the best I could in finding him a blood source, his father's family."

The comparison made Shelby cringe. How could Blaize compare her coming to Grenada to hiring a doctor? Hiring a doctor could be totally impersonal. She had come to Grenada hoping to find family.

"That's right, you told me the young man's father is dead."

A series of affirmations rippled in the room.

Dr. Minor turned quiet before he spoke again. "I

heard Cleophus fainted after his Rites of Passage ceremony."

"What you heard is true," Blaize replied.

"How did it happen?" Dr. Minor looked from one of them to the other.

"We were dancing," Shelby began. "Spinning actually. One minute he was smiling and talking; the next minute he was at my feet. It happened so quickly."

Dr. Minor nodded his head.

Blaize leaned on the desk. "Charles, you said you were going to give us some information. I feel like we're the ones who are giving you information." His impatience was obvious.

"I'm just trying to get a handle on this, Blaize." Dr. Minor squeezed the clump of hair on his chin. "I guess there's no other way to say this than to say it." He paused. "When Cleophus was admitted into the emergency room tonight more blood was taken. The results were quite different from the first time. There were many normal red blood cells. So I thought someone had made a mistake and I tested his blood again, and when I did"—he looked at the medical file—"just about all his red blood cells were normal."

"Are you saying Cleophus is getting better?" Marlene sat at the edge of her seat.

"I am saying not only is he getting better . . ." Dr. Minor closed his eyes. "He is improving at a rate that defies medical explanation."

"Defies medical explanation." Marlene repeated the words as if he were speaking a foreign language. "But Cleophus hasn't had any treatment."

"I understand that full well, Marlene," Dr. Minor said.

Shelby stood up and walked to the corner of the room. "Are you telling us Cleophus won't need a blood transfusion?"

Dr. Minor heaved a huge sigh. "I am telling you that I plan to keep Cleophus here tonight for observation. But if his blood test results are what the current trend indicates they will be, he'll be able to go home in the morning."

Marlene jumped up and planted a kiss on Dr. Minor's lips. "Thank you. Thank you," she cried before she grabbed Shelby, then quickly turned to Blaize.

"There's no need to thank me," Dr. Minor said, standing up. "I sure didn't do it. Nor anyone else, at least not in the flesh."

Shelby didn't think Marlene heard him. She was beside herself with joy.

"Blaize. Can you believe it, Blaize? Not only is Cleophus going to be all right. He's completely healed."

"We're going to have to wait until tomorrow morn—" Dr. Minor tried to interject, but Marlene would have none of it.

"He's completely healed, Blaize." She held on to his neck and he hugged her back. For a moment his eyes met Shelby's before Marlene grabbed him by the hand and said, "Come on, Blaize. We've got to tell the others. They've been out there praying for a miracle and here it is."

Shelby followed at a close distance as Marlene pulled a cooperative Blaize through the emergency room, the waiting room, and onto the property outside.

Some of the people were sleeping, but when Marlene and Blaize emerged they were quickly nudged awake by the vigilant ones.

The crowd began to move in closer, but Marlene could not wait for them to gather round. "We can't thank you enough for coming here tonight," she said at the top of her lungs. "So I wanted to tell you as quickly as I could, your prayers and songs have not been wasted. My brother, Blaize, and I"—she put her arm through his—"were just told by Dr. Minor that Cleophus is healing in a way that he cannot explain. His exact words were what's happening defies medical explanation." An intake of breaths filled the air. "And Dr. Minor says, if things go the way they are going now, Cleophus will be on his way back to Hummingbird Island in the morning and no further treatment will be necessary."

A round of "thank yous" erupted as arms went up in the air and people began to hug and kiss one another. In seconds Blaize and Marlene were engulfed by their friends and neighbors. Congratulations and well wishes abounded.

Shelby watched the exchanges with dual emotions. She was happy because it did appear that Cleophus' body had begun to heal itself, but on the other hand, there was a profound sense of sadness because no one noticed she was not involved in the celebration. Shelby found the more they celebrated, the more she backed into the doorway, until she could barely be seen at all.

"Listen. Listen." Jeannette raised one arm in the air. "There is no doubt in my mind that Cleophus will be returning home tomorrow morning, and I think we should give him something to return to."

A chorus of "yeses" went up.

"If it's okay with Blaize and Marlene, we will prepare a feast for tomorrow to welcome Cleophus back to Hummingbird Island."

Jeannette looked at them expectantly. Shelby could not hear their responses over the cheers and shouts, but she assumed by Jeanette's reaction they had agreed.

"Quiet!" Jeannette shouted, patting the air. "And now, because Blaize and Marlene have opened their hearts and their home to us, we will take care of them tonight, in our homes, in our way."

More shouts of agreement went up as the crowd closed in on Blaize and Marlene as they herded them down the street. The nurse behind the check-in counter came and stood beside Shelby.

"What is all the shouting about? They better be glad they're taking it down the street. I was about to tell them they were going to have to keep the noise down."

"Well, I guess that won't be necessary now," Shelby said quietly.

"Aren't you going with them?" the nurse asked.

"No. I don't think I will. I think it's time for me to go home. My work, as I was so aptly told, is done here."

"What kind of work do you do?" The nurse studied her. "With all the praying and such, are you a minister?"

"No. I'm not a minister." Shelby gave a sad smile. "I'm simply someone who knows when it's time to go home."

0 "And where might that be, may I ask? It's surely not Grenada."

Shelby thought of the boy who had guided her to Carib's Leap. "It's that obvious, huh?"

"I'd say so."

"And I guess it always will be," Shelby said softly.

"What did you say?" The nurse tilted her head to the side.

"I said St. Petersburg, Florida, is my home, and I intend to head back there as soon as possible," Shelby announced. "The airport isn't that far from here, is it?"

"No. Not far at all." The woman looked at the

small bag Shelby had at her side. "You must have known you were going to be coming and going right back."

"Something told me to travel light," Shelby replied. "But if I left a couple of shorts and a few T-shirts it won't kill me. At least I'll have my dignity," she added, her voice trailing off.

"If you say so." The nurse's bottom lip protruded with indecision.

"There is one thing I'd like for you to do for me," Shelby said.

"I can if I will."

"I'm going to write a note for the Blaize family. The man and the woman who just left. That includes the young man Dr. Minor came in to treat tonight. Would you make sure they get it before Dr. Minor checks Cleophus out of the hospital?"

"I will probably be off the schedule by then, but I'll tell the next attendant to give it to them tomorrow."

"Thank you," Shelby said. "Now, I'd like to use your phone to get a ride, if you don't mind."

Chapter 38

Blaize moved with the momentum of the crowd. It had grown larger as they progressed down the street and curiosity seekers learned of Cleophus' miraculous healing. Up ahead, Marlene was being carried. She balanced herself with her arms stretched wide. She held on to two people's shoulders. Her joy was evident by the thrust of her head, and Blaize almost knew how she felt. Almost, because he was not a mother who had discovered her child was totally healthy for the first time in his life.

Still, Blaize could not remember when he had felt so happy, so full. The power of the ancestors' ways had been proven. His nephew, Shelby's nephew, would live to a ripe old age.

No sooner than her name came to mind Blaize looked for Shelby in the crowd. She had not been hoisted up like Marlene, but she had to be amongst them somewhere. He continued to search to no avail. Had she not joined the celebration? Was Shelby not pleased with the proof of his beliefs? The last thought caused a hardness in his chest.

Blaize recalled the last time he had seen Shelby. It had been in the consultation room. He did not recall her standing with them when Marlene made her jubilant announcement. Shelby had not stood by their side to proclaim to his fellow islanders that because Cleophus had gone through the Rites of Passage, healing his spiritual wound, therefore his physical illness no longer had a space to survive.

Blaize's body rattled with the pats on his back and he smiled at the occasional shouts of "Victory," but the gestures no longer felt as sweet. He was certain Shelby had decided not to be there. She could not lend her presence or her support to something she did not, and would never, believe.

Blaize's old demon of American perceived superiority raised its head. Perhaps Shelby considered Dr. Minor to be no more qualified to make an accurate diagnosis than a bush doctor. He had acknowledged the Rites of Passage ceremony. He had determined Cleophus' healing defied medical explanation, the one and only thing Shelby would ever understand and accept.

With a jumble of hands Blaize found himself being lifted up above the crowd as several deep voices began to chant, "Blaize. Blaize. Blaize." Marlene looked back and smiled at him, and Blaize determined he would have to be satisfied with the moment. This exuberant display was probably too much for Shelby's tamed blood. An island thing. No doubt she was finding a hotel room for the night that would be more to her American liking.

Blaize began to sing the song that was gaining favor within the crowd. He would deal with Shelby, and his feelings for her, in the morning, when they returned to the hospital to take Cleophus back to Hummingbird Island.

"We've come to see Cleophus Blaize," Marlene told one of the nurses standing behind the counter.

"Isn't that the young man who is being checked out now?" She turned to her coworker.

"Yes. Dr. Minor is with him right around the corner." She batted her eyelashes at Blaize. "You're welcome to go down there, or wait right here if you like. It's your choice."

Blaize glanced up the hallway. "Has anyone else been here asking for a Cleophus Blaize?"

"No," the wide-eyed one replied, but they both smiled beguilingly.

"I think we'll head down to where Cleophus is being checked out," he said to Marlene.

She nodded her agreement.

"Suit yourself," the eager nurse replied, then

turned her back and started working on the opposite counter.

"So Shelby hasn't gotten here yet," Marlene commented. The heels of her shoes tapped on the floor.

"It appears that way," Blaize replied.

"I hope we don't end up missing her. We should have kept a closer eye on her last night," Marlene said. "But I was so excited, I didn't think about it at the time."

"There's nothing we can do about it now." Blaize's voice was cool. Mentally he had come to terms with Shelby's possible abandonment. Emotionally . . . that was another subject.

"You don't seem to be very concerned." Marlene looked up at her brother.

"That's because I don't think Shelby got left behind. I think she knew exactly what she was doing when she didn't come with us. That was her intention."

They turned the corner and were greeted by Dr. Minor. "Good morning."

"Good morning," Blaize and Marlene replied.

Concern knitted Marlene's brow when she bent over and gave a wheelchair-bound Cleophus a kiss on the forehead. "And good morning to you."

"Good morning, Cleophus." Blaize squeezed his shoulder.

"Good morning," Cleophus replied, smiling.

"Dr. Minor." Marlene's voice trembled. "Did

you find something else? Is that why Cleophus is in a wheelchair?"

Dr. Minor looked at Cleophus and shook his head. "Oh, no. This morning's test results were exactly what I expected. All of Cleophus' red blood cells are normal. He's as healthy as he can be." His expression reflected the awe surrounding the situation. "Any patient who is being checked out must ride in a wheelchair. It's hospital policy."

"I see," Marlene remarked, and smiled down at Cleophus again.

"We're just about done." Dr. Minor rifled through a small stack of forms. "I've got to get all the paperwork together. Oh," he said suddenly. "I nearly forgot. I've got something for you." He reached in his pocket and pulled out a folded sheet of paper. "The attendant from last night told me to make sure the family got this." He handed the note to Blaize.

"What is it?" Cleophus asked.

"It's something your aunt left," Dr. Minor informed him as he tapped the closed file against the counter. "Well, that's it. You're good to go." He looked at Cleophus. "It's cases like yours that keep my feet on the ground. It makes me know I'm not the master healer, I'm simply a tool. Good to meet you, Cleophus Blaize." He stuck his hand out for a handshake.

"You too, Dr. Minor," Cleophus replied, as a sad

note entered his voice. "And thank you for everything."

"You're welcome," Dr. Minor said as he shook Blaize and Marlene's hands. "Until the next time." He looked in Blaize's eyes.

"Let's make the next time a social occasion," Blaize replied.

"You're on," Dr. Minor said before he walked away.

He was barely out of hearing range when Cleophus said, "Aunt Shelby has left."

"What?" Marlene looked at Cleophus, then Blaize.

"She's gone back to America."

Blaize looked at the folded piece of paper he held in his hand.

"Grandfather told me that Aunt Shelby would be going away. He also said he would be leaving. That I didn't need him anymore. That I had a family now. You," he looked at his mother, "and Uncle Blaize and Aunt Shelby."

Blaize stood still as stone.

"Aren't you going to look and see what it says, Blaize?" Marlene asked softly.

Slowly he unfolded the note and began to read.

I can tell the time has come for me to go back to America. I can't thank you enough for your hospitality and all the things that your family

*has opened my eyes and my life to. I will al-
ways remember Grenada, Hummingbird Island, and the Blaize family.*

Shelby Russau

"Why did she leave like that?" Cleophus looked
at them, confused.

"Perhaps she'd had enough," Blaize replied
softly.

"Enough of what?" Cleophus pressed.

"Enough of us." His jaw muscle began to work.
"Things that happened here went against your Aunt
Shelby's reality. She didn't believe in our ways,
and she wasn't willing to change that," Blaize explained.

Marlene put her hands on her hips. "What are
you talking about? Shelby did more changing than
all three of us put together." Marlene's volume rose
with her ire. "Men. You just don't understand anything. She comes here, we turn her life, her beliefs
and her heart"—she poked Blaize in the chest—
"upside down, and she is the one who hasn't done
enough. Huh." She tossed her head. "*We* didn't do
enough. Shelby weathered another country and culture because of us. She weathered threats because
of us, and if it hadn't been for Shelby telling me
what it really means to believe in something, no
matter what it is, I think I would have lost my mind
when Cleophus was lying there unconscious. Last

night we should have showed her that we cared, and not been so self-centered as you are being now," Marlene raged.

"Marlene, I know you grew to like Shelby." Blaize tried to help her confront the truth. "But we've got to face the facts. She doesn't believe as we do. She doesn't see life as we do."

"And what does that matter? She loves you, and you love her. I know it. I see it in your eyes." Marlene stared into them. "You've got to stop shutting yourself off, Blaize, when life is calling you to feel. If I had someone who loved me, and I loved them, I would not let them get away. I was searching for love all those years when I went from man to man to man. And with one failing encounter after another my self-esteem dwindled until I didn't have enough to even hold in my hand. I couldn't even come back home, and share the life that my son deserved, because of it. I felt I had disgraced the family. But family means far more than that. Family means to accept a person as they are with all their faults, and hope in despite of them that you will continue to love one another. We are a family. Shelby is our family. Now it's your job to go find her and tell her so."

Blaize looked at the conviction in his sister's eyes and he knew what she said was true. With all his preaching about living by the dictates of your heart and not your mind, Blaize had turned his back on his own philosophy at a time when it was most important to honor it.

He shook his head and threw his arms around Marlene. "Finally, my strong-willed baby sister is back and on my side."

Chapter 39

Shelby turned on her favorite reading light. It was a replica of a Tiffany lamp she bought at the Cobb-webb auction a couple of years before. She had arrived in Miami that morning, then taken a bus to St. Petersburg. It had been a long day and now Shelby wanted to settle in quietly and continue reading the book she had started the night Blaize showed up on her porch. Her stomach tightened at the thought of it.

Shelby flipped the pages and chided herself for not using a bookmark. The doorbell rang and Shelby got up and peeked through the blinds. It was Linda, who was now standing in front of the window, trying to see inside. They nearly met eye to eye.

"Girl. What are you doing here?" Linda made herself heard without the benefit of the door or window being open.

"Wait a minute," Shelby said. She had mixed

feelings about Linda's arrival. She wanted to see her, but she wasn't prepared to answer the inevitable questions. Shelby braced herself as she opened the door.

"I don't believe this," Linda started as she crossed the threshold. "Here I am driving by your house, trying to make sure nobody has broken in or anything, and I saw a light come on. And I said to myself"—she put her hands on her hips—"I know Shelby has not come back from Grenada and didn't tell me. So I parked the car, not knowing if I should call the police or what, and here you are sitting up in here with your lounge clothes on like you've been doing for the past five years."

Shelby let out a deep breath. "Would you rather that I be wearing something else?"

"I'd rather for you to give me a hug." Linda opened her arms wide and Shelby came to her.

No sooner than they disengaged Linda was at it again. "What are you doing here? You must have known I was about to put out an APB on you. I thought you were going to call me when you got there. You know. Let me know that you were okay."

"Well, obviously, I was and am okay," Shelby replied in a tired voice.

Linda took a step back. "Yes, you look okay physically, but I don't know what kind of sound that was. What happened over there?"

"So much happened, Linda, I don't know if I'd be able to tell you in a single night."

"You can try, can't you?"

"I don't know if I want to." Shelby looked her dead in the eyes. "At least not right now. I've got to sort out a few things."

"Well, at least tell me, was the boy Cleophus' son?"

"There's no doubt in my mind that, yes, Cleophus is my nephew. He is a wonderful bo—young man. Very special in more ways than you could believe."

"Then why do you feel so heavy to me?" Linda's face grew long.

"I guess it's because I went over there with some unreal expectations. What they were, I'm not really sure. I simply know that if they had been fulfilled I wouldn't be feeling the way I feel right now."

Linda took a seat without being invited. She leaned over a bit and looked at Shelby with her head turned one quarter of the way. "This wouldn't have anything to do with that man, Blaize, would it?"

"It's possible," Shelby replied.

"Did things get to going between you?"

"For awhile."

"What do you mean 'for awhile'?" Linda sprang back. "You were supposed to be gone for almost a month. You're back here in a week and you say things got to going between you for a while? That would be one of the shortest 'whiles' I ever heard of."

Shelby placed her fingertips to her lips to stop them from trembling. "I told you I didn't want to talk about this right now, Linda."

"Oh, Shel." Linda came and sat beside Shelby on the couch. "I didn't mean to upset you. This stuff really got deep, didn't it?"

Shelby nodded, because she knew if she spoke she would begin to cry.

"I told that big, handsome"—Linda pressed her lips together for a B word and came up with "—biscuit eater, if he hurt you he was going to have to answer to me. I told him that standing in that airport."

Shelby couldn't help but smile. Linda's tongue could quickly be turned into a weapon for or against her. "I don't think he did it intentionally, Linda. Some things are cultural."

"He's a Black man, isn't he?"

"You know the answer to that."

"That's enough right there. All kinds of folks are able to get together, and I have no problem with it. But when I saw the man that took you on the plane with him to Grenada, he looked like any brother walking on the streets." She paused, then added, "Although a lot better looking. So." Linda crossed her leg. "It couldn't be that big of a difference."

"Sometimes there are differences that go beyond

skin color. The way Blaize looked at life . . . the way he lived, it was so different from anyone I have ever known. Black or White."

"Really?" Linda's jaw dropped.

"Really." Shelby echoed.

"Well, what did the brother do?"

"It was not only what he did. It was the things he said." Shelby counted off on her fingers. "How he believed. How he lived. What he . . ."

"Wait a minute. Wait a minute. Back up. Back up. 'How he believed.' No offense, Shelby, but as I recall I'm the one who goes to church every Sunday. I haven't seen you there except for those special occasions when you think you're going to feel guilty about turning me down."

"That's just it, Linda. It wasn't about church. It wasn't about religion. It was how he looked at life. There was no separation between his spiritual beliefs, nature and his daily life."

"And that made you come back here like this?"

"No. Not in and of itself. I came back because . . ." Shelby searched her thoughts, her heart. "I thought if I found out Cleophus was actually my nephew I would have an instant family. That I would actually belong to and with someone. But it wasn't that simple."

"I don't understand." Linda showed her palms. "What does that have to do with Blaize?"

Shelby scooted to the edge of her seat. "Blaize's way of approaching family is all tied up with his beliefs and . . ." She searched for the right words. "Cleophus is a part of that."

Linda made an "I am clueless" gesture.

"A major part. It's almost like he symbolizes it," Shelby tried to explain.

"All right. I'll take your word for it. So-o, did Cleophus have the blood transfusion?"

"No, he didn't."

"What happened? Your blood type didn't match?"

"It matched perfectly." Shelby drew another deep breath. "It ended up he didn't need it."

"So the man, Blaize, lied."

"He didn't lie, Linda." Shelby looked in her eyes. "Cleophus didn't need the blood transfusion because there was this miraculous healing." A stunned expression surfaced on her face. "There was one unbelievable thing after another happening over there, and Cleophus was in the center of all of it."

"What do you mean, miraculous healing?" Linda turned skeptical and serious.

"After Cleophus went through this ritual that marked his change from a boy into a man, he fell into this comalike state. Blaize felt it might have been the power of what he had experienced in the ritual, but I insisted that he be taken to a hospital."

"That's exactly what most sane people would have done," Linda supported her.

"Well, we took him there and several hours later

it was discovered that Cleophus' sickle cell anemia was healing itself."

"A medical doctor told you that?" Linda asked.

"Yes. A medical doctor."

"Okay." Linda put her fist up to her mouth. "I'm going to take what you just told me at face value. Let's say your nephew, Cleophus, did experience some kind of miraculous healing. You should be happy, Shelby. You should be in Grenada jumping for joy."

"I am happy for him. I am so happy because he is so-o special." Her eyes misted over. "But what became apparent to me after Cleophus' healing was . . . " Shelby paused. "I was no longer needed." She could barely say the words. "I mean they totally forgot about me, Linda. It was as if I had never existed. Blaize and his sister, Marlene, were embraced by their community and they were one big happy family. I was left standing at the hospital door. Just some outsider who had outgrown her usefulness."

"Ohh, Shelby, you don't know that's true," Linda tried to console her.

"Nobody came back for me." Shelby's eyes were wide with disappointment. "I left a note for the family, meaning Blaize, Marlene and Cleophus, saying good-bye and telling them I planned to leave this morning. I even called a hotel from the hospital and booked a room, just in case someone came back that night looking for me, the attendant would have been able to tell them where I was staying. But nobody came back. I flew back to Florida this morning without a single soul caring." Shelby wiped away a tear before it fell.

"M-m-m," Linda sounded, patting her friends knee.

"M-m-m, is right," Shelby replied. "So you see why I had to come home? Nobody really cared about me there. Except for Cleophus," she added quickly.

"Why didn't you stay to say good-bye to him?" Linda searched Shelby's face.

"Because we said our good-byes. Cleophus knew I would be leaving and he told me not to forget him."

"He knew you were going to leave early?" Linda scrunched up her face.

"Um-huh. I told you he was a very special young man. And I will never forget him. Never."

Shelby knew she would never forget Blaize either.

Chapter 40

"After all you've told me my head is spinning."
Linda finished the can of soda Shelby had given
her. "What time is it?"

Shelby looked at the clock on the table. "It's
almost midnight."

"Well, I'm worn out. And you look like you've
been rejuvenated now that you've dumped all that
stuff on me."

"You know you can be something else," Shelby
remarked. "You practically drug everything out of
me, and now you're complaining that I dumped the
stuff on you." The phone rang. "I don't know who
this could be." She picked up the receiver. "Hello."

"Hello, Shelby."

"Yes." Shelby's rich brown skinned turned
ashen.

"Who is it?" Linda mouthed from the couch.

"It's Blaize." Blaize's voice traveled over the
phone line.

"I recognize your voice." Shelby's voice sounded breathy.

"Who is it, I said?" Linda repeated with exaggerated mouth movements.

"We were surprised to find out that you left so quickly," Blaize continued.

"Well, I thought it was time for me to go. We have an old saying here in the States . . ."

"It's him, isn't it? It's him." Linda came over and stood by Shelby, who nodded and turned her back.

"Never overstay your welcome," Shelby continued.

"You could have given us an opportunity to determine if you had," Blaize replied.

"It really doesn't matter," Shelby hurried on. "Did Cleophus get checked out of the hospital this morning?"

"Yes, he did. With a totally clean bill of health."

"I knew he would." Shelby's eyes misted over but she put a smile in her voice. "That's fantastic."

"Give me that phone. Let me talk to him," Linda whispered, reaching for the receiver.

"Stop." Shelby whispered back, slapping her hand.

"What did you say?" Blaize asked.

"I'm sorry, I was talking to someone else," Shelby replied.

"So you've got company." Surprise and disappointment was in his voice.

"It's only Linda. You met her at the airport," Shelby reassured him.

"You didn't need to tell him that." Linda wagged her finger. "See, I need to talk to him, you don't know what to say."

"But she was just about to leave." Shelby looked at Linda pointedly.

"So you don't normally have company this late?" Blaize stated.

Shelby looked at the receiver. "I'm thirty years old. I can do whatever I want."

"Now that's talking." Linda stuck her thumb in the air, and Shelby pointed toward the front door.

"Then I'm on my way over," Blaize said and hung up.

Slowly, Shelby returned the phone to the charger.

"He hung up on you because you said that?" Linda clicked her tongue. "Honey, he isn't like any brother I know. You'd have to say far worse things than that to get him to hang up. Especially calling long distance."

"He's on his way over." Shelby looked at Linda with blank eyes.

"You got to be kidding." Linda replied.

"I'm not kidding." Shelby started walking in circles. "That's what he said. He must have been calling from somewhere here in St. Pete."

"Well, you need to hurry up and go put something else on," Linda advised.

"Why?"

"Because look at you. You've got on some lounge sweat pants and a little fuzzy top that's showing your belly button. That's not the kind of outfit you wear to hook a man."

"I am not trying to hook anybody." Shelby lifted her head. "If he's coming over here on such short notice, he's got to deal with me as I am."

"O-o-h, I hear you, girl. That's right. Be strong. He's on your turf now." Linda cocked her head. "Even though he's come all the way from Grenada." She looked at Shelby as if she had lost her mind.

"You're right." Shelby started to run to the back. "I've got to put something else on."

A knock sounded at the door.

"He's here already," Shelby exclaimed.

"He must have been calling from the pay phone on the corner," Linda surmised.

Shelby covered her mouth with both her hands. "All right. I'm going to be calm. I can do this," she talked to herself as she walked to the door.

"Yes, you can." Linda rushed to the couch and picked up a magazine as though she had been looking at it all the time. "And I'm going to make sure I stay to see it."

"Who is it?" Shelby called through the door.

"Blaize," Shelby heard him say before she took one last breath and pulled.

"Blaize." She stepped to the side. "Why didn't you tell me you were here in St. Petersburg?" Shelby thought she sounded like someone on a TV sitcom, she was trying to be so matter of fact.

"I thought I'd come by and tell you in person." He stood in front of her and looked deep into her eyes.

Shelby squeezed by him and closed the door. "Well, you know I'm more than surprised." She put on her most accomplished smile. "You remember Linda, don't you?"

"Yes. Hello, Linda," Blaize said, without taking his eyes off of Shelby.

Shelby could feel a flush coming on, but she did her best to control it. "We were just sitting here chatting when you called."

"I see." He continued to watch her.

"Would you care to sit down?"

"I'd appreciate that. I've come a long way," he said, his voice like silk.

"You sure did." Linda had to get into the conversation. "Everybody else is going to bed and you're making late-night calls."

"I'm ready to settle in for the night as well," Blaize replied. "That is, if Shelby will extend to me the same hospitality that we extended to her on Hummingbird Island." He looked at Shelby, who was just about to sit at the other end of the couch.

"So you're saying you plan to spend the night here?" Linda clarified the situation.

"If Shelby will have me," he replied, his voice like raw honey.

"Oh my," Linda said, crossing her legs.

"Linda." Shelby stood up again. "I know that I have kept you up way past your bedtime, and I'm really sorry about that." She started walking toward the door. "So why don't you come by tomorrow before we go to the Juneteeth Celebration? You should be well rested and in a better state of mind by then."

Reluctantly, Linda followed Shelby to the front door. "Are you sure you can handle this?" she asked real low when she reached Shelby.

"Positive." Shelby threatened her with her eyes, and opened the door.

"Well." Linda took a step forward. "Just in case." She gave a decoy smile to Shelby before she called over her shoulder. "Remember what I said in the airport; you're going to have to answer to me."

Shelby gently pushed Linda through the door. "With friends like you, who needs a bodyguard?" She smiled a fear-filled smile before she closed the door, and donned her hostess mask.

"So what brought you back to St. Petersburg?" Shelby asked with as much courage as she could muster.

"You did," Blaize replied softly.

"I did." Shelby glanced at him, then hid her eyes

with downcast lashes. "What do you mean by that?" She could feel his gaze boring into her. She started to sit at the end of the couch, but sat in the overstuffed chair instead.

"You left Grenada without saying a word. Yes, you left a note, but considering all that we have been through together, all of us, you would have to admit it was a little inadequate."

"It didn't feel inadequate at the time," Shelby replied softly.

"Why did you leave, Shelby?" His accent lingered on the L of her name.

"I felt it was time for me to go. That my reason for coming to Grenada had been fulfilled." Shelby tried to look at him with confidence. "It was quite obvious you all didn't need me anymore," she added, then wished she could take it back.

"Need you." Blaize's voice vibrated. "Not only do we need you, we want you. I need and want you now." The words were rich and husky.

This time, when Shelby looked at him, she could not pull away. Blaize stood up and started toward her. For a second Shelby couldn't move, then raw fear took hold.

"Look. I don't know what all of this means." She made a circular motion with her hands. "Your coming to St. Petersburg and the things you are saying now, but it's a little too much, too fast."

"Seems like we've had this conversation before," Blaize replied.

"But not in my house at nearly one o'clock in the morning," Shelby said. "So why don't I just show you the guest room and we can take this up later." She got up and started down the hall. Blaize followed.

"This will be your room." Shelby opened the door. "There is only one bathroom and it sits right here in the middle." She pointed to the end of the hall, then crossed her arms. "If you need towels, they're in there," she said as she backed away. "I hope you have a good night's sleep."

Chapter 41

Shelby closed her bedroom door, put on a long gown and slipped between the sheets. Her heart was racing and her head spinning. *Why has Blaize come here? I can't take any more emotional strain. It was easier being alone and knowing it. Being on the verge of having a man, and a possible family, was excruciating. I would rather be alone than be abandoned again,* Shelby confirmed deep inside herself.

She got out of bed, lifted her blinds and gazed at the sky. This time the stars and the moon seemed so far away. Was it a sign that she would never have the love in her life that she had always wanted?

The door creaked behind her. She turned to see Blaize standing just inside her room.

"I decided this was later," he said, crossing the floor.

"Blaize, what are you doing?" Shelby heard herself say as he put his arms around her and his lips came down on hers.

Every fiber in Shelby's body tingled. His lips were so soft and smooth. His tongue an invitation. Shelby could hear a deep purr in his throat like a restless animal that was coming awake. She opened her mouth and allowed him further entry as her arms went around his neck. She pulled down ever so slightly.

A little voice in the back of her mind asked Shelby the same question she had asked Blaize only moments before. *Shelby, what are you doing?* But he pressed his body against hers and the feel of him drew her away from logic and into total desire.

Under the influence of Blaize's kiss, and his touch, Shelby could not back away. She could only go to him as her body and her mind recalled the joyous pleasure they had last shared by the waterfall.

Shelby heard the blinds come down behind her, and then felt her satin gown rising up her thighs. Gently Blaize encouraged her to raise her arms, and the gown was over her head and on the floor.

The bedroom was so small, Blaize took only a few backwards steps with Shelby in tow before he lay back on her sheets, then pulled her gently down beside her. Shelby felt as if she were in a dream as she stared into his eyes.

"My Shelby," Blaize whispered, and rained

kisses near her lips before he sought the wholeness of them again. "Did you really think our lovemaking at the waterfall would be our last time?" he breathed. "Did you really think I would do without you?"

His heady words made her moan as he guided her beneath him. "I didn't know what to think. I just had to get away. I had to come home to what I know."

"But you know this, Shelby." Blaize rubbed against her and made himself known. "Why did you leave that way? Did you want to see if I would come after you?" He shifted to the side so he could touch her, and his hand found her wet and willing.

"I didn't feel wanted." Her words came in spurts. "I didn't feel needed there," Shelby whispered.

"I need you, Shelby." Blaize began to kiss her neck, her breasts. "I need you more than I have ever needed anyone." He looked up at her with dark eyes before his face descended lower, and he made his need known.

Shelby's body sparked with pleasure as he drank of her being. She could not speak. She could barely breathe as Blaize discovered and explored every part of her. Finally, Shelby found her voice and she called his name over and over again as she drew his body upwards. "Oh Blaize," she murmured. "I need you too."

It was what he needed to hear to go inside her, and once there, Shelby and Blaize's pleasurable journey together had just begun. He took her to the peak over and over again, and each time she would reach it, Shelby thought there could be no more, but there was; and her body would respond anew. When they began their final climb Shelby could feel Blaize tense as his movements grew in force. This time he would meet her there, and Shelby opened and thrilled to him like never before.

"I love you, Shelby," he said. The words were deep and true.

"I love you too," she cried, and she ached with the pleasure of it and the possible pain of never seeing him again.

Blaize awakened to an empty bed. He sat up. Shelby's nightgown was hanging on a hook behind the door and he could hear voices coming from the front of the house. He slipped on his pants and entered the hallway. Shelby and Linda were standing at the front door.

"Good morning," Shelby said.

"Good morning," Blaize replied.

"Hi there," Linda quipped, her eyebrows rising meaningfully.

"I didn't know how tired you were or how long you were going to sleep," Shelby began. "And I'm a volunteer for the Pinellas County Millennium Celebration. Remember? That's what I was doing when you met me."

Blaize looked at her purse on her shoulder and

the berry color of her lips. "Yes. I remember."

"Well, Linda and I had already agreed to support the Juneteenth Celebration at Campbell Park. So if you're hungry there's food in the kitchen. I shouldn't be gone long."

Linda took another hard look at the half-nude Blaize. "Maybe you should stay here, Shelby."

"No, it's fine," Shelby replied quickly. "You'll be okay, won't you?"

"I didn't come all this way to be left in your house alone."

The silence was palpable.

"I won't be gone long." Shelby walked past Linda and out the door.

Linda looked at Blaize, shrugged her shoulders, and closed the door.

Blaize didn't move. He thought of the flight he'd scheduled for that afternoon. He planned to be on it. And he planned for Shelby to be on it as well.

"What in the world is wrong with you?" Linda asked as she started the car.

"Nothing." Shelby glanced at her and looked away.

"Nothing? You just left a half-nude, gorgeous man standing in your hallway. And here you are in my car on your way to Juneteenth."

"Thanks for explaining it to me, Linda," Shelby replied.

"Look, don't get smart with me. You're the one with the problem."

"Yes. I do have a problem. I admit it."

"And pray tell me, what is it?"

"I don't know what he wants," she said with exasperation. "If he wants to play here today gone tomorrow, I can't play. I'm not open for, 'Come visit me every blue moon on my tropical island and then go back to Fifth Avenue South here in St. Pete.' "

"I could play that," Linda quipped.

"Sure you could." Shelby looked at her hands. "And James would break your neck."

"Seriously, Shel," Linda began. "How can you expect guarantees from the man this early in the relationship? It's not logical."

"Well I don't want to deal with logic. I don't want to deal with any of it." Shelby held on to the dashboard. She looked at Linda with all of her past in her eyes. "I can't take being left alone again, after belonging, Linda. The things that happened in Grenada touched my life so deeply I wouldn't be able to take just toying with it. I left on my own. I made a clean break of it."

I understand that, Shel," Linda replied as she parked the car. "But Blaize is here. What are you going to do about that?" She removed the key from the ignition.

"I haven't decided yet." Shelby looked at her friend.

"Did you make your indecision known last night?"

"No. He didn't give me a chance." Shelby got out of the car.

Shelby and Linda crossed the street to Campbell Park. Shelby's eyes scanned the adoption material at the One Church–One Child booth. It reminded her of her past.

"Isn't this great?" Linda took her first taste of homemade sorbet made by one of the merchants. "This event just gets bigger every year. Jeannie helped organize the first Juneteenth celebration in 1992, and look at it now. I think it is one of the best events of the Pinellas County Millennium celebration."

"They have done a wonderful job," Shelby replied as she smiled at a little boy getting his face painted like an African mask, but her mind was back at home, with Blaize.

"Take a look over there." Linda pointed. "They're about to start a reenactment."

A group of men dressed in Civil War garb took their places, while women dressed in the same period style stood by. "It says here they are the Sons of the Confederate Veterans. They do this kind of thing so we won't forget our racial history. So we will be able to embrace it. Come to terms with it. And hopefully do something about." Linda spooned more sorbet into her mouth.

"Let's stand over here." Shelby pointed to a

stand that was shaped like a ship. Men dressed like pirates were behind it selling jewelry made of sea-shells.

"That's a good idea," Linda replied. "It is kind of crowded."

They walked over to the stand and faced the reenactment.

Suddenly, people began to turn around and look in their direction. Shelby turned to see a black-and-red taxi that had been driven into a prohibited area.

"I don't know what he thinks he's doing," Linda sparked.

The back door of the vehicle opened and Blaize stepped out.

"Wait right here," he told the taxi driver.

"I know you're paying me," the driver shouted, "but I still don't want to get in trouble, so hurry it up please."

Blaize strode across the grass and over to Shelby.

"I've got a flight this afternoon back to Grenada and I want you on it."

"Blaize, what are you talking about?" Shelby glanced at the crowd that had begun to gather.

"I've got to get back to Hummingbird Island. I want you with me. We're a family now. It's where you belong."

"I can't make a decision like this so quickly." Shelby began to shake her head. "What if you change your mind later? I don't know—"

With that Blaize swept her up in his arms and started past the ship-shaped booth toward the taxi.

"Put me down, Blaize. Don't do this!" Shelby exclaimed. "You're causing a scene."

"You can't make up your mind. I live an ocean away, Shelby. I've got to make it up for you."

"It's not your decision to make." She squirmed in his arms. "You're an ocean away, and so are our lives. I won't go, Blaize."

He stopped walking and looked down into her eyes. "I've come all this way to get you, Shelby. If I leave now, I am never coming back."

Shelby looked at him and swallowed. "I've already made it up."

Slowly, he let her down. Blaize looked at Shelby one last time before he turned his back and began to walk away.

Shelby looked at him, then looked back at Linda and all the people who were watching. Somehow the scene was familiar. A crowd. A ship. People from various cultures. Some wearing costumes. A woman resisting. A man walking away. It was the vision she had seen on the mound as a child. It had been her own future that she had foreseen. Her own future that she was about to destroy.

"Blaize," Shelby called and ran after him.

He turned and opened his arms, and Shelby went into them. "Take me home to Hummingbird Island, Blaize. Take me home to my family."

The crowd cheered as they walked over to the

red-and-black taxi. Shelby waved to Linda, who shouted, "You better be back here for my wedding." Then Linda threw Shelby a kiss as the car door closed.

Epilogue
A day later

Shelby sat down next to Cleophus, who was wearing his father's cap.

"It feels kind of funny not being special anymore." Cleophus looked at her with wide eyes. "You know what I mean. Not knowing things anymore, because Grandfather is gone."

Shelby put her arm around him. "You don't need your grandfather in order to be special. You are special just as you are. You are special because you are my brother's son, my nephew, and a Blaize." She gave him a slight squeeze.

"I heard that," Blaize said as he and Marlene approached. "Why does he have to be a Blaize last of all?"

"Because from my point of view," Shelby explained, "his connection to me is through my brother. I am not a Blaize."

"No you're not," Blaize confirmed. "But we're

going to have to rectify that re-eal soon." He gave
her a kiss.

Cleophus threw up his cap. "Oh boy! Talk about
one big happy family."

They all laughed.

Q. Who was your favorite "Mystery Date?"

1. The Playboy
2. The Beachcomber
3. The Bum
4. None of the above

Don't miss the fun as Lauren Stevens opens the door to love . . . and meets her

PERFECT MATCH
by **Hailey North**

He's not exactly what she expected, but he sure is irresistible . . .

Coming in August
From Avon Contemporaries

Dear Reader,

What if you had to get married but there were no good prospects in sight? That's the problem facing Lady Gillian in Victoria Alexander's newest Regency-set historical THE HUSBAND LIST. Gillian and her friends make a list of the *ton's* most likely bachelors, but they're all unacceptable to her—until she meets the very sexy . . . and wildly unattainable . . . Earl of Shelbrooke.

It's evening, you've just settled down, there's a knock at the door—you open it, and could it be Mr. Right? In Hailey North's PERFECT MATCH pretty Lauren Stevens not only has one man vying for her affections . . . she has two—and to make matters more complicated, they're brothers! But for Lauren, Alistair Gotho is nothing but trouble . . .

Go west, young woman! And Rachelle Morgan's MUSTANG ANNIE is the perfect western gal—sexy, sassy . . . and determined not to fall for any old cowpoke that comes her way. But handsome Brett Corrigan is anything but old . . . he's completely irresistible.

Maximilian Chartwell made a promise he'd always protect his young cousin the duke, and he's not about to let an upstart American heiress trap the impressionable lad into marriage. But in Marlene Suson's NEVER A LADY it's Max himself who just might get trapped.

Enjoy!

Lucia Macro

Lucia Macro
Executive Editor
Avon Romance

AEL 0800